D1090101

Advance Praise for *Swinging Doors*

"It's often said that there's a book in everybody. Maybe. But not everybody can write as well as Quinlan Michael Hampston—known to his friends as Mike—or recall details of their lives as vividly as he does in his memoir, *Swinging Doors*. Here is an unvarnished Duluth life the likes of which you're unlikely to encounter on any other printed page. His unflinching willingness to recount in detail his failures in school, painful marriages, tough careers in baking and bartending along with a lot of drinking in Duluth's less polite establishments makes compelling reading."

—Jim Heffernan, author of *Cooler Near the Lake* (2008), a collection of columns originally written for the *Duluth News Tribune*. Heffernan's writing appears regularly in *Duluth-Superior Magazine*.

"If carousing and bonhomie were Olympic sports Mike Hampston would surely be a gold medalist. Whether brawling his way into a navy brig or making a booze-run on a seaplane, there are no half measures in the baker turned barman's vivid no-holds barred, yet frequently funny, slice of working class life."

—Seamus Kelters, BBC News Editor and co-author of *Eyewitness: Four Decades of Northern Life*.

"I laughed out loud at this funny, poignant and sweet book about a boy in Duluth and his road to becoming the man he is today. You will love this story! Big thumbs up!"

—Lori Barghini, co-host, *Lori and Julia Show*, broadcast on myTalk 107.1 (FM 107), Minneapolis-St. Paul.

"Mike Hampston's book is terrific. Who knew The Prince had such great stories and could tell them so well? I had several laugh-out-loud moments. Mike comes off as a genuine character with a remarkable group of friends as a supporting cast."

—Dick Daly, first General Manager of MPR stations in the Minnesota Arrowhead and the Michigan Upper Peninsula; former News Director and Anchor, KBJR Radio & TV (WDSM).

"'Writing is easy. All you have to do is sit down at your desk and slit your wrists.' Several writers are credited with that memorable statement but Mike Hampston would not be one of them. It's evident that Mike loved putting these memories on paper—tales that were not all fun and games but were a real part of who he is. No wrist-slitting here. He has so perfectly, so colorfully, so honestly captured the era. The Navy, bar and Desert Storm tales—so alive! And the later chapters—they capture the warmth and pure emotions of the events. Mike has written a book that brings to mind Woody Allen's *Radio Days* and Neil Simon's *Brighton Beach Memoirs*."

—Gregory A. Bonovetz, Senior Administrative Law Judge, State of Minnesota (Retired).

"I was impressed by Quinlan Michael Hampston's tolerance, even affection, for human frailty—and the absence of malice in his writing. Mostly, *Swinging Doors* is a book about the power of love and redemption in a life and a world full of hazard."

—Mark Salo, essayist and memoirist, Brisbane, Australia.

"I couldn't put *Swinging Doors* down and read into the wee hours of the night. Mike's wit and attitude carry the story. His crowd of characters brought me right into the book. I knew many of them as customers from my own bartending days in Duluth. Finally, his tale brought me back to Japan, where I hung out at the same bars a couple of years after Mike blew through. This book should go to the top of the charts."

—Neill Atkins, former Duluth City Councilor, talk show host 610 KDAL, Duluth, Minnesota.

I was shocked and pleased by the raw details of Hampston's life. I found myself rooting for him through the entire book. And his mother—what an amazing woman!

**—Susan Nash, Market Manager,
Midwest Communications, Duluth, Minnesota.**

MEMOIR

Swinging
DOORS

Quinlan Michael Hampston

Copyright © 2011 by Quinlan Michael Hampston.

All rights reserved, including the right to reproduce this book in any form, except for reviewers, who may quote brief passages in critical articles.

This story is based in part on actual events. Some incidents, characters and timelines have been changed for dramatic purposes, and may be composites.

FIRST EDITION · 2011

15   14   13   12   11   5   4   3   2   1

Library of Congress: 2011912241

ISBN 13: 978-0-9821405-5-0
ISBN 10: 0-9821405-5-X

Manufactured in the United States of America.
Designed by James Monroe Design, LLC.

Typeset using Livory, LHF Indian, and LHF Naylorville

For information about special purchases or custom editions, please contact:

James Monroe Publishing, LLC.
A Division of James Monroe Design, LLC.
7236 Bald Eagle Lane
Willow River, Minnesota 55795

www.jamesmonroedesign.com

For my mother, Marguerite

To my old friend
Ross Frarcier
(Mike)

Quinlan M. Hampton

Preface

A dozen or so premiere storytellers gathered on a late afternoon along a bar rail in Duluth, Minnesota. They were spinning one hilarious tale after another until everyone's sides ached with laughter. It was happy hour. Round after round of drinks were ordered up as each story, featuring the harebrained exploits of local friends and fellow carousers, topped the last one and the belly laughs just kept rolling.

One guy halfway down the bar wiped the tears from his eyes and insisted, "Someone should write this stuff down."

"Hey, Ray, you majored in journalism. You should write a book!"

"Maybe I will someday."

But someday never came, so it fell to me—the least likely and most ill-equipped guy of us all—to think, *Maybe I'll pick up a pencil someday and give it a go.*

When I told my wife about my cockeyed idea to write a book, she asked, "What will the title be?"

"*Swinging Doors*, and it will be about all the craziness that happens in the bar business. Maybe I'll throw in something about my life, both as a kid and then as a bartender."

A year or two passed. Now and then I would find a thick spiral notebook with "*SWINGING DOORS*" printed in a wavy blue graphic on its cover that my wife placed on the breakfast table along with a supply of orange mechanical pencils. I'd push it aside and grumble, "I can't fit that in right now—maybe some other time." More time would pass and there would be that damn notebook again. Then one long weekend, my bride was out of town and I was snowed in. She had left me a reminder by the coffee pot.

I opened the blue spiral notebook and picked up a pencil.

Book
one

1

New Year's Eve at the 402

I walked three or four steps behind my father down the stairs and through the swinging doors of the 402 Bar in West Duluth. It was New Year's Eve, 1948. I was five years old.

As Dad walked through the double doors, he let them swing behind him. Thankfully, I ducked underneath and avoided being bonked on my head. He was dressed in a black wool jacket with the collar turned up. His dark wavy hair glistened from the driving sleet we'd just walked through getting to the 402. Bar patrons arose almost on cue as if a movie star had just walked in.

"Johnny, Johnny!" they yelled. I remember thinking, *Wow, my dad must be a very important guy.* He was handsome and clever and easily drew people to him. Everyone wanted to be Johnny's friend.

My dad came to the 402 almost every day after work. This afternoon he moved directly to the bar for a drink. I hurried to stay close. Then suddenly, Dad's best friend Jimmy Murray scooped me up, put me on his shoulder and announced to everyone, "Here's Johnny's son, Loverboy, who last week I caught kissing the neighbor girl in John and Marg's back yard. A more lovable kid you'll never meet."

"Mike," he asked me, "will you have the usual?"

"Sure, Jimmy."

"Orange Crush and some cheese popcorn," yelled Jim to the bartender. George Schwartz, the bar owner, scooted around the waitress station to deliver my goods.

"Here ya go, Mikey my boy."

Dad was busy shaking hands and kissing girls and didn't even notice that I was having a swell time. My father's friends, one at a time, stopped to say hi, every one of them telling me what a terrific guy they thought Johnny Hampston was. Women with bright clothing and lots of lipstick tried to kiss me. I ducked as much as I could.

Friends quickly closed in around him and soon my dad forgot about me. I found myself sitting in a booth along the wall, looking around at the tiled floor stretched below a dome curved into the ceiling. It looked like a huge upside-down bowl with dim lights glowing behind its rim.

This was New Year's Eve, a very special night. Decorations and mistletoe hung over the dance floor and a set of drums sat ready at the back of the bandstand. Grown-ups were very excited—laughing loud and smoking and drinking. Even a little kid like me could feel the excitement.

I was really enjoying the party, but I was five and didn't have the staying power I would develop in years to come. After my fourth soda and my third bag of cheese popcorn, I curled up in my booth and went to sleep, my damp parka folded to make a lumpy pillow.

Somehow through the bar noise, I was awakened by a call from the barmaid. "John Hampston! Phone call. John Hampston."

I heard my father holler from the other side of the bar. "If that's my old lady, I'm not here."

I jumped out of my booth and ran to the barmaid to ask if it was my mom. She gave the telephone to me and remarked,

"You shouldn't be here anyway, kid. Here's your mom."

Pop took me home soon after the phone call. When we stomped through the back door into the kitchen, Mom wrapped her arms around me, gave me a big kiss, and helped me off with my boots and wet jacket. Hanging it near the register to dry, she scolded Dad about taking me into a bar. Soon tight-lipped words were met with hot responses and a full-blown argument erupted. Watching from the living room doorway were my siblings—Jack, a year-and-a-half older than me, and eleven-year-old Claudia holding the baby, Kitty.

Just as Jack started whining that he had been left at home and Kitty started wailing, Dad pushed by Mom and headed up the stairs, yelling, "Alright, Marg, alright, I won't take your 'dear little angel of the Lord' into any goddamn bar ever again."

It was a promise he didn't keep. On those few occasions when he did take me back over the next few years, Mom was kept in the dark. I was sworn to secrecy by the implicit threat that if Mom found out, I'd never again be permitted to be a part of that special society that existed in the taverns where guys gathered to drink, laugh, and tell dirty stories. So I kept quiet about it and soon enough, all too soon really, as my father drank more and enjoyed my company less, it all came to a halt. By the time I was ten, my father stopped taking me anywhere.

The bar life had made its mark on me. Even at a tender age I understood that there was a sort of magic there, and it wasn't just the booze that attracted all those people frequenting the bars, pubs, and saloons that my father loved so dearly. It was camaraderie—a feeling of belonging to something—that makes a person believe that life isn't just work and bills and day-to-day struggle. So I thought anyway, a wise-ass little kid who could hardly wait to be old enough to join the crowd of fun folks who had made such a great impression on me.

Decades later, I was a new owner of one of those magical places. On September 15, 1990, my old friend Ray Ward and I turned a key that opened the door to our saloon, R.T. Quin-lan's, in Duluth, Minnesota.

But before that happened, I had a lot of growing up to do.

A Hot Time in the West End

The late spring and summer weather is beautiful in northern Minnesota. If the wind cooperates and blows from the south or even from the west, the weather can be sensational.

It was one of those grand mornings in May when I came across a box of Diamond stick matches. I hid them in the pocket of my bib overalls and casually asked my mother if it was all right if I went over to my friend Dean's house. Dean was also five years old.

"That's fine, but don't go off the block and be back in an hour for lunch."

Dean Raymond lived directly across Chestnut Street from us and was my best friend. I looked both ways before I ran across the street and pulled up at the foot of the stairs to his house.

"Deeeean! Deeeeean!" I yelled at the bottom of their front steps. Nobody knocked on another kid's door in those days. You just stood in the yard and hollered his name. I heard his mother telling him to "stay close."

Dean came out. "What do you want to do?"

I whispered in his ear and told him what I had in my bib pocket.

"Oh, no! My mom will beat the tar out of me if I even touch

5

a match!"

"It'll be okay. I'm just going to start a little fire. Come on. Let's go down to the Jungle."

The Jungle was a wooded area about a block or so away from our house. It was my favorite place in the whole world with all the raw materials we needed to construct bows, arrows, sling shots, and rubber guns. It was also the perfect place for Tarzan swings. Because we were just kids and not jungle kings, at least one boy each summer suffered a broken arm from underestimating the distance between makeshift tree shacks.

Next to the Jungle was the Dump, a deep ravine where the city tossed dead Christmas trees. Both were places of endless fascination for any little troublemaker who had the courage to pass Old Man Pinski's house, perched at the edge of the Dump on one side and overlooking the Jungle on the other.

Old Man Pinski was also known to us as "Shaky Fred." I don't think we really meant to be disrespectful but we didn't understand his affliction, Parkinson's disease. It scared us so we steered clear of him and his one-eyed three-legged dog named Doc. We were as much afraid of that dog as we were afraid of shaky old Fred Pinski himself, yet the allure of a dangerous adventure often drew us as it did now, hearts pounding, sneaking through the Dump, past his house and into the Jungle, along a narrow creek bed.

Often the creek would be bone dry, as it was this day. Dean and I wandered along its banks searching for kindling and a likely spot to build our little bonfire. I took out the box of stick matches from my bibs, knelt down, struck a match against the box, and held the flame to our pile of twigs and leaves. Nothing. The leaves and sticks were too green.

Three more tries and I said, "Dean, this isn't working. I've only got two matches left and this stuff is never going to light. Let's go over to the Dump. We'll have better luck there."

We retraced our trail along the creek, emerged from the

Jungle, again swinging wide of Shaky Fred's house, and clambered up the slope. From there, we had a good view of the Dump, stretching out for a long block with at least a thousand dried Christmas trees lying below our feet. At its edge was the Skelly gas station on Superior Street; beyond were the Standard Oil and Como Oil storage facilities where a dozen oil containers took up the entire block. The perfect place for our project.

Once down in the ravine, we pulled one of the crispy dry trees from the pile and dragged it what we figured was a good and safe distance away from the mountain of other trees— about twenty feet.

As I prepared to strike my match, Dean asked me, "Mike, how are we going to put it out?"

"Oh, that's simple. We'll just pee it out." I let my match fly.

The tree started to burn, slowly at first, but then there was a sort of whoosh sound and the whole thing was engulfed in flames. Our eyes popped wide open. We looked at each other and both yelled, "PEE!"

There we stood, our little beanos in our hands, desperately trying to stop what we both knew was now beyond our control.

"I'm running out of pee!" cried Dean.

"Me, too!"

The fire raced through the quack grass seeking a new fuel source which it found about twenty feet away. One after another, dry trees went up like Roman candles, the flames shooting fifty feet in the air. Smoke billowed far higher and was caught by the wind. The fire was spreading—heading straight for the Skelly gas station.

"RUN!" I shouted.

As Dean and I struggled to the top of the hill, we heard the sirens—lots of them—coming from every direction.

Then I spotted mean Mrs. Nelson and her grown daughter, neighbors of Shaky Fred's. They had stopped hanging laundry on the line to watch the fire, and were now pointing at us.

Dean ran for his house and I ran for mine.

For an hour or more from inside the house, I could hear the wavy squeal of sirens. Then, our doorbell rang.

A policeman asked my mother for Michael Hampston, no doubt expecting a young thug as Mrs. Nelson must have described me. Mom asked them to wait. She found me hiding behind some coats in our kitchen closet and brought me by my hand to the front door.

Mother and I rode together in the back of a squad car to the police station where the fire chief and a bunch of policemen with stern faces told me that I had put many firemen in great danger and, furthermore, had cost the City of Duluth thousands of dollars to put out the blaze I had so recklessly started, apparently without the least regard for the catastrophe that I might have caused by starting that fire, not to mention the possible loss of life if the explosion...it went on and on.

Then they went into a huddle—the fire chief, the cops, and my mom.

I couldn't tell what they were saying. It was all whispering. When the huddle broke, the fire chief spoke.

"Well, it looks like we will have to send you to prison for about ten years, isn't that right?"

"Yes," affirmed one of the cops grimly. "Ten years is usually what we give in a case like this."

I started to cry. "Mama, please don't let them send me to prison!"

In fact, my sentence was reduced to a week's grounding, a good spanking, and a promise that I would never again play with matches.

I kept that pledge—until I was eleven and started smoking.

3

Confessions of a Sinner

I was a student in Sister Mary Ambrose's second grade class at St. Jean's Catholic School and very excited about the fact that in two short weeks, after what seemed like forever, I would finally receive my First Holy Communion.

The spring sun felt good on my face as I started home along Second Street on my six-block hike. I carried my catechism and my reader under my arm, being careful not to step on any cracks as I was concerned about doing any harm to my mom's back. Just as I was circumnavigating a big puddle, I heard footsteps rushing up behind me, fast and hard. I started to turn but it was too late.

I felt hands on my back and a big shove. The books went flying out from under my arm and I went falling straight into the mud puddle. Elbows and knees skinned up and bleeding, I looked up and saw Tom Leroux, the class bully, leaning against the fence in front of his yard, laughing at my humiliation. He had failed second grade the first time around and was older and a head taller than anyone else in the class.

I was crying as I picked up my books from the dirty water. They were ruined! I knew I'd be in trouble with Sister Ambrose for letting them get damaged. I threw them onto the grass along the curb and went after Leroux, which won me a punch

9

in the eye, but I came back like a tiger and went for his legs with enough force to knock him backwards into the water. We rolled back and forth, flailing away at each other with lefts and rights. Soon we were both crying and soaking wet.

Tom's mother came out of their house and pulled us apart. Leroux told his mother I had started it and she dragged me back to Sister Superior's office at St. Jean's where she demanded I be punished for attacking her poor little Tom.

I put up the best defense a seven-year-old could muster but was found guilty and sent home with a note to my parents about my vicious attack on innocent Tommy Leroux. My father was all for swift punishment but my mother stuck up for me even though she knew that she would have to pay for the replacement books; no small matter. Like most families in the West End, ours didn't have much money.

Sister Ambrose, who had witnessed Tom's playground behaviors, suspected that Mrs. Leroux had not given a proper account of the brawl in front of her house. She understood that Tom was a bully. I told her that Tom and the other kids teased me all the time about my unusual first name, Quinlan, and wished everyone at school would just call me Mike like they did at home. Sister told me that she would speak to Father Savoie about it, but regardless of the reason for the fisticuffs, she assured me that when I went to my First Confession, God would forgive all my sins and that I must not hold a grudge against Tom for that would also be a sin. I tried, but couldn't find a way to let it go. I was worried, and I would have to make my First Confession in a few days.

Waiting my turn that Saturday, I prayed that Father would give me absolution and that I would be forgiven for the ill feeling I felt toward my schoolmate. In the confessional, as I knelt, I heard the wooden door slide open, then the soft, slow voice of Father Savoie saying, "Yes, my son." I made the sign of the cross and began, "Bless me, Father, for I have sinned. This is my First Confession."

I listed and numbered all my sins as we were taught by Sister, explaining to Father my feelings of anger about the fight and what had happened as a result. His kindly voice promised that God would forgive me if I was truly sorry. I made the best Act of Contrition I could find in my heart and he absolved me of my sins. My penance was three Hail Marys and three Our Fathers and after I finished those prayers, I ran home—this time on the other side of the street from the Leroux house.

As I entered our kitchen, Mom was checking a cake in the oven. The screen door slammed hard just as she warned, "Don't slam the door!" The cake fell flatter than an ironing board. I looked at that fallen cake and blurted, "Oh, hell!" It took less than a second to realize that what I had just said was a sin on my recently cleansed soul. Before she opened her mouth to scold me, I burst out, "I'm sorry, Mom. I've got to go."

I flew down the back stairs through the yard and, turning on all the speed I had, raced down Second Street back towards St. Jean's Church. I stumbled up the concrete steps, breathing hard. Too late! Confessions were over. How in the world could I receive Holy Communion now? I had a sin on my soul.

I'm going to Hell, I thought, *or maybe Purgatory*. I wasn't sure what the sentence was for saying "hell," but I knew it was a sin, venial or mortal. I was positive, though, if I received the Body of Christ with this indiscretion on my soul and got run over by a bus before I could get back to confession, I would either burn in Hell for eternity or suffer in Purgatory until my family and friends could have enough Masses said to pray me out. I wasn't sure how many that was but I knew it was a lot and Masses cost money. I didn't think my father would spend much of his hard-earned cash on a filthy-mouthed little sinner such as myself.

I looked around for the priest but found only the parish janitor, Louie, in the church basement. "Have you seen Father Savoie, Louie?"

"I think he's over at the rectory."

I went out the front door and sat down on the steps of St. Jean's Church with my chin in my hands. I wasn't allowed to cross busy Third Street unless I was accompanied by an adult. So there I was, stuck until I could find someone to escort me over to the other side. After about twenty minutes my patience was beginning to wear thin when out of her house on the corner came Eddie Knutson's mother.

I ran down the stairs and told her that I needed to get over to the rectory and pleaded with her to help me. She took my hand and we went to the corner where she looked both ways to check traffic, and walked me across. I thanked her and dashed up the long stairs.

The rectory was a huge, old brick home with a large front porch. I reached up and pushed the doorbell. It gave a loud *bing-bong* but nobody came. I waited a minute or so and tried again. This time I got results. The big wooden door opened and towering over me was Mrs. Girard, a very tall, heavy-set woman.

"Yes? And what can I do for you, young man?"

"I would like to see Father Savoie, please, Mrs. Girard."

"Father is very busy," she said. "He's writing tomorrow's sermon and is not to be disturbed."

"Please, ma'am," and I started to cry. "I have to see Father. It's very important."

"Can't it wait until Monday?" she asked, her voice softening.

"Oh, no, that would be too late. I've got to see Father today!" By now, the tears were streaming down my cheeks.

"You wait here," she instructed. "I'll ask him if he'll see you." She disappeared into the rectory. I dried my eyes with my shirt sleeve and in a minute, Father Savoie came to the door.

"Yes, Quinlan. What can I do for you?"

"I need to talk to you, Father. It's about my confession."

"Well, come in and tell me why your confession could cause all these tears."

In Father Savoie's study there were two large, overstuffed leather chairs. He asked me to sit in one and when I had done so, he took the other. He gave me a long look over his glasses. "Now tell me, what is this trouble that has brought you to me so upset?"

I told him about the bad language I'd used when my mom's cake collapsed. He smiled gently and asked if I would like him to hear my confession again.

"Oh, yes, Father," I beamed. "Would you, please?"

"I'd be happy to," he replied. He got out his stole, put it to his lips, placed it around his neck, and made the sign of the cross. "You may begin, my son."

I made the sign of the cross. "Bless me, Father, for I have sinned. It has been one hour since my last confession." I then confessed to the bad word I had said and made an Act of Contrition even more heartfelt than the one I'd prayed earlier. Father granted me absolution and, giving me a penance of three Hail Marys, told me to go in peace. He removed his stole, kissed it, and put it back into the wooden box on his desk.

"Father, can I ask one more favor?"

"What is it, Quinlan?"

"Well, I can't cross Third Street by myself."

"All right," he smiled. "Come on." He took my hand and walked me down the front steps and across the street. In front of the church he told me sternly, "Now go home and don't get into any more trouble."

I thanked him and for the second time that day ran the six blocks from St. Jean's to our house on Chestnut Street, careful upon entering the house not to slam the screen door. I apologized to my mother for ruining her cake and went to wash up for supper.

That night I went to bed early with a sin-free soul, thanks to our kindly old parish priest. There would be many more sins to confess in the coming years but most were not brought to church for absolution.

Timmy Tyler

Going through my early life was difficult and school was torture. I was (and still am) severely dyslexic. When I was in school, dyslexia wasn't understood; most teachers and some parents diagnosed its symptoms as either stupidity or sheer laziness.

Bringing my report card home was a real knee-knocker. My dad would take one look at all the red marks on it and yell, stomp, and pound his fist on the table. Then he'd snarl, "Well, boy, you know what this means!" I wasn't always sure but "this" usually meant a minimum six-week grounding, plus whatever else he thought might make me "toe the mark!" Mom always stayed on my side and insisted that I was neither stupid nor lazy, but for all her love and protection, she usually was unable to derail the wrath of my father.

When I was ten years old, my older sister Claudia came to my rescue. She had an idea that not only saved my own self-esteem but also reassured my mother that her son had a bright mind in spite of his poor grades. Claudia was a copywriter for KDAL TV, our local CBS station, and one day she opened the door to my salvation. She asked me if I would like to host a Saturday morning cartoon show called, *Poppo the Clown*. With few of the necessary academic skills, I was very sure I would never be able to pull this deal off, but with Mother and Claudia's encouragement I agreed to try.

The following Tuesday afternoon, Claudia and the producer, Tom Cassidy, delivered my script. My immediate job was to memorize it by the end of the week. The first show was set to air live on Saturday morning. Mom helped me by reading aloud every commercial at least a hundred times and very late on Friday night, she looked me square in the eye and said, "Michael, you have all this material down pat and I am very, very proud of you."

Saturday arrived as I feared it would. Tom picked up Claudia and me and dropped us off at the front door of the Bradley Building on the southeast corner of Lake Avenue and Superior Street. Traffic was buzzing by and shoppers roamed the sidewalks of downtown Duluth. I stood for a minute, a knot in my stomach, looking up at the huge white building where I was to give my first performance. I was sure I would throw up.

"Come on, let's go," my sister called, pressing the button to summon the elevator. When the doors of the ancient contraption opened, there was Jenny, its operator, almost as old as the elevator itself. Wordlessly, she admitted us.

"Two please, Jenny." Claudia and I stepped into the elevator through huge iron gates, like the ones seen in old movies. The elevator chugged, ground, and bumped its way up to the second floor.

At the end of the hallway, past the unemployment office and beyond a set of glass doors, was the KDAL TV studio. In the production office, Claudia introduced me to several of her co-workers.

"This is my little brother, Mike!" Everyone was very nice, especially a handsome lady with ash blonde hair named Milly. I liked her instantly.

Someone stuck his head in the doorway and called to my sister and me, "So this our next TV star. Welcome aboard, kid." He told Claudia that things were just about ready in the studio.

"Mike," Claudia said, "you sit here and brush up on your copy. I'll come back for you in a few minutes."

I looked over my many pages of typewritten copy, six commercials in all, and once again was fairly sure I would puke. Where was the bathroom anyway? I wanted to run, quit, get the hell out of there, and was just about to bolt when Claudia and Tom came into the office. Tom, sensing my distress, tousled my hair and said, "Relax, kid, this is going to be a piece of cake. Come on. Let's just go do it."

We entered the studio. I was wide-eyed, rubbernecking around the room. The evening news desk was on one wall and next to that was Carl Casperson's weather tower. I was very surprised to learn that the tower wasn't really sixty feet in the air as it appeared on TV but built of six feet of plywood that stood on the floor inside the studio. One side of the room was lined with large windows of the control room where the director and engineers worked the magic of television. My set was a mock-up living room with a television set as the focal point. Tom got the cameraman into position and asked for the studio lights.

LIGHTS! Oh my God, what lights—blinding brilliant rows of lights pointed directly at my poor sensitive eyes. Almost anything would send a flood of tears down my cheeks. My older brother Jack loved to think of things that would open the floodgates. He'd smile and say, "Onions! Big yellow strong onions rubbed in your eyes!" or whisper in my ear, "Guys sticking their axle grease-filled fingers in your eyes!" The worst was, "Lemon juice squirting into your swollen red eyeballs!"

"Take it easy," said Claudia. "I'll get you some tissue. Don't worry. You'll get used to it." And to some degree, I did, but I must say that KDAL probably spent more money on Kleenex than on my talent fees during the months that we taped those shows.

With the waterworks temporarily controlled, Tom ran through how he wanted me to introduce the first show. Besides the introduction at the top of the show, there were six commercials for grocery products. I would do both the intro and the commercials, live, from memory. Once he was fairly confident that I knew what to do, Tom again asked the director for lights and camera. When everything was ready, he'd snap his fingers and that would be my cue for action. This was the final run-through.

At 10:00 straight-up, right after the station ID, the director rolled the titles and credits of the film, *Poppo the Clown*. Then studio cameras turned on and I got my cue.

Sitting cross-legged on a hunk of carpeting with the big old console TV in front of me, I was pretending that I had been watching Poppo, just like the kids at home. When the cue came, I turned from the TV, looked into the red light of the camera, beamed a huge smile, and announced to everyone in TV Land, "Hi, there! My name is Timmy Tyler!"

I put on my costume, a blue and white checked shirt, and got there on my own the following Saturday. Arriving at the Bradley Building that morning at precisely 8:00, I rang for the elevator but it didn't come. Then I noticed the sign—Out of Order. I took the stairs three at a time. Hurrying past one of the TV station offices, I heard a voice call, "Excuse me, son." I stopped and saw a small man, not much more than my size. "Are you Claudia Hampston's brother?"

I nodded my head. "Claudia is my sister. I'm Mike." He shook my hand and somehow I managed to get out, "Nice to meet you—but, I think I may be a couple of minutes late and I don't want Claudia and Tom to worry."

He gestured for me to come into his office. "Sit down, son, for just a moment. I'll make sure they know you're here." He dialed a number and I heard him say, "Milly, Dalton here.

Michael Hampston is with me. I wanted to have a few words with him before they get started today."

Mr. LeMasurier asked me how I liked my new job and the atmosphere at KDAL in general. He seemed particularly interested in the fact that I was reciting the commercials from memory. Most of the regular announcers read their copy off something called an "idiot sheet" he told me with a little smile. We spoke for a few minutes and then he said, "Run along now. It's been nice talking to you. Stop in any time. My door's always open."

In the following months the president of KDAL, Dalton LeMasurier, and I became good friends. I reported to him first on Saturday mornings and gave him a run-down on that week's work. He'd often ask his secretary to bring coffee for himself and hot cocoa for me. I sat on his immense oak desk, swinging my legs, drinking hot cocoa, and shooting the breeze. One time I heard some guy in the hallway grumble, "Claudia's brother is in there making points with the boss, I see."

The show was a hit with the Saturday morning cartoon set and throughout the Channel 3 viewing area, kids tuned in to watch the boy in the checkered shirt sell IGA grocery products and talk about the latest exploits of *Poppo the Clown*. Pretty soon, wherever I went, kids would say, "Hey, isn't that Timmy Tyler?" Once when Jack and I were at the movies, a kid came over and asked for my autograph.

Eight short months later, the show was cancelled and my days in the limelight were over. But Timmy Tyler had a good run—watching TV and being on television, drinking hot chocolate with a president, and making some nice bucks. For a while, I *was* somebody. But now my stardom was a thing of the past, and I returned to my regular life as an underachieving, dyslexic lump.

5

The Bike

One great result of my job at KDAL TV was that I got the courage to ask my parents if I could have a bike. I could take some of the money I earned from my TV gig. Pop said he would allow me to buy a used bike but only with the stipulation that I would also pay to have Jack's bike rebuilt and repainted. The rest of the money would go for school clothes in the fall.

I made a list of all the bike shops in Duluth and for the next month hopped the bus to each of them, plus a couple across the bridge in Superior, Wisconsin. Finally, after my third visit to Stewart's Wheel Goods, I saw it. The bike was blue and white with chrome fenders and red, white, and blue streamers on the handle grips. It was a Schwinn and the most beautiful thing I had ever seen in my life. I gave the man a five-buck deposit, carefully counting it out one dollar at a time.

Waiting for the bus, my head was swimming with anticipation over my new bike. Then a terrible thought came to me. What if Pop had changed his mind? He never had to work hard to come up with reasons why I couldn't do something. All the way home, I searched for answers I could say back to him and rehearsed them a hundred times, praying I would come up with just the right words when I needed them.

I also prayed that he would come right home after work

and not stop at the bar for drinks, knowing far too well that booze always put him in a foul mood, and if he came home with a load on, I didn't have a chance in hell.

I waited on the back steps for Pop's car to roll into the driveway, thinking how glad I was that it was yet two weeks until report cards were due. A bad report was one sure thing to blow me out of the water.

I waited and waited. It was already 3:30, and still no Pop. I figured by this time I was screwed. He was probably belly up to the bar at the 402 getting a snoot full. Then out of the corner of my eye, I saw his maroon 1940 Ford come around the side of Garon Knitting Mills at the end of the alley. I ran out to the driveway and when the car came to a stop, I was right there waiting for him. I gave him a long hard look trying to determine whether or not he had been drinking.

He switched off the motor, turned, and looked back at me. Then he smiled and asked, "What are you doing, knucklehead?"

Thank God, I thought. *He's sober.*

Stammering, stuttering, and boiling over with excitement, I told him about the bike and asked if we could take a drive to Stewart's so he could check it out.

"Maybe tomorrow," he said as he started to get out of the car.

Tomorrow? Oh, no! I thought, *Tomorrow is Friday. He'll get drunk and I won't have a prayer of ever seeing that bike again.* My father got drunk every Friday and the whole family dreaded the moment his shoe crossed the threshold on the back porch and all hell would break loose. I had to think of something quick.

"But Pop, the big sale ends today!"

Amazingly, my inspiration worked. "Well, okay. Let's run over there and take a look."

He caved! He caved! I couldn't believe it. I had never talked him into anything before in my whole life.

My father and the salesman settled on a price to include the refurbishing of Jack's bike and the next day I rode it to Stewart's Wheel Goods with one half of the money and a letter from my pop that listed what he wanted done with Jack's bicycle—paint job, brakes, new fenders—and better put on white wall tires and handle grips with streamers, and a mirror.

The bicycle repair guy said it could be done in a week and I could pick both of them up then.

The next week dragged by. I couldn't sleep. My appetite was shot. Mom was sure I was sick but I convinced her it was only that I was so excited about my bike.

When the big day came, my brother Jack and I boarded the bus heading downtown early so we could be at Stewart's when the store opened. In my pocket was the rest of the money I owed them. At the shop, the man checked my receipt. "Yup, they're ready," he said as he took my final payment. Handing me a new receipt—paid in full—he told us to go into the back and show it to the fellow there.

We walked past the counter, through the shop door and there they were. I had never seen such a sight; two beautiful, freshly painted bicycles with little white tags on them that read, "SOLD! HAMPSTON!"

Jack and I rode all over town that day. I was having the time of my life. At suppertime, we roared down our street and into our yard, threw down our kickstands, and ran into the house, shouting for Mom to come out and see our new prizes. She beamed a big smile and congratulated me. "You worked hard for that new bike, Mikey. Now take good care of it." She gave Jack a significant look and a nod that told him, "And that goes for you, too."

I promised Mom I would be responsible and went in to supper.

That night, as happy as I was, I had a foreboding feeling. The dreaded report cards would be out in a week and if I didn't show improvement, my father now had one more weapon in his arsenal to use as a punishment for bad grades—my Schwinn!

I knew for sure that a bad report card would mean losing the use of my prized possession. But I tried to put it out of my head and hoped for a miracle.

The next week I rode the wheels off that bike. From morning till night I cruised up and down the streets of Duluth, knowing that when I got my grades on Friday, it could come to a screeching halt.

It was 3:00 on the last day of school before summer vacation and the school was buzzing with electricity. Everyone felt it, except for me. I felt like a man on his way to the gallows. When Sister Rock passed out the report cards, mine came with a letter for my parents. My death sentence, I presumed. I mustered the courage to look at my card. It was just about the same with plenty of Ds and Fs although I did show some improvement in geography and history, scoring Cs in both, and a B in religion. The rest was not pretty, not unless you really like the color red. The letter to my parents informed them that I was to attend summer school for both arithmetic and spelling. Spelling! Me! Go figure.

Well, I was right. I was grounded to the house for two weeks and lost riding privileges for a month. I'd have to walk to summer school. The last thing my mom needed was an eleven-year-old boy underfoot for two weeks in June, but as usual, she cut me as much slack as she could; the two weeks ended up being only one. And miserable as I was, I took solace in the fact that eventually I'd have my wheels back.

Then one day, I walked in the back door to find my mother and Jack in the kitchen. Mom's face looked white. Jack ran upstairs.

Mother said, "Sit down, Mikey. I have bad news for you."

"What, Mom? Is Pop okay?"

"Oh, it's not anything like that, honey. Mike, I don't know another way to say this. Your bike's been stolen."

My heart sank to my stomach. "What?" I screamed. "How could that be? It's in the garage!"

"No, it isn't," she said. "Jack and Tommy Tester took both bikes to the YMCA to swim and when they came out your bike was gone."

"No! No!" I sobbed. "Geez, Ma, I only got to ride it for a week!" Mom hugged me and said that the police were sure to find it. But I knew better. I knew I'd never see it again.

That night when my father heard the news, he remarked, "Well, now he'll have more time for his school work."

Mom began to ask Pop if he would buy me another—but he cut her off. "He can earn money for the new one."

I don't think I ever forgave him. He didn't seem to care at all how heartbroken I was over the loss of that bike.

Schilla's Bakery

I never did get another bike, but turning twelve, I figured, what the hell, I'd have a car soon. So I got myself a paper route and started once again to save my dough, only this time I set my sights much higher than the lost two-wheeler.

In Duluth, Minnesota, in the 1950s, a newspaper route was not easy for a kid, especially in winter. During those months when the temperature sank to twenty-five degrees below zero, I rose at 5:00 a.m. seven days a week, and piled on many layers of warm clothing. I must have looked twice my size wearing all that padding as I marched out into the frigid morning. Five blocks up the hill I picked up my papers outside the IGA grocery.

I had sixty-five daily papers to deliver and ninety on the tough Sunday route. The strap from my newspaper bag dug into my shoulder as I climbed over snow banks and trudged along unshoveled sidewalks—a struggle for a smallish twelve-year-old carrying a full bag of thick Sunday papers. After one winter of this drudgery I became convinced that there must be a better way to turn a buck.

The following summer, as I was on my way home from Garon's Grocery with a sack of things Mom had ordered, a man standing in the doorway of Schilla's Bakery yelled to me,

"Hey kid!"

I turned and saw a heavyset man, forty or a little more, dressed in a white shirt, white pants and a white apron. He had a cigarette hanging out of the corner of his mouth. I stopped. "Yes, sir?"

"Ya want a job?"

"What kind of job?"

"Oh, just cleaning up the bakery after we get done for the day, usually about four hours."

"I don't know. I'd have to ask my folks."

That night, after supper, I told my parents about my conversation with Mr. Schilla, the baker. Mom was against it, saying that it was too hard a job for such a young boy.

"Aw, Mom," I said, "I was breaking my back hauling those Sunday papers up and down snow banks all last winter and no one ever said that was too hard for me."

Dad liked the idea. "It'll make a man out of him," he commented, lighting a smoke. Pop was forever trying to "make a man" out of me.

Even though my mother continued to have reservations, it was decided that I could take the job. The next morning, before the sun was up, I walked through the double screen doors that led me into Schilla's Bakery and the start of a career.

Mom was right, of course. The job was terribly hard. There were endless stacks of black pans needing to be scrubbed clean every day and huge mixing bowls to be scoured out. The floors had to be scraped on hands and knees with a wooden-handled bench scraper, then swept and mopped. Bread pans required greasing. Finally, the big bins had to be filled with flour, sugar, salt, and all the rest of the ingredients the bakers would need for the night's work.

During that summer, I got stronger; my hands were calloused from the endless scraping of the floor, and although it was physically exhausting work, I did my best. Ed Schilla, the bakery owner, was very nice. He told me that I was the best clean-up kid he had ever had, and raised my pay to fifty cents an hour.

I couldn't spend that much money. I was rich, rich, rich. But my success didn't come without strings, not in my family.

Five dollars a week! That's what my father decided I should pay to the family fund for my board and room. *Extortion!* I thought it, but I couldn't say it. My father was the law, so I paid him his pound of flesh—reluctantly, but I paid it.

I began to go to the bakery earlier and earlier. I enjoyed talking to Mr. Schilla and the other bakers. They loved to swear and whether they realized it or not, they taught me every filthy word in the book. I became proficient in cussing, a talent that came in handy throughout my life. The bakers also started to give me little chores that would make their jobs easier. I'd hear someone call out, "Hey, Mike, caramel the pans for caramel rolls," or, "Ice the Danish and cinnamon rolls and then scale bread loaves, would ya?"

I remember Mr. Schilla asking, "When do you go back to school, Mike?" He was planning my work schedule for fall.

"Tuesday, I replied, "but the Republicans don't start until Monday." You see, I was brought up in a very devout Catholic, DFL family and hadn't yet learned to distinguish the difference between a Republican and a Protestant, thinking they were alike and in the group of kids who didn't attend Catholic schools.

The sixth grade at St. Jean's wasn't any easier for me than all the previous ones. I dragged my way through each school day like a boy with cement in his shoes and an anvil on his back. When my school day was done, I would run to my job at the bakery where a guy didn't have to be good at English, math, or science. I just had to do my job. When bakers asked me, "How's it going?" I'd just shake my head.

"Hey, kid, I only went to the fifth grade, and look at me now," one of them might say, or, "Ya know, the world needs bakers, too!" Little did I know how these words would ring true for me for the next thirty years.

In the middle of a December night's sleep, our phone rang. Mom woke me, saying that Mr. Schilla wanted to talk to me.

"Einar has had a heart attack," Mr. Schilla said urgently. "He'll be okay but we're really busy here and I wonder if you can come in and fry doughnuts for me?"

I asked him what time, and he said he needed me right away. Mom had heard our conversation and she nodded in agreement. She'd tell my father when he got up for work in a few hours.

For the next several months, Ed Schilla and the other bakers taught me all they could about baking. I was a quick study and soaked in everything they threw at me. I was now thirteen and as accomplished as anyone who had spent two years in an apprenticeship program.

Sometime in June of that year, Ed himself was the one who was hospitalized. He died from a brain aneurism and his wife closed the shop. Einar and one other baker went over to Johnson's Bakery.

And when September rolled around, I went to public school feeling a new self-confidence. With my bank account full and a swagger in my step, I entered the uncertain but thrilling world of adolescence.

7

Three Hoods and Roxie

I started at Lincoln Junior High School in 1957 and probably wasn't the only student going through a teenage upheaval, but puberty hit me like a category five hurricane. Lincoln was boiling over with blossoming young girls in tight sweaters and skirts. I now stood a towering five feet six. I'd grown my hair and, with a formula of half Brylcreem and half butch wax, fashioned a jelly roll hair-do that rested big curls over my eyebrows. It was a D.A. (a "duck's ass") that would have made Gene Vincent, the singing heartthrob of all teen girls, jealous. That hair stood up against wind, rain, and snow with never a lock out of place.

I spent a good portion of my savings on a new wardrobe—black pleated wool slacks, one of those skinny silver belts, and shirts with silver or gold threads running through the cloth. But my coolest purchase was a pair of black loafers with white leather lightning bolts cut in along the sides, and...a black leather jacket. I was too cool for school!

I walked through the front door of Lincoln Junior with my leather jacket hooked on my finger and slung over my shoulder. Pretty girls in snug skirts wiggled by me hurrying to their first class. I smiled to myself and couldn't help thinking, *I am going to like this place.*

Going to junior high didn't improve my scholastic standing but my social life sure took off. It was generally known that at Lincoln you fell into one of three groups—jocks, brains, or hoods. I was athletic enough, but to be on any school sports team you had to have pretty good grades, and that wasn't going to happen. The brainiacs belonged to the student council, wore button-down collars and got straight As. So I was a hood! I tried my best to fit into my new group and found that I was a natural.

One of my classmates, Al Drang, was a kid who could have fit into any social circle. He was both very bright and athletic but Al chose to hang out with the hoods and it didn't take long before he and I became fast friends.

After school we hung out at the Korner Dairy Bar where we met the third part of our inner circle, Johnny Starkey. He looked like a rock star and girls were crazy for him. Johnny was more than a year older than Al and me, and he had dropped out of school. The three of us became inseparable. We played pinball, shot pool, and smoked a million Lucky Strikes.

At night we three would cruise up and down Superior Street in Johnny's 1939 Plymouth looking for girls. Johnny usually had two or three girlfriends on the line but he was always on the lookout for new talent. Although we dressed the part of really cool guys, Al and I were not in Johnny's league. We were still inept at talking to the opposite sex.

Al was first to attract a full-time girlfriend. Helen was a tall, willowy blonde with a pretty smile and friendly way about her. Soon he saw more and more of Helen and less of Johnny and me.

One Saturday, Johnny called me. "Put on your lightning bolts, pal, we're double dating tonight." He assured me that the girl he was fixing me up with was a knockout. They would be waiting for us at his best girl Janet's house.

Jan answered the door and invited us in. Seated on the couch was my date. She had inviting eyes and strawberry-blonde hair.

Right away I could tell she was built like a starlet. Slowly, slowly she unfolded long legs that had been tucked underneath her and stood up to meet me. It had quite an effect. She was at least five feet ten and Johnny wasn't kidding. She was a knockout.

"Mike," said Janet, "this is Roxie."

It took me a little time to catch my breath but finally I managed to stammer out, "Hi, there, stretch, how ya doin'?"

"Not bad. How 'bout you, shorty?"

Dancing at the Meth—the Methodist Church—that Saturday night was a pleasure and a challenge. It is quite a trick twirling a girl who is four inches taller than you. When it was time to spin her, I'd have to get up on my tiptoes. The slow dances were a hoot. I had to rest my head on her breasts as I hummed along with Bobby Vinton to "I'm Mr. Lonely."

After a few dates, we weren't just dancing and I learned the pleasure and pain of addiction. After having sex, my Amazon girlfriend would slap the crap out of me and cry that I had taken advantage of her love for me.

I just figured that she was nuts, but I thought, *What the hell! My old man slaps me around all the time anyway. At least with Roxie, I'm getting something out of it.* And I went back for more, as often as I could.

This went on for about a year and a half until two incidents brought it all to an end. The first was Roxie telling my parents we wanted to get married.

"Married?" my father yelled. "Get the fuck out of my house! Mike is only fifteen years old."

"Yes," argued Roxie, "but I'll be seventeen next week and we can get jobs and a little apartment."

"I told you to get the fuck out of here!" my father screamed again.

Mom remembers that she was so flabbergasted by Roxie's cockeyed idea that she couldn't speak. We were both taken aback by Dad's using a word we had never heard him say before.

The second event that brought about our demise happened later that afternoon. Infuriated by my father's enraged reaction to her marriage proposal, Roxie went berserk. She unleashed a barrage of left-and right-handed slaps to my head and face. It was plain scary and I thought, *Screw this*! and took off running. I never saw her again.

Linda and the Genius

Not long after the breakup with Roxie, I began to see a girl from school. She was sweet and cute, and closer to my own age. There were two other qualities that attracted me to her. She was a much more manageable size, five feet-two, and she wasn't given to violent fits of anger. Her name was Linda. She was the best friend of Al's girlfriend and Linda liked the four of us to go out together. A bonus was that Al and I got to see more of each other.

We went to dances, movies, and to the beach at Park Point. Linda was a good girl and only fourteen so I couldn't even try anything sexual; some kissing and holding hands was all that I could hope for. But I was older and having already tasted forbidden fruit during the time I spent with Roxie, I thought of little else. Morning, noon, and night, I was driven mad by the raging hormones that tormented my developing body. Some mornings I thought that I'd roll over in bed and pole-vault right into the closet. Linda was wise enough to know she shouldn't give an inch. After six months, she barely allowed me to approach first base. For the time being, that held me at bay.

At Christmastime, I turned sixteen. When September next rolled around, I enrolled for the third time in the eighth grade.

I know that sounds impossible but here's what happened. I flunked every class the first try. My second go at eighth grade was looking like a repeat performance. The first reporting period of that year showed straight Fs and Incompletes. I'd also logged twenty days of absence, quite a feat when you consider there were only six weeks in a report period. In a stroke of creative genius, I stole a blank report card out of a teacher's desk drawer and put myself on the B Honor Roll.

My parents were elated and for the rest of that school year, my father finally let up on me. But my scam, like my real report card, had failure written all over it. Just before the end of the school year, my parents received a call from Wayne Hammer, one of the vice principals at Lincoln Junior High. He wanted to see them.

"What the hell do you mean, failing?" Pop yelled and Mr. Hammer showed him and Mom the actual report cards my teachers had prepared.

Mom told me later that it was a good thing I wasn't there at the time because I surely would not have lived through it. That afternoon, when I walked into our driveway and saw Pop's car sitting there, I wondered, *What the hell is he doing home?* He was working the afternoon shift that week.

Jack sat on the back porch, a huge grin on his face.

"What's going on? Why's the old man's car here?"

He laughed and slapped his knee. "Little brother, you are so totally fucked."

"What?" I felt my heart sink and a lump blocked my throat. Jack chuckled. He loved to see me in trouble. I suppose he figured that as long as the old man's attention was turned on me, he could get away with anything he wanted.

"Your report card, asshole. The old man knows everything!"

After taking my ass-kicking all over the kitchen, I was banished to my room and told that I was grounded for the rest of my life. Mom brought me a couple of towels and some ice and began to apply them to my bloody nose and split lip.

'Sure, mollycoddle the little son of a bitch," Dad yelled from downstairs. "Dear little angel of the Lord, my ass!"

I spent most of that summer "under hack" with a few exceptions when Mom could manipulate my father and get some time for Linda and me to go to a movie or to her house for dinner. Sometimes, when Dad worked the afternoon shift, Linda and Al and Helen came to our house to play records or listen to the latest hits on WEBC Radio. We would move the front room furniture around to create a dance floor and rock and roll our hearts out. My sister Kitty loved to dance and always wanted to get in on our home-style rock 'n' roll parties. Despite my grounding, I had some good times that summer.

Soon it was September again and I was back at Lincoln Junior about to try for the eighth grade hat trick. I had become such a part of the school folklore that my fellow students were placing bets that once I was able to buy a car, I'd get my own spot in the faculty parking lot. A couple of the teachers actually called me "Uncle Mike."

Mr. Hammer had warned my folks that one more infraction of the rules and I'd be expelled.

And that gave me a great idea.

Wise Guys

The very next day I walked into the school office and asked to see Mr. Hammer. The secretary told me to sit and Mr. Hammer would be with me shortly. I was very nervous. I was pretty sure that the stunt I was about to pull had never been done before.

The door to Mr. Hammer's office opened and he walked out and over to the secretary's desk.

"Yes, Mrs. Brannigan, what is it?"

She pointed me out. "This boy would like to see you, sir."

He strode over to me, stopped and asked, "What do you want, Hampston?"

I stood, looked him in the eye and did the last thing he ever would have expected. I reached into my shirt pocket and came out with a pack of Lucky Strike cigarettes, popped one into my mouth and lit it. "Mr. Hammer, there's a couple of things I'd like to get straight between us."

His eyes went wide. His jaw dropped. He started to say something but couldn't seem to get any sound to come out. He reached out and snatched the smoke from my mouth, threw it on the floor and stomped it out.

"You! Into my office!" He pushed me through his office door and slammed it, pulled the shade and charged. I sidestepped him and the roundhouse he threw missed. Unfortunately for me, the next two didn't but I shook it off. Hell, he didn't have nearly the punch my old man had.

"Mr. Hammer, you hit me again, I'll defend myself."

"You're expelled!" he screamed. "Sit there and don't move a muscle!"

He strode out the door and was back in three minutes, shoving an expulsion notice into my face. "Now get the hell out of here and if I ever see you around this school again, I'll have the law on you."

I walked out the front door of Lincoln Junior High, and half-way down the stairs to the sidewalk, turned around to see Mr. Hammer standing in the doorway with his hands on his hips. I guess we were both thinking, *Good riddance,* probably the only thing we ever agreed on. As I headed down the street toward Lincoln Park, I thought to myself, *Well, Michael my boy, that's it for school. If you want to learn anything more, you'll have to learn it on your own.*

Curiously, Pop didn't seem very upset when Mom broke the news that night. I think he saw it coming and I think that he was embarrassed to have a nitwit son who was spending his third year in the eighth grade. He merely said, very matter-of-factly, "You have thirty days to get a job and start paying board and room or I'll kick your ass out into the street."

I found some work with a man named Krashinsky who owned a truck and picked up loads of flour at a railroad siding and then delivered them to the big Master Bread plant. So four days a week, I lifted, hauled, and threw hundred-pound sacks of flour from eight in the morning till four in the afternoon. After work I would come home dog-tired, eat supper and go right to bed. Pop raised my room and board from the five dollars a week I had paid him during the Schilla bakery days to twenty. I only made ten bucks a day, and giving my father half of what I made by busting my ass ground on me. But I still had a double sawbuck for myself every week and for the first time ever I was out from under the misery of the report cards that had tormented me all my life.

I'd always looked forward to Friday nights. Now I liked them even better. The whole day was mine. There was no flour pick-up and Linda had to babysit on Friday nights. It was my night to howl and I could start as early as I liked.

One particular Friday in the second week of December—a very warm day for that time of year—I met Johnny and Al for a lunchtime burger at the Korner Dairy Bar. Over a game of pool and some Cokes, a brilliant plan was devised. Al, the only one of the three of us still in school, had given himself a day off and he'd had a brainstorm.

"Today is steel plant payday. With Christmas coming, the West Duluth bars will be nuts. Here's my plan. When the steel plant changes shifts at 3:00, we'll be ready for action. Mike, you and I can dress up in our dads' work clothes. Johnny's got his own from the gas station. Then we'll slip into the Kom-On-Inn, belly up to the bar and have a few beers."

"You must be nuts. Johnny looks old enough 'cause he's eighteen, but we look like we're twelve."

"No sweat," says Al. "They'll be so busy, if you reach the bar they'll give you a drink."

And so it happened that on the second Friday of December, two weeks short of my seventeenth birthday, I walked through the swinging doors of the Kom-On-Inn. Al was right. It was perfectly easy. The place was packed to the hilt. We squeezed and pushed our way to the bar where the barmaid, a little on the chubby side, flashed a smile at Johnny. "What'll it be, handsome?"

"Three Schlitz and three shots of bar brandy," replied Johnny. Obviously, he'd done this before.

Just then a booth opened up. Al jumped in and signaled for us to follow suit. Johnny asked the barmaid if she would deliver the drinks. "Sure thing, good-lookin'." She brought a tray with our three beers and three shots. Johnny paid her and added a quarter tip. She thanked us and scurried back to the bar.

Al laughed out loud. "I told you, Mike. She didn't even think about asking us for an I.D."

We toasted Al for coming up with a great idea and soon all three of us were well on the way to getting plastered. A couple of drinks later, Al and I were out in the parking lot projectile vomiting, with Johnny spitting in disgust. "Jesus Christ, you guys. I thought you were tough."

We went back into the bar and cleaned ourselves up a bit in the men's room. Al looked in the mirror. "I'm going home, guys. I've had it."

Under the threat of death if Al puked in his car, Johnny agreed to drop him off at his house. "I'll see you guys tomorrow," muttered Al as he got out of the car. We watched as our mastermind zigzagged his way up the stairs to his front door.

I was feeling a little better so Johnny and I cruised around for a while until he stopped in front of his house, telling me to wait in the car. He went around back toward the garage and reappeared a couple of minutes later. Johnny opened the trunk and put something in it before he got back into the car.

"Ya got any dough?" he asked.

I fished around in my pocket. "About five bucks. Why?"

"I've got an idea how to make some quick easy cash. But first we're gonna make a little trip to the hardware store." He turned the key and shifted into first gear.

I should have had a bell or a whistle or a warning light go off in my head at this remark, but I was always interested in making a quick buck and with the brandy and beer still buzzing in my brain, I probably wouldn't have noticed if an alarm had sounded anyway. So I only asked, "Yeah? How?"

"Parking meters."

"How do you figure to do that? You got a key or something?"

"I've got something just as good as a key," he smiled. "I've got a hacksaw."

"You've lost your goddamned mind."

"No. No. It'll work. Listen! We pick a quiet street. We take turns keeping watch while the other whacks off a meter. Then we move to another part of town and do the whole thing over again. It can't miss, and by morning, we'll be rich."

"Got any extra blades?"

"That's what we're gonna get right now."

If Paul Newman had made the movie *Cool Hand Luke* a decade earlier than he did, I probably wouldn't have gone for this nutty idea. But when you add booze, stupidity, poor judgment and greed together, you've got a formula for belief in the success of pulling off the perfect crime. That's what we figured.

Our prowl through West Duluth brought us to a perfect spot where some streetlights were busted out and we went to work. The job was much harder than we had anticipated. It took at least a half-hour before the first meter clanked to the curb. Johnny threw it in the back seat and we sped off in search of our next hit.

By midnight we had eleven parking meter-heads wrapped up in a blanket and we were running low on hacksaw blades. The booze had all but worn off by now. I was worn out from all the sawing and had a raw blister on my right hand. Johnny suggested hauling the meter-heads to Lincoln Park to bust them open. Three hours later, having exhausted ourselves and our supply of blades breaking the locks on ten of the eleven meters we called it quits and headed to an all-night restaurant where we could count our loot.

Under the harsh fluorescent lights of the Greyhound Bus Depot café, we regarded a pitiful pile of pennies and nickels. The meters had apparently been emptied earlier in the day. After counting our haul we found that, minus the expenses—hacksaw blades and burned up gas—our grand total put us fifty-four cents in the hole.

"Next time, Johnny," I said, "let's just burn our money and go home to bed. That way we won't have to work our balls off and we'll get a good night's sleep to boot."

Johnny just gave me one of his big, toothy grins and said, "What the hell, we had fun, Mike. What are you bitching about?"

When we pulled away from the curb in front of the Greyhound building it was close to five in the morning. Johnny squealed his wheels as he always did, probably not the smartest thing to do on a deserted downtown street at the crack of dawn. From a block behind us I heard a siren and turned to see the red lights flashing. As Johnny pulled over, I yelled, "Where's the eleventh meter?

"It's in the back seat on the floor covered with a blanket."

We looked at each other, panic stricken. "WE'RE FUCKED!"

10

Devil or the Deep Blue Sea

Johnny Starkey was tried in adult court and sentenced to six months at the county work farm. There was no Juvenile Hall or its equivalent in Duluth in 1959 so I was put into Cell Three on the second floor of the St. Louis County Jail. That was the longest weekend of my life. The lukewarm beans with baloney sandwiches on stale bread brought twice a day sure didn't stack up to my mother's cooking. The cell was damp and cold and the one dirty blanket and flat, used-up pillow didn't give me much comfort.

But my personal discomfort and anxiety were nothing compared to my worry for my mom. She had stood by me and protected me from my father's wrath all my life, and now I knew she would have to endure his ranting, raving, fist-pounding fury because of me.

Monday morning, still wearing my dad's work coveralls, they brought me down by elevator from my second floor jail cell and into the sheriff's office. Mom was there and I could tell she had been crying. Another pang of guilt shot through me as she stood and came toward me with outstretched arms.

"Michael, Michael!" She cried. "Are you all right? Did they give you enough to eat?"

Mom always figured a good meal could fix just about

41

anything and the first thing she would ask anyone who came to our house was, "Are you hungry? Can I fix you a bite?"

"Yes, Mom, I'm fine." The deputy told me to sit down on the bench where she had been sitting, saying a bailiff would be there soon to escort me to the courthouse across the street. He instructed my mother to go to the courtroom on the third floor, where the judge would convene court proceedings at 9:00.

The bailiff marched me and several other juvenile offenders, handcuffed, across the street and up the stairs to the third floor. We filed in and took seats in the front row where we were instructed to sit until His Honor entered through the door behind the massive oak bench.

"When the judge enters, I will say 'All rise' at which time you will all stand until I tell you to sit," announced the bailiff.

I saw my mother sitting with the other parents, red-eyed, and once again felt the weight of my guilt. The judge entered and when the bailiff barked, "All rise," we stood in unison.

One at a time, the judge heard complaints that had been filed against the other boys who were being prosecuted and one after another, he sentenced most of them to the State of Minnesota Reform School at Red Wing, a couple of hundred miles from Duluth on the Mississippi River. Some got probation. Mine was the last case to be heard and by the time he had finished dealing with eight or nine other juvenile delinquents before me, it seemed to me the judge was fed up with teenaged evildoers and ne'er-do-wells. He would throw the book at me, I was certain.

"The chair," I imagined dramatically. "He's going to give me the chair!"

As he finished with the case before mine, his gavel banged on the desk. To me it sounded like the falling blade of a guillotine removing some poor unfortunate's head, probably for a lesser offense than knocking over parking meters.

The bailiff's voice boomed loudly. "The City of Duluth vs.

Quinlan Michael Hampston." He motioned for me to rise. I stood up and the judge told me to approach the bench. I stood before him, shaking a little, and waited. With his glasses on the end of his nose, he read through the police report, drummed his fingers on the desk, and after what seemed like an eternity, took off the glasses, pushed the papers aside, and cleared his throat.

Pointing to the stack of paperwork, he spoke. "It says here that you and some fool friend of yours sawed off eleven parking meters. Is that correct?"

"Yes, Your Honor," I heard my voice squeak.

"I guess I feel compelled to ask, what in the world were you were thinking?"

I was fairly sure that I would be on the bus to Red Wing that afternoon, but suddenly I felt a calm come over me and I answered in a friendly kind of way, "Well, Your Honor, it seemed like a good idea at the time."

A chuckle echoed through the courtroom. The judge's gavel fell. He glowered menacingly. "Don't get smart with me, you little punk."

I apologized and he asked me if either of my parents were in the room. "Yes sir, my mother's here."

Mom rose and he asked if she would please approach the bench. Again, he perused my paperwork. After some time, he asked, "Mrs. Hampston, are you having trouble handling Quinlan at home?"

"No, sir. He is a sweet boy and he has always been very cooperative."

"Well, due to the fact that he hasn't been in trouble before, I wouldn't want to send him to Red Wing. However, he has dropped out of school. Is that correct?"

Mom nodded sadly. "Yes it is, Your Honor."

"The boy is on a fast track to prison," said the judge, "and something must be done! I see here that his seventeenth birthday is coming up soon."

"Yes, on Christmas Day."

"Well, he went on, "if you and the boy both agree to his entering the military service, I will forego a term in the reformatory, provided that he is on a bus on his way to boot camp by New Year's Day."

Whew! At least he didn't say, "by sundown."

Again his gavel banged and I was instructed to go with the bailiff across the square to the recruiting offices where, as the judge had said, I could pick my poison. He gave the bailiff an envelope for the recruiter of whichever service I selected. Mom and I followed the bailiff from the courtroom in a somber mood. Besides dealing with my sentence to military service, she and my father would have to make restitution for half of the parking meters Johnny and I destroyed. I knew that would go over like a lead fart with the old man, but I promised Mom I would repay them when my military checks started coming in.

At the Federal Building, the bailiff asked me, "Which one will it be, kid?"

"Marines," I said without hesitation. I'd always thought the Marine dress uniforms—blue and red with the white cap—were very cool. Besides, *Sands of Iwo Jima* was one of my favorite movies and I always fancied myself kind of the John Wayne type anyway. Into the Marine recruiting office we went.

The staff sergeant behind the desk looked up and said to the bailiff, "Another one, huh, Bill?"

"Yup. You're doin' good business today."

The sergeant gave me the once-over and asked, "How much you weigh?"

"I'm 125 pounds."

"Forget it, kid. We take men, not babies. There's a height and weight requirement and a half-pint 125-pounder like you won't make it. Why don't you try the Navy?"

The Navy recruiter was much more agreeable. He read the note from the judge waiving any aptitude tests recruits were required to pass before entering the Navy and nodded. Looking up, he gave me an unimpressed appraisal as he handed me a thick stack of papers to fill out and sign.

Nine days later, on December 27, I slid into a rear passenger seat, happy and relieved to be making my jail break, not from Red Wing but from my father's house. I was on a Greyhound bus going up Thompson Hill, with Duluth and my checkered past disappearing out the back window.

Book
two

11

Boot Camp

Looking out the airplane window down through puffy white clouds I could see the hills surrounding San Diego. It had been a tiresome journey first by bus and then by plane, but now a kind of electricity started running through me, an excitement mixed with fear, uncertainty, and joy.

A bus for the Naval Training Center (NTC) picked me up along with the other young men outside the terminal and rolled out to the access road that serviced the San Diego International Airport. The bus driver told us we would be at NTC in about ten minutes and pointed out several interesting sights along the way. I had never seen palm trees before. They were more beautiful than I had imagined.

Arriving at our destination, the bus slowed to a stop outside the main gate and a guard stepped aboard. "I have twelve recruits for receiving," the driver announced. The guard glanced at the passengers, hopped off, and the doors closed. We proceeded through a tall arch, anchored on each side by a yellow adobe guardhouse. Coming to a building marked Receiving & Outfitting, we filed off to be greeted by a large sign that read:

WELCOME ABOARD
YOU ARE NOW MEN OF THE UNITED STATES NAVY

A chief petty officer in dress blues, with his hands folded behind his back, barked out the order for us to form a straight line in front of the bus by height, from left to right. There I was on the end, 125 pounds of twisted steel and sex appeal, proud to be a member of the US Navy.

He called us to attention and I did my best impression of Gary Cooper standing at attention for the commanding general in the movie *Sergeant York*. As the chief paced back and forth in front of us, I thought how glad I was that I had recently applied some fresh Brylcreem and butch wax mixture to my hair. First impressions are very important. My jelly roll lay perfectly in the center of my forehead and I was sure that the chief would be impressed with my good grooming.

He started on the left with the tallest man, asked him his name, where he was from and welcomed him into the Navy. The chief repeated this, moving down the line with each new recruit. "What's your name, son? Where ya from? Welcome aboard." Expecting the same, I prepared the answers in my mind. As he approached I popped out my chest, my thumbs pointed straight down the seam of my trousers, and went over my answers in my head. "Hampston, Sir. Duluth, Minnesota, Sir. Thank you, Sir." I was ready.

Chief Willis M. Flynn stopped in front of me, his teeth set tight in his lantern jaw, his steely blue eyes boring into me as if he were trying to figure out just what the hell I was.

There was no "What's your name, son?" No "Where ya from?" No "Welcome aboard."

"Well," he said after a long silence, "and just why has the Department of the Navy chosen to send me a greaseball midget?"

The answers I had ready were gone.

"Answer me! I asked you why the hell you're here, punk!" he shouted.

"Well, sir," I choked, "the judge said I had to go to reform school or to the military."

"And why was the Navy so lucky as to land a prize catch like you?" he demanded, his eyes narrowing and veins popping out in his neck.

A shudder ran through me. I had been off the bus ten minutes and had already made an enemy of the Navy's equivalent of Wayne Hammer. So I said the first thing that came to mind. "I couldn't get into the Marines," I replied.

His eyes opened wide, his face flushed a crimson red. "You smart aleck, greasy, midget bastard! I'm going to personally see to it that you never graduate from this training center and you are put back on a bus to your mommy!" he screamed.

So all in all, my first day of boot camp went pretty well.

In the next few days, more recruits poured into receiving and outfitting and when it was deemed we had reached the correct number, Company 090 was formed. Company petty officers were picked. Naturally, I wasn't to be chosen but then again, I had tried to stay under the radar and was just happy to have survived that first day.

Clothing issue came next; then haircuts. I didn't really mind watching my curly locks hit the floor. My hair had gotten me in trouble from the moment I arrived and I was already a little tired of the name "Greaseball" that Chief Flynn had bestowed on me. With my head shaved and my acne in full flower (probably due to nerves), I appeared to be about twelve and stuck out in formation like a small sore thumb.

During one inspection, Chief Flynn's assistant company commander stopped in front of me with a look of disbelief and asked, "You in the Navy, kid?"

"Yes, sir!"

"Ours or theirs?"

"Well, ours," I stammered.

As he moved down the line of sailors I heard him say, "Un-fucking-believable."

I wasn't aware until much later that it is a common practice for company commanders or drill instructors to pick out the weakest, smallest, most unlikely boot camp recruit and ride him as hard as possible to break his spirit and make him quit. The theory is if they can make this weakest link into a sailor, the rest will fall right into line. And if they can't, good riddance! Either way, the chief's job becomes much easier.

Most of the other guys didn't seem to mind the horseshit treatment I got. I suppose they were just happy that they hadn't been singled out to be the goat. But there was one thing I knew that Chief Flynn didn't. There was no way in hell that I was getting on a bus heading home to go back under my father's thumb. If they wanted me gone, they would have to kill me and ship me home in a body bag.

Chief Flynn picked a clone for his recruit chief petty officer (RCPO). They had the same steely blue eyes and the same square jaw. Hell, he could have been the chief's son and no one would have been surprised. His name was Wendall R. Hutchings, Jr. and he was a twenty-four carat prick. When Flynn wasn't on my ass, Hutchings was right there to take his place. Hutchings was one of those football-captain, prom-king, class-president assholes I might have run into in high school—if I had ever made it to high school. Between Flynn and Hutchings, my life in boot camp wasn't much fun. So I did the only thing I could do. I lowered my head, dug in my feet, and with the tenacity of a pit bull, I hung on.

With my newfound stubborn streak, the next few weeks got a little easier. Although Flynn and Hutchings still rode me hard, I muddled through, studying the Bluejackets Manual in the head until all hours. I labored over my locker prior to inspections—one small mistake would have me with my M1 over my head circumnavigating the parade ground at double time.

My mistakes became fewer and fewer. Although most days I would screw something up, even Chief Flynn noticed a difference in me. Then service week came.

Each company of recruits, in its fifth week of training, was required to provide some sort of service to the NTC. The company commander assigned each recruit his job. It might be mowing lawns, messenger duties, buffing floors or galley work. Chief Flynn had saved a very special job for me.

When all the other recruits in Company 090 had received their envelopes containing their assignments, Chief looked at me with something like a smile but more like a sneer and said, "Come with me, Hampston."

The chief's car was parked outside the barracks. "Get in the car." I got in.

As we sped away from the barracks, he began to hum some undistinguishable tune. This worried me. Hearing the chief hum seemed like a prelude, kind of like the warning of a rattlesnake's tail. He drove to the back of the gigantic number one mess hall, parked the car and snapped, "Get out and follow me."

We entered the galley through double screen doors at the back of the building. Chief shot me a look and ordered, "Wait here." The galley was enormous. It fed 15,000 men every meal. Cooks and mess cooks by the dozens zipped by me as I watched Chief Flynn cross the galley and open a glass door marked Commissary Office. Five minutes later he came back accompanied by a fat man dressed in whites. Chief was laughing and I was pretty sure that wasn't a good sign. I hadn't seen the mean bastard smile before, much less let loose with a belly laugh like I'd just heard. He motioned me to come and I hurried across the galley, stopped and stood at attention. "Yes, sir."

"Hampston, this is Chief Ballbricker. You will work for him." He shook Chief Ballbricker's hand, turned, and walked out the back door.

Ballbricker spoke briskly, "Follow me."

"This," he explained, "is the grease pit. The run-off in this pit comes from the scullery where the food trays are rinsed after every meal. Your job is to load up the slop down there into those buckets." He pointed toward a line of pails along the scullery wall. "Haul them up and empty them into the truck you find outside. It's easy to spot, marked Kelly Garbage Service. Any questions?"

"Do I have to get right down there into that stuff, sir?"

"Unless you can find a way to get it to come up to you," he snickered. "In this locker you will find hip boots. Remove your shoes first. That grease will eat up a pair of shoes in no time flat. You can store your leggings and shoes in the locker. There are also a shovel, broom and swab in there. When you have emptied the pit, it must be swept and swabbed out until it's shiny clean. Understood?

"Yes, sir." Suddenly, I was wishing I had never lit up that Lucky in Mr. Hammer's office.

"Now get to work. I'll be back in a while to check up on you." He strode away.

Now, there's possibly a shittier, dirtier job in the world, but for the life of me, I can't think what it could possibly be. For the next seven days I stood up to my waist in the most vile muck you could imagine, twelve hours a day. Then when my day was done, I worked for hours on the cement scrub tables outside the barracks trying to get the grease and grime from the pit out of my clothes.

I survived the week-long grease trap ordeal but my dungaree uniforms unfortunately didn't fare as well. The repeated scrubbing and re-scrubbing had taken most of the color from them and the navy blue pants that had been issued to me were now a pale powder blue. My light blue dungaree shirts had turned almost white.

The following week, Lieutenant J.G. Jennings, Battalion Commander, conducting an inspection tour, moved through the ranks, noting discrepancies and infractions the sailors had committed as he went. When he got to where I stood at attention, he paused, looked me up and down for what seemed like a very long time and asked, "How long you been in the Navy, son?"

"Five weeks," I answered.

"What in God's name has happened to your uniform?" he asked in bewilderment. I explained the beating my uniforms had taken under the scrub brush.

"Are all your dungarees faded like this?" he quizzed.

"Yes, sir."

The battalion commander turned to Chief Flynn. "How long did this recruit spend on grease-trap duty?"

"Seven days," responded the chief.

"Chief, report to me in my office immediately after this formation."

"Yes, sir."

As it turned out, a recruit was only supposed to be assigned to clean grease-traps for one day and then only as punishment for a serious infraction of the rules.

The next day I was sent back to receiving and outfitting for a new issue of dungarees. The only trouble was that now, after five weeks of washing, the rest of the company's dungarees looked faded compared to mine which were brand new. I still stuck out in formation. So there I was, back at the scrub table, working my ass off trying to get my uniforms to match the others.

I think Chief Flynn must have gotten *his* ass chewed out because he and Hutchings both let up on me. I started to blend in. My work clothes were the right color. My seamanship tasks seemed easier and I began to think maybe I'd live through boot camp after all.

12

Freedom

Liberty call came the following Saturday. At the end of the sixth week of training, recruits who earned the privilege were granted a twelve-hour liberty in San Diego.

At 11:00 on the Saturday morning after my sixth week, my cousin Gail Jacobson who attended Santa Monica City College and one of her girlfriends picked me up along with my shipmate Marvin Maxwell who hailed from Mankato, Minnesota.

I hadn't seen a girl for six weeks and was very taken with Gail's friend Judy. She was tall, blonde, and as pretty as girls can be. I remember fantasizing over this lovely California co-ed but somewhere in the back of my mind I had a flashback of everything that had happened with Roxie and decided that perhaps it wasn't a good idea to pursue her. *Geez,* I thought, *maybe they all kick the hell out of you after sex.*

Marv and I were now trained sailors but we were still teenagers and we spent a terrific day of fun with Gail and Judy at Mission Beach Amusement Park riding the roller coaster and eating hot dogs.

The liberty ended too soon. When the girls dropped us off at NTC at 10:30 that night, Judy gave me a little kiss goodbye. Marvin talked Gail into a brush of the lips as well and then they drove off, leaving us waving "so-long" at the front gate.

The last three weeks of naval recruit training passed without incident and suddenly it arrived. Graduation day!

We stood in formation as Chief Flynn passed by each sailor congratulating him and shaking his hand. I couldn't help thinking of that first day getting off the bus at receiving and outfitting. When the chief stood in front of me I thought to myself, *I did it! I did it! I beat the son-of-a-bitch!*

"Well, Hampston," he said, "I finally made a sailor out of you. Congratulations and welcome to the Navy." He stuck out his hand. I took it and felt that he was sincere. Unexpectedly, I smiled. "Thank you, sir."

"Chief! You don't call me sir anymore, Hampston. You're a sailor now. You call me chief."

On the parade ground, as we passed in review, Hutchings barked out, "Eyes right!" and 120 heads of Company 090 snapped right. I couldn't believe my eyes. There on the podium stood Chief Petty Officer Willis M. Flynn, his steel blue eyes gleaming and wearing the biggest shit-eating grin I had ever seen.

Well, I'll be damned! I thought. *Isn't life a mystery?*

I had fourteen days' leave but the fifty bucks a month I earned in boot camp wasn't enough for round-trip airfare home, so the three-day bus ride half-way across America was my only option.

At the Greyhound Bus Depot, the baggage man reassured me, "Don't worry, sailor, there'll be no snafu on my watch. I'm putting your bag on the right bus." I stopped at the gift shop and bought two packs of Luckys and a magazine, *San Francisco, the City by the Bay*, then jumped aboard.

We drove past the road to the airport and I saw an NTC bus heading to the training center. Man, did I feel sorry for the poor, pimple-faced, runt-of-the-litter, son-of-a-bitch who was about to step off that bus and be selected as Chief Flynn's new goat. I sat back, chuckling to myself as we headed east out of San Diego. I pulled out my duty orders from the large manila envelope on my lap and read that I was to report to the USS *Vesuvius* (AE-15) anchored in Port Chicago, California by 1800 hours on March 15, 1960.

I lit a smoke and opened my magazine to see what it could tell me about my first port of call. Port Chicago was located ninety miles upriver from San Francisco, just past the beautiful island of Alcatraz where I surely would have ended up if Chief Flynn had been successful in his effort to drum me out of the Navy. There were several other promising tourist attractions I might explore when I came back to join my ship. Until then, I was a sailor on leave.

The trip home was uncomfortable but after basic training, I wasn't used to much comfort anyway. To relieve the boredom, I slept as much as I could and made the best of it. Three days later we made the last passenger pick-up at Hinckley, Minnesota, the half-way mark on the Minneapolis-to-Duluth run, where we were told we would have thirty minutes for breakfast.

I grabbed a cup of coffee and a piece of apple pie and went into the head to clean up and do the best I could with my rumpled uniform. I wanted to look squared away when I saw my family. There were just seven of us passengers traveling the last leg of the trip to Duluth so I made my way to the front and sat by the driver.

"Going home on leave, huh?" he asked.

"Yes, sir. I just graduated from boot camp and have two weeks. Say, any chance you can let me off at Grand and Chestnut Street? It's just a block from my house."

"Not a problem. I'm fifteen minutes ahead of schedule."

At 10:30, the Greyhound pulled to an unscheduled stop in the West End of Duluth. The driver opened the big luggage compartment, retrieved my sea bag and wished me good luck. Grinning, I shouldered my bag and began to walk down Chestnut Street to my parents' house. I'd grown up here but hadn't really noticed the working-men's houses so distinctly before. As I passed Bryant School, a car slowed, the window lowered, and a girl called, "Hey, sailor! Want a ride?" It was Arlene Schweitzer, a girl who had gone to St. Jean's School with me.

"No thanks, Arlene. I've been riding all day."

I wanted to savor this moment. I remember to this day the feeling of joy I felt walking down my street, filled with a tremendous sense of accomplishment. Mom made a big fuss over me and even my father seemed to look at me in a new light. He even asked how I was fixed for cash. "I'm fine, Pop, but thanks."

He fished twenty bucks from his pocket and gave me the keys to his prized 1959 white Thunderbird. "Take Linda to dinner or something."

Pop gave me the use of his T-Bird whenever he could and when it wasn't available, Linda's dad let us use his car. The time flew by. In what seemed like the blink of an eye, I was packing to return to California and my new duty station. This time I was traveling in style. Mom had paid for my airfare from what she used to call her pin-money, asking me not to tell my father.

Linda and I had spent almost every waking hour together during my leave. I was crazy about her. Though eager to board my first ship I knew that I was really going to miss her. We kissed good-bye and promised to write often. I hoped that she would wait for me.

13

Going to Sea

Port Chicago was a flat, desolate, and lonely place. A long expanse of chain link fence bordered three sides of a vast pastureland that was the Port Chicago ammunition dump. For safety's sake, all of the buildings were spaced far apart to spread out the potential targets. There wasn't a tree in sight. On the other side were docks where the ammunition ships were berthed.

The marine at the gate looked over my orders and passed me through to a Jeep parked nearby that took me to the pier where the *Vesuvius* lay at berth. As I ascended the gangplank, I wondered if there was a Chief Flynn or someone of his ilk waiting for me on board this bucket.

I played it out just as we'd learned in boot camp, saluting the ensign and then turning to salute the officer of the deck (OD). "Request permission to come aboard, sir." The chief boatswain's mate who was that day's OD returned my salute.

"Permission granted." I stepped off the gangplank onto the quarter deck and gave him my orders. He opened the folder and looked at them briefly. "Welcome aboard, Hampston."

I blew out a long breath and thought, *Well, so far, so good.*

The OD called for the messenger of the watch who would show me to the second division berthing compartment. We walked along a passageway and then down a ladder to my new home. Bunks stacked four-high lined three small corridors. Alongside each was a six-foot-high stack of footlockers. Seated at a table in the center of the compartment was a first class petty officer.

"Hi, ya, Rodriquez," said the messenger. "Here's your new guy." Rodriguez took my paperwork, glanced at it, and looked up.

"Hampston. Yeah, we been expecting you. Welcome aboard." I blew out another breath and thought, *Patience, Mike, there's bound to be a pecker-head lying in wait aboard this ship some-where.* Rodriquez assigned me a bunk saying, "You'll like this one. It's right near a fresh air vent."

Then he showed me to an empty locker. "You can stow your gear here. If you haven't got a lock, I have an extra that you can use until you buy one at the ship's store. Three hatchways down on the port side you will find the issue room. Tell the guy there—his name is O'Brien—I said to issue your bedding. I'll take your packet to personnel. In the meantime, make yourself at home. Chow is at 1700h. If you can't find the mess deck," he said with a chuckle, "just go back topside and then follow the stampede."

Life on board the *Vesuvius* was a snap compared to boot camp. Second division's job on board was to take care of all the topside center portion of the ship. First division had the fore section and third division, the after portion.

Topside sailors are bo'sun's mates, third-class petty officers or above. If you are below that rank, you are a deck ape. That was me—a deck ape. All day I chipped paint and repainted bulkheads haze gray. I primed the decks with red lead and then gave them a coat of deck gray. I got to know those decks inti-mately, scrubbing and swabbing them daily.

In addition to his day-to-day duties, each sailor is required to stand four-hour watches that might be anywhere from the fo'c'sle to the fantail, or from the bridge to the engine room.

My first watch came two days after I came on board. It was the midnight to 0400h watch on the bridge. The quartermaster of the watch stood behind me instructing me in how to operate the helm, right to such and such degrees, left to so and so, steady up on this or that many degrees. Here I was steering a multi-million dollar ship when a short year ago I wasn't even trusted to drive my dad's car.

While our ship was in port we were granted port and starboard liberty; one half of the crew had every other day and every other weekend off. Port Chicago didn't have much to offer a sailor for recreation, so on my days off I went into a nearby town called Walnut Creek and took in a movie or two. Sometimes I just hung around the soda fountain where I could be around other young people. On weekend liberties I would take the bus to San Francisco with a few of my shipmates.

I'd made a new pal aboard ship, Kevin Arrowsmith. One liberty weekend, we went to visit his dad's business partner Carl in Daly City. Carl's home was perched on the hill overlooking San Francisco with a beautiful view of the city and the Golden Gate Bridge. Carl was a great guy and obviously quite well off. Believe it or not, Kevin's dad and Carl were actual arrowsmiths. Imagine that, a guy name Randolph Scott Arrowsmith who manufactures arrows for a living!

What I learned on that first weekend in Daly City was that the Arrowsmiths were members of the Navajo tribe—a people with a history both tragic and inspirational. Forced to surrender to the US government and following the brutal forced march known as the Long Walk, the Navajo were resettled in the area now known as Navajoland—a vast tract of land that extends into New Mexico, Arizona and Utah. In the 1920s, oil was discovered within its borders, but long before that, Kevin's family had gone into the business of making and selling both targets and hunting arrows. After several generations, they were still doing very well.

Learning this, I couldn't resist asking Kevin, "Well, why

the hell aren't you working for your dad in the family business rather than going into the Navy?" He explained to me that after the Navajo resettlement, the Arrowsmith men had always served in the military, initially as scouts. His father had been a marine Navajo code talker in the Pacific during the Second World War, translating military codes that were undecipherable to the Japanese. Without the code talkers, it's unlikely that the Marines would have taken Iwo Jima.

I asked him, "So, why not join the Marines?"

"Well," said Kevin, "I got in trouble with the law and the judge told me I had to go into the military or to jail and I couldn't get into the Marines because I was too small, so I joined the Navy."

I laughed till my sides ached. Kevin didn't see the humor, but he laughed along with me when I told him my story.

The following week we got under way on a West Pacific cruise. When we departed Port Chicago, we could expect to be at sea for the next nine months. The *Vesuvius* threw off mooring lines and the ship slipped away from the pier as the 1-MC, the ship's public address system, cracked out, "The Ship is Underway. Set the Special Sea and Anchor Detail. On Deck, Section One."

We steamed past Alcatraz and under the Golden Gate Bridge at 0800h. I was off watch and had a couple of hours free so I had positioned myself on the fo'c'sle for a better vantage point to say goodbye to San Francisco and the US mainland. I could see Daly City, high on the hill, the sun brightening the red adobe rooftops. I waved and wondered if Carl and his wife might be up there watching our departure.

Steaming south by west, ten days later we dropped anchor at Pearl Harbor.

14

Attack on Pearl Harbor

At 1700h the bos'un's mate of the watch announced over the 1-MC: "Now Liberty Call, Liberty Call. Commence Liberty of Section One to Expire on Board at 2400 hours. Section Two, Relieve the Watch."

Section one was ready. We gathered on the quarterdeck in dress whites, starched and pressed, with shoes spit-polished to a mirror shine. Saluting the OD and ensign, we requested permission to go ashore. Walking single file down the gangplank and through the front gate of Pearl Harbor Naval Station, we were about to make our frontal attack on the unsuspecting civilian population of Honolulu.

At 2300h that night, the paddy wagon of the Hawaiian Armed Service Police (HASP) pulled to a stop on the pier. Five other *Vesuvius* sailors and I piled out of the back, uniforms bloodied, filthy, and torn. Shore patrolmen escorted us up the gangway to the OD.

The next morning, at captain's mast, I stood at attention in front of our skipper, Commander Cooper Porter. The captain was reading the complaint that had been filed against me and my shipmates as a result of the previous night's shenanigans.

"Hampston," he said, "can you tell me in your own words just what the hell happened last night?"

My right eye was swollen shut and my lower lip was split, making it difficult to speak clearly, but I cleared my throat and to the best of my ability gave my account of the donnybrook that took place at the Palace Bar on Hotel Street.

"Well, sir, we were playing shuffleboard, minding our own business, when a group of marines came in. After a few beers they challenged us to a game of shuffleboard for fifty bucks."

Commander Porter nodded, "Go on."

"Well, sir, after beating them flat three games in a row they became kind of unfriendly and made a couple of not very flattering remarks about sailors and the Navy in general. Then, sir, one of our guys returned the compliment and the next thing I knew, one of those...pucks, I think you call them...came sailing across the room toward my head. I ducked and the puck went right through the window behind me and then all hell broke loose, sir, and the next thing I remember was being loaded into the back of the HASP paddy wagon."

"Hampston, I see that according to your 201 file, you have served on the *Vesuvius* for just over four months. Is that correct?"

"Yes, sir."

"Are you aware that the legal drinking age in Hawaii is eighteen?" he shouted.

"No, sir," I said, my knees beginning to shake, "but no one asked for an ID."

"Are you aware that gambling is illegal in Hawaii as well!" he shot back.

"No, sir. I didn't know that either, sir."

He tapped his pencil on his desk, looked back down at my 201 packet and finally looked back up at me and said, "Hampston, I don't like troublemakers in my ship, nor do I like troublemakers in the Navy. I am restricting you to the ship for two weeks which just happens to be the duration of our stay in Pearl Harbor. I am also forfeiting your next month's pay and, in addition, you and the rest of the thugs who participated in the brawl in Honolulu last night will make restitution for the damage done to the Palace Bar. Is that clear?"

"Yes, sir," I answered, thinking to myself, *Hell, my dad would have just taken my bike away and sent me to my room.*

He glared at me for a second and said, "Hampston, if I ever see you here before me at captain's mast again, I'll get you off this ship so fast it'll make your goddamn head swim." He banged a gavel on his desk and barked, "Dimissed!"

I did an about-face. The master at arms opened the door of the captain's cabin and I marched out. In the passageway outside, Kevin Arrowsmith and the rest of the offenders waited their turn before the skipper. As I passed, I shot a look at Kevin and said, "You're screwed, pal."

Out on deck, as the soft trade wind blew against my face, I lit a Lucky and felt a tremendous feeling of relief, thinking, all in all my first liberty in Hawaii had gone pretty well.

I didn't get to see Waikiki Beach or the hundreds of bikini clad college girls splashing in the surf. But so what? There would be other liberty ports. The next would be Guam in eight days and although liberty in Guam wasn't famous for its night life, there would be swimming, surfing, and some time to just relax. It was unlikely that I'd get into trouble in Guam.

15

Brig

Everything doesn't always go as I imagine. Guam wasn't all swimming, surfing, and relaxing. What Guam actually turned out to be was two weeks in the Marine Corps Brig.

At the second division beach party, an annual event, I drank too much beer and when I was hauled back aboard, drunk as a lord, it seems I took a swing at Chief Mattson who was the OD on watch at the time.

Sure as God made little green apples, bright and early the next morning, there I stood in front of the captain again. Commander Porter was a fair man, but I hadn't made much of an impression on him during our first meeting and he didn't seem too happy to see me again. I thought he would never stop ranting and raving. Finally he declared that he was sentencing me to fourteen days of hard labor at the United States Marine Corps Brig right there on Guam.

"And furthermore," he went on, "upon discharge from the brig you shall be transferred to some other USN duty station. Now," said the captain to the master at arms, "get this piece of shit out of my sight and off my ship." The MAA escorted me to my locker where I packed my sea bag and took a long, last look around.

"Come on, Hampston," he said. "Move it!" He took me to

the quarter deck where the OD handed me my packet. I saluted. I requested permission to go ashore and it was granted. I saluted again before I passed the ensign. Then I walked down the gangway into the welcoming arms of two lance corporal marine brig guards. They grabbed my sea bag and packet, cuffed my hands behind my back, and loaded me into the back seat of a station wagon marked USMC Brig.

The USMC Brig in Guam was a large cement block structure approximately one hundred yards square. The capacity of this facility, I learned later, was three hundred prisoners although when I arrived, the inmates numbered around 140. Marine Corps brigs were not designed to rehabilitate prisoners but to punish them for whatever laws they had broken. The brig's term for cell was "box." As luck would have it, I was assigned Box Thirteen. Then I was issued dungarees and white hats with corresponding numbers stenciled on them. In addition to the number thirteen, a large P for "prisoner" was stenciled on each item of clothing.

It seemed to me that most brig chasers were lance corporals from either West (by God) Virginia, or Alabama, and I figured that they had never owned a pair of shoes until entering the Marine Corps. They probably thought I was a hardened Yankee punk from a rough slum neighborhood. Needless to say, the guards and prisoners did not hold one another in high regard.

Brig boxes had no doors, only a red line painted on the deck in the doorway. If a prisoner crossed this line without permission, he could be shot. The food we were fed was left over from the other military installations on the island, and believe me when I say it was nothing to write home about. In fact, if I had written home about any of this, it would have brought my mother to tears.

The work was brutal. During the Second World War, the Americans and later the Japanese built hundreds of buildings, airstrips, and bunkers on Guam. The island was an important piece of real estate during the war in the Pacific. Now it was home to a make-work program that assigned brig rats the job of swinging sledgehammers against these structures to break them down into gravel.

At 0500h every day of the week, we were roused by the turnkey of the guard sounding a Klaxon horn. We stood at attention with our toes on (but not over) the red line to hear the roll called in order from the first to the sixteenth box. When my turn came, I would pop my white hat on my leg and shout, "Turnkey of the Guard, sir, Prisoner Hampston, Box thirteen, US Marine Corps Brig, Guam, present, sir!"

If a prisoner screwed this up, he received a nice jab in the stomach with a nightstick and then had to try it again, repeating it until he got it right. Each screw-up earned another application of the nightstick. Once a guy was successful, the turnkey would say, "Step across, pri'nor." My dad would surely have been glad to know that I was finally learning to "toe the mark."

When all sixteen prisoners stood at attention in the passageway outside their boxes, the turnkey would bark, "Right face!" We were then escorted to the head to wash up. After that we had a half hour for chow. The rest of our time we spent out at the rock pile making little ones out of big ones.

It was a new and unpleasant experience for me, passing long stretches of empty hours grinding away on work detail—and there was plenty of time for thinking as I lay at night on my bunk. For those two weeks I tried my level best to keep a very low profile and made myself a promise that if I lived through it, I would never again get in trouble.

Upon completion of my sentence, I was driven to the naval air station and put on a transport plane bound for Okinawa. I was billeted in a Quonset hut on the air force base outside the city of Naha. The sign above the Quonset hut door read X-Division, marking it as a transit barrack that housed servicemen moving from one duty station to another. I would be in transit there for one month, and after that time I'd be reassigned to the Essex-class aircraft carrier USS *Ticonderoga* (CVA-14). An aircraft carrier! I was very pleased with my new assignment and counted the days until her arrival in Okinawa.

While serving my time in X-Division, my job was to sweep and swab the deck of my Quonset hut each morning after chow. Next, I emptied the trash into the Dempsey Dumpster located behind the building. That was it. It took me all of an hour to complete these tasks and the rest of the day was my own to do as I pleased. It was like being on vacation. I'd go to lunch, take a nap or drop into the recreation center and shoot pool until 1600h. When liberty commenced, I'd put on my dress blues and go into town.

I wrote long letters home during this time, omitting the details of my having busted rock for the last fourteen days, of course. Linda and my folks wrote back to let me know they welcomed news of my activities.

My favorite haunt in Naha was the Sleeping Tiger Bar where most of the sailors, soldiers, and airmen from X-Division hung out as well. At that time in Okinawa, you weren't required to be eighteen to drink so I wasn't breaking the law by having a few beers. One night, shortly before I was to meet my new ship, I was in the Sleeping Tiger drinking beer and shooting pool when four of the largest special forces soldiers I'd ever seen darkened the doorway. They were in dress greens with spit-shined jump boots and berets laid low just over their eyes.

I was pretty impressed and thought that these guys could really do some damage if they took a mind to it. Just then, a big, dumb, second-class gunner's mate who was also in X-Division, made a stupid remark. "Hey, where'd you guys get those funny hats?"

I hit for the back door and made it into the alley just as the shit hit the fan.

The following morning I learned that half of X-Division was on report for everything from inciting a riot and destruction of private property to assault and battery. *Well, this time I finally dodged the bullet,* I thought. I was beginning to learn that discretion really is the better part of valor.

A few days before my transfer, about a dozen more sailors who were also being transferred to the *Ticonderoga* came into X-Division. One of these was Kevin Arrowsmith. The *Vesuvius* was scheduled to return to San Francisco for decommissioning and had dispersed some of the ship's company to other ships already in the Far East. Arrowsmith had drawn the *Ticonderoga.* We shook hands, slapped backs, and were both very happy to see each other. I filled Kevin in on my two weeks in the brig and the month's long vacation I was enjoying in Okinawa.

Kevin had been promoted from seaman apprentice to seaman and proudly pointed out the three white strips on the left sleeve of his dress blue jumper. I congratulated him, feeling a slight pang of jealousy.

Liberty call was announced and we headed into town to celebrate his recent promotion, passing by the Sleeping Tiger and grinning at the sign that was now nailed across the door, CLOSED FOR REMODELING.

16

Deep Sink

I looked up at the gigantic aircraft carrier that was to be my new home and thought, *How in the hell can that big son-of-a-bitch float?*

I knew nothing about this four-city-block-sized haze-gray monster resting at the pier. The flight deck towered about one hundred feet above the pier and the super structure rose seven stories above the flight deck. I felt like a four-year-old kid in a museum looking up at the skeleton of a Tyrannosaurus Rex.

"Here we go, buddy," I said, turning to Kevin as we both shouldered our bags and walked up the after brow. On board, we were brought to personnel where we received our division assignments. Kevin was a bo'sun's mate striker and I also hoped to train for a new technical duty.

The chief yeoman, examining my packet, looked up and said, "I see you've been in some trouble."

"Yeah, chief. Seems like I'm always in the wrong place at the wrong time."

"Well, you better keep your nose clean here. This skipper takes no prisoners. I see here you are recommended to strike for commissaryman." He thought for a minute and picked up a phone.

"Good morning, chief. This is Chief Elkins in personnel. I

71

have a seaman apprentice here and his 201 recommends him to strike for CS. Can you use him? OK. I'll send him down."

I was assigned a bunk and locker in the S2 Division berthing compartment and then informed that I was to relieve my section counterpart at 0930h the next morning.

I had no idea what my apprenticeship would be when I made my way to the mess deck the following morning. I only got lost four times. The door to the commissary office was open and a first class petty officer commissaryman sat at a desk reading a newspaper. I knocked, but there was no reply. I knocked again. He didn't even look up. I cleared my throat. That didn't seem to work either.

Finally, a little timidly, I said, "Excuse me?" Nothing.

I tried again. His paper clenched in his fist, he pounded the desk, looked up and shouted, "Can't a man even read the *Stars and Stripes* around this place without some asshole kid bothering him? What the fuck do you want?"

I couldn't speak. I just stood there shaking, thinking, *Oh, God, no! It's happening again!* I was deep in the middle of a Chief Flynn flashback when his voice came back to me.

"I asked you what the fuck you want?" I still couldn't speak. I wanted to, but I couldn't make any sound come out. I just stood there like some sort of an idiot.

"If ya can't talk, just get the fuck out of here and let me get back to my newspaper."

I stepped from his office out onto the mess deck and was thinking, *Well, another nice beginning, stupid,* when I heard a voice call, "Sailor!" I turned to see a khaki-clad lieutenant junior grade looking at me with raised eyebrows and a slight concern.

"Yes, sir," I answered. He crooked his finger motioning me to come toward him. I walked to LTJG Andrew Johnson and stammered, "Sir?"

"Had a little trouble with Petty Officer Seeley, did you?"

I stuttered, "No, sir, I was just trying to find out about my job, sir. I'm supposed to start work here at 0930h."

"Relax, son," he said, "and get yourself a cup of coffee. I'll straighten this out." He turned and entered the commissary office.

A guy in whites with a cook's hat brought me a cup. "The coffee is in that copper over by the hatch. There's a ladle hanging on the side."

I ladled out a cup of joe and lit a smoke. The cook that brought me the cup said, "You're the new guy, huh?" He stuck out his hand. "My name's Rodrick."

"Hampston. Glad to meet you."

Just then I heard the ass-chewing First Class Petty Officer Alfred D. Seeley was getting from my new Division Officer LTJG Andy Johnson. Five minutes later, Seeley exited the commissary office, giving me a look that would have made one of Chief Flynn's glares look like a smile from my kindly old parish priest, Father Savoie. Unfortunately, Seeley was to be my new galley watch captain.

The next morning I relieved my S2 counterpart. My new job in the main galley of the USS *Ticonderoga* came with its own name. I was called "deep sink" while on duty. In a tremendous three-compartment stainless steel sink, I was to wash every piece of cooking equipment used to cook the food for 2,400 men. The guy I relieved introduced himself as Ron Jenkins and told me he was from Eugene, Oregon. He handed me his rubber apron and said, "Burgers for lunch. They do them on the grill. You'll have a pretty easy first day."

Once we got underway, the ship went to "port and starboard duty" which meant a shift going on duty in the morning at 0930h had a twenty-four-hour watch. Every day, I relieved Jenkins and wopped pots until after the galley was secured for the day—a task that took at least ten hours. Then I swabbed down the galley, got a quick shower and hit the rack around 2200h for six short hours of sleep until 0400h the next morning when our watch was wakened by the night cook. We would work the breakfast meal until 0930h when we were relieved, and it was my turn to hand the rubber apron back to Jenkins.

I worked hard, but nothing I did was right in the eyes of Seeley. He was on my ass every second, shouting, and screaming, and finger-pointing. That pit in my stomach was back, but there wasn't anything I could do—at least as far as I could tell. So once again I lowered my head, dug in, and hung on.

The next two months were spent at sea. The long, hard hours working at my deep sink job took its toll on my morale, and one day, when Seeley had been particularly hard on me, I snapped and started screaming back.

"You're on report, you little fucker!" he shrieked.

Here we go again, I thought. *They're going to slap my ass back in the brig, sure as hell.*

Seeley stormed from the galley and into the commissary office.

I was caught up on my pots and pans for the moment; I stepped out of the galley and across to the big kettle where the coffee was steaming, grabbed a cup, and lit a smoke. The door was closed but I could hear the muffled sounds of shouting coming from inside the office.

I had just finished my smoke and was on my way back to my deep sink when the door to the office opened and Chief Sargeant—honest to God, that was his real name—walked out and called me. "Hampston, step into the office for a sec, will ya?"

I followed the chief in and shut the door. "Sit," he said, pointing to a chair. I obeyed.

Seeley sat at the desk where I had first seen him reading the *Stars and Stripes*.

"Now," said the chief, "just what the hell is going on between you two?"

Seeley began a rant that went on for five minutes, explaining to the chief just what a piece of crap I was.

"Hampston, what have you got to say about what's been going on here?"

"Well, chief, Seeley just doesn't like me. I'm doing my best but since my first day aboard he has been on my ass."

"Seeley," said the chief, "I've heard your constant shouting and bitching coming from the galley whenever you're on watch, night and day. You can be heard all over the mess deck. You ride your people too hard, Seeley, and it's having an adverse effect on the efficiency of your entire watch. Now, I want you to lighten the fuck up on your entire crew! *Understood?* Hampston, you and Seeley obviously have some sort of personality clash going on so I'm going to split you two up. Seeley, for tomorrow's shift, grab a mess cook to work the deep sink until I can find you a permanent replacement. Hampston, tomorrow you will report to Petty Officer Dunning at 0930h in the bakery."

"Bakery?"

"Yeah. Red Dunning is short one guy over there and they can use you."

"Okay, chief," I smiled.

"What are you grinning about?" he asked.

"Well, I used to work in a bakery back home in Minnesota. It was a good job. I liked it."

"Why didn't you tell us that before?"

I shrugged. "No one ever asked, I guess."

I didn't sleep well that night. My mind flooded with memories of Schilla's Bakery and the nice old guys who took me under their wing when I was just a boy and I remembered the warm, clean smell of bread baking. I was still tossing and turning when the night cook woke the watch at 0400h. I showered, shaved, put on clean whites and went topside for a cigarette. I leaned against the port side rail of the sponsor deck and lit my Lucky.

Ticonderoga cut through the sea, silently turning up folds of blue phosphorus that reminded me of the blue bubble lights my mother hung on the Christmas tree each year. Flying fish leaped into the air trying to keep up with the ship, and about fifty yards off the port side, a school of dolphins played and jumped, racing our vessel.

I felt as if I had been reborn. I was getting another chance. Surely this time things would go my way.

And go my way, they did.

17

Mr. Johnson

I finished off half a pack of smokes waiting to report to the bakery. I didn't want to seem overly eager by showing up early so about 0800h, just before the chow line secured, I went below and jumped on at the end. I moved down the line getting my scrambled eggs, bacon, and fried potatoes. Seeley was supervising two cooks working the grills. He spotted me and shot me a dirty look. I ignored it and got my cup of joe and moved to a table on the mess deck.

Unable to wait any longer, at 0900h, a half hour early, I lifted my leg over the hatchway that led to the bakery and there it was—that smell—that wonderful, welcoming smell that only a bakery can have.

I'm home, I thought. *Damn it, I'm home!*

Two guys sat on the bakery bench. "Is Dunning around?" I asked.

"Nope," one of them answered, "He's on the next watch. He should be here in about fifteen minutes though."

"Hey," said the other guy, "you're the deep sink on Seeley's watch, aren't you?"

"I *was*. I'm coming to work here on Dunning's watch."

They jumped down off the bench and one extended his hand. "Hi. I'm Lopez—Dave Lopez. This here's Tino Sanchez.

We're the Chicano watch." He flashed a toothy grin.

I shook both their hands and was telling them some about my brief naval career when a tall redheaded man sporting a perfectly groomed red handlebar mustache walked in. He pointed at me. "Hampston, right?"

"That's me."

He put out his hand. "I'm Red Dunning. You can call me Red. Chief Sargeant says you have some experience. Is that right?"

"Yeah, I worked in a bakery for about six months when I was a kid."

Red was in his early thirties and smiled at the "when I was a kid" remark.

"Well," he said, "I sure can use a guy that knows his way around a bakery bench. The new kids they send me—I usually have to teach 'em to tie their shoes."

The *Ticonderoga* bake shop, with eight bakers, four on each watch, supplied bakery products for 2,400 officers and crew, three meals a day. My new watch captain Red was an absolute joy to work for. He treated me as an equal, although he was a first class petty officer and I was a lowly seaman apprentice. He was soon impressed with my baking abilities and it wasn't long before I was his go-to-guy. I had learned a lot at Schilla's that Red hadn't learned in navy bakeshops and he was happy to hear about tricks that Ed had taught me to make the work go faster. I guess you could say that was the happiest time in my life. I had a job I loved, a boss who treated me with respect, and for the first time I could remember, I didn't have anyone on my ass.

Three sailing days out of Manila, I heard Red scream in pain. He had been spinning a run of bread from the barrel mixer and was pushing the advance button with one hand and grabbing and pulling the dough out with the other. The advance had stuck and the dough grabbed his hand and pulled in his arm, breaking it in three places. But he had been lucky—guys have been killed in just that sort of accident. We got Red to sick bay where the medics put a pin in his arm and wrapped it in a cast from his armpit to his wrist.

A few days later, we dropped anchor in Manila Bay. The chief, on Red's recommendation, had made me temporary watch captain even though two other guys on our watch were senior in rank. Chief talked to Mr. Johnson. He, in turn, talked to Commander Calloway, the head of the supply department, about getting me a promotion; that is, above the three new stripes on my left sleeve I would wear a crossed keys and feather insignia. I would now be Commissaryman Striker Seaman Hampston. A big deal. A real big deal.

My promotion was approved that afternoon and when Red walked into the bakery, his right arm in a sling, he handed me a package of stripes and the designation insignia for both blues and whites. "Ya better get these sewn on, kid. You have liberty tomorrow and you wouldn't want to be out of uniform." He smiled broadly as he stuck out his left hand and said, "Congratulations, Mike." I was sorry about Red's arm getting broken up so badly but I was as pleased as could be about what had come to me because of his injury.

One man short, there were only two other shipmates on our watch, John Green and Steve Lewis. Green was a well-built, good-looking kid from Kalamazoo, Michigan, a high school football star who had been in the Navy a year and a half. Lewis hailed from Pittsburgh; he was heavyset with a ruddy complexion and a hearty laugh that could be heard from the fo'c'sle to the fantail. Day after day, the bakery was a beehive of activity, and working so many hours together we quickly formed a tight-knit crew. While we rolled dough and cut biscuits, we laid our plans for the next day's liberty.

Because of our odd working hours, cooks and bakers had

watch standers' liberty cards that allowed us to go ashore as soon as we were relieved from watch. At 0930h, the day we arrived in Manila Bay—after the requisite shit, shine, shower and shave—I donned my dress whites, sporting my new rank and insignia.

We hit the beach.

Actually, we hit every sailor bar we could find that day and drank oceans of San Miguel beer and had more fun than any three sailors should be allowed, and for once it didn't include getting my ass into some sort of a jam. A full hour and a half before liberty expired, half in the mitt but still upright, we ate monkey meat on a stick outside the gate and caught the liberty launch back to the ship.

We were in port for six more days, every one better than the last, but I emptied my wallet pretty damn quick. I was glad to learn of a barber in the ship's service department who lent money and I borrowed ten dollars with the agreement to pay him back fourteen on payday. On the last day of liberty in Manila, I went through that ten bucks as fast as green corn through the new maid and then cringed the following payday when I had to pay back the fourteen dollars I'd promised. That taught me a valuable lesson—at our next port of call, I stayed aboard and saved my cash.

The day before we got underway again, I let it be known that I now had some money to lend.

At our next liberty port, I loaned out all the money I had, holding a few bucks back for cigarettes, soap, and a few candy bars from the ship's store. Now I was the guy standing at the end of the pay line collecting the cash. I repeated this scheme at the next two liberty ports and soon had plenty to lend and plenty to spend. It was just as my illegal-as-hell slush fund had really taken off that a mess cook came into the bakery and told me that Mr. Johnson wanted me in the commissary office.

"On my way."

My first thought was, *I'm caught.* I told Green to watch the ovens and walked to what I expected would be my doom.

Mr. Johnson was sitting at his desk when I knocked. "Oh, it's you, Hampston. Come in and shut the door."

My throat tightened. In front of him lay my 201 Service Record.

"Something has come to my attention," he said, looking down at my packet.

"Yes, sir?" I swallowed hard.

"You sent me a list of things needing either repair or replacement in the bakery."

I wondered what the hell that had to do with my slush fund.

"Well, it's your list. Did you write this?" he asked, handing me the three pieces of paper he held in his hand.

"Yes, sir. Those are the things that should be fixed in the bakery."

He motioned for me to sit and I took the chair that faced his desk. He paused, searching for the right words, and then said slowly, "Son, I don't want to offend you." He hesitated again. Finally, he said, "Hampston, you write like a third grader. How in the world did you ever pass the test to get into the Navy?"

Hell, I was just happy I wasn't going to jail. I didn't mind if he thought I was a dumbbell. A little sheepishly, I answered, "I didn't exactly take the test, sir."

I told him the whole story, the three tries at eighth grade, Mr. Hammer, the parking meters, the judge. Everything. When I had finished, he just looked at me, astonished. He rummaged through his desk and handed me a book and asked me to read a passage for him out loud.

Well, I tried, but I don't think I did very well because when I finished he said, "Just what I suspected. You *write* like a third grader because you *read* like a third grader. Hampston, do you know what dyslexia is?"

"No, sir."

"Well, son, you're as dyslexic as the day is long." I had no clue what he was talking about, but as Mr. Johnson explained what it meant, the word didn't seem so worrisome.

"People with this problem have trouble with symbols and words. The brain sometimes either turns letters or numbers upside down or around and sometimes, like when taking a test or tackling something else that's stressful, everything gets jumbled all together. Does that sound familiar, Hampston?"

I nodded, and he continued. "It makes it very difficult for a dyslexic to distinguish between what he's reading or writing and jibberish. But you know what, Hampston? We can do something about that." He had been a special education teacher before entering the Navy, he told me, and he added that he was going to help me to become a better reader.

"Go back to work and we'll talk soon." I thanked him and returned to the bakery.

A week and a half later, Red came back to work. His arm was out of its cast, but it was skinny and still weak so at first he couldn't do anything very strenuous. Over the next two weeks he got stronger, and once again we were working shoulder to shoulder. It was nice to have him back to his old self, and our watch was back to running like a brand new Hobart bread mixer.

One morning, returning to the bakery after replenishing the bread on the chow line, I found Red and the chief talking in the passageway outside the shop. Chief Sargeant informed me that the out-of-commission ice cream machine had been fixed and the skipper wanted us to start serving ice cream as soon as possible.

"Yeah, so?" I said.

"Mr. Johnson and I think you're the man for the job," answered the chief.

"Gee, chief, I'd rather stay in the bakery."

"Well, you don't call the shots around here so report to the ice cream room when you're done here and the wrenches will show you the mechanics of how the contraption works."

I was pissed about leaving the bakery. I felt as though I'd been double-crossed by Mr. Johnson and the chief. But as the man said, I didn't call the shots around there so after we secured from watch, I did as I had been instructed and reported to the ice cream room. There were two machinists' mates there, a chief and a second class. They gave me a half-hour class on how the thing worked and a few pointers on troubleshooting.

The ice cream machine sat in a small storeroom caged with wire. The machine itself was a huge, metal, rectangular rig, five feet high and twelve feet long. Tucked alongside were a table and two chairs. Lining the bulkheads were wire shelves filled with the ingredients necessary to make almost any flavor of ice cream imaginable.

After the chief machinist's mate finished, I said, "So what you're saying, chief, is that I pour powdered ice cream mixture, milk and flavoring in here, push this button that says, START and in an hour and a half, it comes out here. Right?"

"Right. If you have trouble with the machine, let me know." He wished me luck and the two of them left.

I was sitting at the table in the storeroom familiarizing myself with the inventory sheet, still crabby about having to leave the bakery, when Mr. Johnson came in carrying a leather briefcase. I stood. "Good morning, sir." He returned my good morning and told me to sit down.

"How's it going?" he asked.

"Fine, sir. The wrenches got me all squared away on the ice cream machine. I've been looking at this ice cream recipe book. This is pretty easy stuff, sir."

"Good," he said, opening his briefcase. "Then you'll have plenty of time on your hands, right?"

"Yes, sir, I guess I will."

"That was my whole idea," said Mr. Johnson as he extracted from his briefcase half a dozen books. "This storeroom is not only going to be your workplace, it's going to be your classroom."

He stacked the books in front of me. "Hampston, by the time this cruise is over, you will be reading at a high school level."

I shuffled through the books and looked up at him. "Well... well, sir, these are little kids' books."

"I picked these up at our last liberty port. They are third-grade level books because you read, now, on a third-grade level. We will start there and move up to harder books as you improve."

He patiently taught me how to read for meaning and to pay attention to punctuation. I relaxed and slowly, my brain began to unscramble words as I went along. What had eluded me all my life seemed now to be in my grasp. My ice cream job was so easy I had at least eight hours a day to read if I wanted. As time went on and my reading ability improved, I read every book he brought me—children's classics and adventure stories like *Lassie, Come Home* and *Black Beauty*. Before too long I was flying through the pages of Ian Fleming and traveling the world with James Bond as *Ticonderoga* steamed from one port to the next.

Mr. Johnson would stop by the ice cream room some evenings and ask me to read aloud to him. When I'd stumble, he'd remind me, "Slow down, kid. It's only me."

Then one night, as I was finishing my ice cream cleanup, I looked up to see a smiling Mr. Johnson standing in the doorway.

"Hello sir," I said, standing my broom against the bulkhead.

"I don't think you need me anymore, Hampston. Your reading is greatly improved and you have a pretty good handle on how to deal with your dyslexia. I brought you a graduation present," and he handed me a paper bag filled with books.

I thanked him for the books and all he had done for me.

"It was as much fun for me as it was for you," he said. He turned to leave, then stopped and turned back. "That reminds me. You will be replaced here tomorrow. You go back to the bakery on Red Dunning's watch in the morning."

A year after I left the *Ticonderoga*, I heard from another

shipmate that Mr. Johnson had resigned his commission and returned to teaching kids with learning disabilities. They were lucky to have him and I wondered how my life would have unfolded differently had there been a Mr. Johnson at our school during my early years.

18

Foreign Women

While Mr. Johnson and I were hard at work on the reading project, the *Ticonderoga* along with the rest of Task Force 77.7 was continuing its Far East cruise with goodwill stops in several ports of call. The Naval Air Station at Subic Bay was most sailors' favorite liberty port in the Pacific and I would soon discover why.

Outside the gate of NAS Subic Bay was the Filipino city of Olongapo. This oasis of sailor bars and whorehouses was the Sodom and Gomorra of the Far East and as I stood on the flight deck at parade rest with the other sailors, it seemed as if I heard it calling to me. Bars lined both sides of the single street that was Manila Boulevard. Names like Texas Saloon and Minneapolis Bar flashed on neon signs as sailors made their way past the main gate to the city center fountain where a huge statue of a World War II Filipino war hero stood, rifle in one hand and machete in the other.

It was here on Manila Boulevard that I discovered the attractions that had been luring other sailors for years.

I was on the beach that morning—our first liberty in Subic Bay—with a new addition to S2 Division. His name was David W. Devereaux and he was destined to become my best friend for the duration of my naval career. Dave was born and raised in Cut and Shoot, Texas. You may doubt there is such a place, but I've seen the proof—postmarks on mail he received. Dave was a charmer, but he could turn the most innocent situation into a mess of trouble—for himself and anyone near him.

We were walking along the boulevard and noticed a large neon sign with an arrow pointing the way up a wooden stairway at the side of a building that read D Stars Bar ~ Servicemen Welcome.

Ascending the stairs of the D Stars Bar a couple of steps behind Dave, I looked up and noticed double bamboo swinging doors. Suddenly, I thought of the 402 and laughing a little to myself, wondered if they had any cheese popcorn. The D Stars was a wooden addition to an original building, an older stone structure. The addition seemed like an afterthought—no glass in the windows and only bamboo shutters that could be lowered and fastened with a rope when it rained or the wind came up. A long bar lined the inside wall. On each outside wall were booths, and tables sat in the middle of the room in front of a bandstand and dance floor. It was all pretty primitive.

We pushed our way through the doors and up to the bar. Ordering up a couple of San Miguels, we turned around to take stock of our surroundings. It was early afternoon and there weren't many GIs around. Dave and I held watch standers' liberty cards and had been permitted to leave the ship early that day.

Along one wall, seated in the booths, were the D Stars B-girls, probably a dozen or so. One of them played the juke box and Johnny Horton's voice began to fill the room with "The Battle of New Orleans." Two at a time, the girls got up to dance with each other. Dave looked at me and grinned, "I can hardly wait for a slow dance." The girls were of all sizes and shapes but what they did have in common was that they were all pretty and all young, with the exception of one short, round woman who looked to be about fifty. She turned out to be the Mama-san.

"You want meet my girls?" she asked.

We were adolescent boys and the excitement of it all seemed irresistible. But I had a girlfriend at home and wasn't really on the hunt. Dave's face, however, lit up like a Christmas tree. "Sure, bring 'em on."

We brought our beers over to the table and Dave ordered a drink for all the girls. Mama-san brought each of them some sort of pink cocktail in a tall frosted glass garnished with a lemon and a cherry as they all gathered around us. Overtaken by lust, my pal took one of them by the hand and pulled her onto his lap.

"My name is Marie," she giggled.

One girl stood out in the bevy. She was a very small, delicate thing with a face so sweet that I couldn't help staring. Mama-san noticed my interest and nudged her toward me, speaking softly in Tagalog, or Filipino.

In broken English, she told me her name was Baby Carisco. I could see why they called her "Baby." She looked very young but I believed Mama-San when she said, "She sixteen...she legal to work bar. She cute, no?"

Through that afternoon we drank beer, danced, and had one hell of a time with these two little Filipino flowers. Soon the bar filled up with sailors and marines from the *Ticonderoga* and other ships in the harbor. I was returning from a trip to the head and found Baby dancing with a third-class gunner's mate. I felt a pang of jealousy but was certain if I made an issue out of it, a fistfight would likely result. I'd been there before and had no interest in another tour in the brig so I waved at Baby, drank down my beer and headed for the door.

She caught up with me as I was halfway down the stairs. Baby explained that unless I was her full-time boyfriend she was supposed to dance and drink with any GI who asked. But if I were to give the Mama-san 100 pesos she could be my full-time girl and any time I came in she would spend all her time with me. And for ten more pesos we could go to her room in the building behind the bar.

Without a thought of the girl back home, I leapt at this deal like a northern pike after a chub minnow and for the next three days I spent my afternoons in the D Stars, drinking San Miguel and my evenings in Baby's room, learning that not all girls found it necessary to beat you up after sex.

On our first day back at sea I woke with a burning feeling in my groin. In the head I stood at the urinal thinking, *I'll be fine after I piss.* But no, I wasn't fine. I must have left my fingerprints indented in the pipe above the urinal as it seemed to me someone was pulling a rusty chain at lightning speed from my pecker. *Damn it,* I thought, *I've got the clap.*

In sick bay, a medic that I knew quite well confirmed the suspicion.

"Yup, pal, you got the clap," he said as he jabbed me in the ass with a shot of penicillin.

He told me if I would make him five gallons of rocky road ice cream, he could keep this quiet and give me my penicillin on the sly. I agreed, dodging the two-week restriction I would face for contracting a venereal disease and the mandatory and very boring VD classes.

I didn't tell anyone other than Dave about my medical condition. He laughed. "What the hell did you expect? The real pretty ones all have VD. You're lucky it was only the clap and not something worse. Next time go in covered and for Christ's sake, check their shot card." I wrote to Baby to inform her that she was infected and should have it taken care of before she gave the whole fleet the clap, and I heeded Devereaux's advice. The problem never arose again.

After a stop in Hong Kong we were once again underway, bound for Yokosuka, Japan. During our sea maneuvers, somehow a signal was misread from our ship to a naval destroyer on our starboard side. When our signal was flashed to turn to starboard, the tin can turned to port instead. The destroyer hit us forward on the starboard side and bent the whole of her bow section over like a boxer with a severely broken nose. One man was killed on the tin can and many were injured on both ships.

Now, it takes a lot to roll an aircraft carrier. But the *Ticonderoga* rolled to port like a kid's toy in a bathtub. A cruiser from our task force towed the crippled destroyer to Yokosuka but *Ticonderoga* had to wait for relief from the USS *Ranger* before going back to the States for repair. First we headed for San Diego to get our bow patched up. Then we could proceed up to the Navy shipyard at Bremerton, Washington for full repairs.

While in San Diego, *Ticonderoga* tied up to the carrier pier on North Island. We took on stores and replacements during that stay. One of the replacements was my brother, Jack.

Bremerton

Jack had recently graduated from boot camp at the Great Lakes NTC in Chicago and he had requested duty with me on the *Ticonderoga*. He was assigned to second division as a deck ape and hated it like nothing else on earth. My brother was, and for the rest of his life continued to be, allergic to manual labor. Being stuck with this affliction, he had developed an uncanny talent for finding ways around anything and everything that might cause him to break a sweat. Somehow, in that first week, he conned his way into the undemanding job of cleaning the head outside the chief's quarters. It would take him an hour out of each day. With all his free time, not wanting to be noticed by the NCOs in his own division, he would disappear to either the cook's compartment or his new hide-out in the bakery where he moved flour bags around to make a place where he could sleep his days away.

About a week before we left San Diego there was a stores working party. Every man on board who was not rated (seaman and below) and not on watch was required to become a link in a human chain starting at the number three elevator doors. Cranes unloaded food and supplies that had just been delivered by trucks parked alongside the *Ticonderoga*. A relay of hands passed the cartons through the ship's passageways and down ladders to storerooms, refrigerators and freezers in the below deck. Being in commissary, I was in charge of one of these human conveyer belts, checking invoices and keeping the line moving.

Unfortunately, my brother Jack was assigned along with the rest of second division to my line. He whined and complained some but in the Navy, I outranked him and explained, "Jack, as Dad would say, 'Ya gotta put something on the bar besides your elbows.' *Everyone* has to do his part on these working parties."

Grumbling, he continued to pass cases of canned goods to the next sailor in line and privately I felt a small amount of vindication for all the times Jack had conned me into doing his lawn mowing and shoveling chores. Checking back and forth, up and down the line, I noticed a sudden slowdown and followed it back to its source. It was my brother, lying on the deck, holding his ankle and screaming in pain.

I stayed with Jack throughout his admittance to sick bay, marveling at the lengths he would go to in avoiding real work. But an x-ray revealed that his Achilles tendon had become partially detached. It would take two surgeries to mend Jack's leg. The first was at Balboa Naval Hospital in San Diego, two days after the injury. He was fitted with a walking cast and sent back to the *Ticonderoga*, relieved from all duty. The second surgery was to be in six weeks at the Naval Hospital in Bremerton, Washington. Once we got underway, it was a week's steaming time to Bremerton. Jack was like a little kid; he was so excited to be at sea for the first time. He got around pretty well with the aid of a cane. With no job to do, he now spent almost all his time in either the cook's compartment playing cards or hanging around the bakery and I have to admit that it was great to have him around.

One day I had just finished browning the meringue on the lemon pies we were going to serve for supper when Jack came into the bakery.

"Hey, Mike, can I have a piece of pie?"

"Big brother, there are 380 pies on this rack. Eat them all if you want and I'll make 'em all over again."

So the knucklehead sat at the bakery bench and ate six whole ten-inch deep-dish lemon meringue pies. As he gobbled up pie after pie, I shook my head and warned, "You're gonna get sick."

I was right—he got sick and how! He puked up lemon meringue pie for twenty-four hours. It might have been my imagination but it seemed his face even turned a little yellow.

Jack never again touched a piece of lemon meringue pie or anything else lemon, for that matter. He wouldn't even wear a piece of yellow clothing.

Ticonderoga spent the next six months at the shipyards in Bremerton repairing the fender bender she'd received in the collision. They also added an angle deck to the flight deck to accommodate the new jets we were supposed to receive.

Jack got his second operation and was assigned temporary duty at the Naval Hospital where he brought ducking out of work to a new level. I saw him a couple of times with a broom in his hand but I think he was using it as a cane more than anything. On board, the mess section went to three-section liberty, one day on and two days off, and working only every third weekend. Our crew was cut by one-third because the air squadrons were transferred off the carrier until work was completed. With the smaller work load, we could finish the day's baking in about eight or nine hours, with one baker staying aboard and the others free to come and go as they liked.

I was getting kind of bored with all the free time I had on my hands. I couldn't explore the area because I didn't have a car and I found myself wishing we were back at sea. One day I was walking up the street outside the shipyard and passed the Crow's Nest Bar. I noticed a sign in the window—Help Wanted.

The place was empty, I suppose because it was only 9:00 in the morning. An old white-haired guy came from the back room and said, "Sorry, sailor, we're not open yet."

"I saw your help-wanted sign."

His name was Mike Flannigan. A retired chief quarter-master, Chief Flannigan had owned the Crow's Nest for ten years. After ten minutes of conversation it was decided that I was the Crow's Nest's new swamper.

My job was to clean and stock the bar. I started at 5:00 in the morning on all the days I didn't have duty on board ship. When I was done cleaning, I'd hang around the bar and Mike would tell me sea stories about his Navy career. He was a fine storyteller and one hell of a guy.

He had a destroyer blown out from underneath him at the Battle of Leyte Gulf where he won the Navy Cross. During that battle, he had saved a bunch of guys from burning to death by getting them into the water while being severely wounded himself. Mike took a liking to me and after about a month, he asked me to watch the bar one day while he went to the doctor. He gave me a crash course on bartending, wished me good luck, and left for his appointment.

The bar started to fill up and I struggled to stay even with the drink orders. Mike returned from the doctor an hour later and laughed when he saw the full bar. "Hell, I shouldn't have come back, kid. You're doing great."

Before long I was bartending two out of three weekends when I was off duty from the ship. There were plenty of girls around the Crow's Nest, especially on weekend nights. Most of them were WestPac widows (wives of sailors who were at sea in the West Pacific). One of them was Donna. She was drop-dead beautiful and had the morals of an alley cat. On a Saturday night, half-way through my shift, she walked in and slithered onto a barstool.

"Well, you're new. Who are you?" I told her my name and that I was a baker on the *Ticonderoga*. She caught me checking the diamond ring on her left hand, laughed and said, "Yeah, I'm married but I'm not a fanatic about it."

Donna flirted with me through the rest of my shift and at closing time asked if I'd walk her home, explaining that she didn't like walking alone at that time of night. She lived in navy housing six blocks from the bar. On the walk to her place, she told me she had two kids but they were back home with her mom and dad. Her husband was on a ship that was bobbing around in the Pacific somewhere.

I shouldn't have accepted the offer to come in for a drink. I knew it was wrong for a couple of obvious reasons—my girlfriend and her husband. But it wasn't my first wrong move in life and it surely wouldn't be my last. She told me to get us a couple of beers from the fridge while she freshened up and then she wiggled up the stairs. I found a church key in a kitchen drawer and popped open the beers just as she walked down, dressed in one of those Chinese dresses. It was red silk with a high collar and slits up the side. Well, I tried to tell her I wasn't the kind of guy who would sleep with another man's wife but by the time I got the words out of my mouth, I was.

Sunday morning, I left Donna's house and walked back toward the ship. I was feeling guilty for what I had done and made myself a promise to never put myself in that sort of situation again—well, not with a married woman anyway.

Jack and I took the ferry to Seattle to visit an old friend from the neighborhood, Marty Askelson and his wife. We spent a weekend with them and while there, Jack met and fell for a friend of theirs named Janice Christiansen. I saw an opportunity and came up with a plan to convince Jack to buy a car. I sold him on the idea when I pointed out that anytime he had liberty he could drive to Seattle to visit Janice. He didn't catch on to my ulterior motive. I had a lot more time off than Jack did and I figured that when he couldn't use the car, hell, somebody should.

The next week Jack purchased a 1951 Chevy Deluxe Torpedo Back from a used car lot in Bremerton and I was in business. I don't think Jack drove that car more than five or six times during the rest of his tour in the Navy—while I ran the wheels off it, from Seattle to Tacoma and back to Bremerton.

When repairs to the ship were completed, Jack received orders to NAS Sand Point, Washington. *Ticonderoga* was headed back to the West Pacific. I left the car—out of gas and parked on a side street near the hospital. And I left a note with a buddy to give my brother; it told Jack goodbye and where the car was parked.

Ticonderoga got underway, heading to San Diego for replenishment and then bound for the Far East. Unfortunately, Jack never did get my message. He spent half a day in a taxi searching all over Bremerton before he found the car. He was less than pleased to learn that it was out of gas and made a mental note to kick my ass the next time we met. Ten miles out of Seattle, as Jack headed to his next duty station, the driveshaft fell off. Steam must have come whistling out of his ears as he pushed the car to the side of the road. He took off the license plates and abandoned it, no doubt planning how he would take his revenge.

Jack wasn't at Sand Point long. He got a medical discharge shortly after reporting for duty and was offered a 20 percent disability pension for life or the option of an $800 buyout. Being the clever businessman he was and thinking he could avoid work for a long while, he opted for the latter. Six weeks later, he was broke.

Meanwhile *Ticonderoga* steamed west to Pearl, then on to Subic Bay, Manila, and finally to Yokosuka, Japan. I had passed the test for third-class petty officer and was promoted just before we reached Japan. As my new rank came with a substantial pay increase, I decided to close down my slush fund operation and leave the usury business to some upstart with a bigger tolerance for risk. I had plenty of money set aside and I didn't want to take a chance of jeopardizing everything I'd worked so hard for.

But I was, in fact, about to put life and limb, not to mention my Navy career, in jeopardy one more time.

20

Chase Scene

Getting ready to go ashore in Yokosuka, Japan, my buddy Devereaux, that red-blooded Romeo, was all pumped up to meet a beautiful woman—even if he had to pay for the pleasure of her company. I reminded him of the advice he had given me. "Don't forget the shot card and go in covered, pal."

Yokosuka was a great liberty port. Like any great city, its cultural offerings ranged from high to low. There were plenty of sightseeing tours on either buses or trains where a sailor could learn a great deal about Japanese culture. But Dave and I, like many others from the ship, were not wise enough to take advantage of these rich cultural opportunities. We headed straight for Thieves Alley.

Thieves Alley was a half-mile strip of neon-lit bars, noodle houses, and shops where you could buy almost anything you could imagine. The street wasn't open for traffic with the exceptions of Japanese police and shore patrol vehicles—all pretty busy due to three aircraft carriers being in port—one American, one British, and one Australian. I recognized the possibility of a tri-nation donnybrook.

Dave found a bar with a huge bucking horse lit up in red and yellow neon and a star of Texas above it. "Look at that sign, Mike—The Dallas Bar!" A cowboy through and through, he insisted we check it out. It was packed to the rafters with sailors and marines from three navies. Shore patrolmen were everywhere, stopping fights and hauling drunks out to the waiting paddy wagons. "What a great joint!" Dave laughed as we elbowed our way through the crowd to get a drink.

"Yeah, but five bucks says we're in a fight before we're through with our first beer."

Just then, an Aussie sailor the size of an oak tree clapped a massive hand on my shoulder, smiled broadly and inquired, "Aye, mate, ya wanna fight?"

"No, thank you. But there are some Brits over in those booths that would probably love to."

"Thanks!" He grinned, turned, and strode over to the booth where he picked up a Limey and threw him over the bar.

"That's it, pard'ner," I said. "I'm the hell out of here."

We found another place a little less rowdy and got down to the business of getting loaded and finding some girls. We learned that the bar hookers were very expensive, but one of them told Dave if we came to her house, she would give him a better deal.

Now about this time, Dave was kind of drunk and wasn't using his best judgment. He told me he'd be back in an hour.

"No goddamn way am I gonna let you go off into the boonies with that whore, pard," I told him emphatically. "Jesus, Dave. This has mugging written all over it—you'll end up dead and stuffed in a dumpster!"

"Well," he smiled, "you'd better come with me and watch my back then. Otherwise I'm going by myself."

Since I couldn't stop him, I went along. I figured there's safety in numbers, even if our number was only two.

It was against Japanese law and military law for sailors to go wandering off into the toolies. A block past Thieves Alley, we were out of bounds and soon found ourselves a mile or so out on a dimly lit street with no idea where we were. We told the cab to wait and he agreed to wait half an hour for a thousand yen—almost ten bucks. Haggling wouldn't budge him. Ten bucks, half an hour. That was it. The hooker opened the door and we walked into a small but neat house. She turned to me to ask, "You want girl, too? I have friend. Very beautiful."

"No thanks," I told her, thinking I would rather go back and fight that big Aussie than get the clap again.

Kimako was her name and I could see why Dave was so attracted to her. She was a very good-looking woman and had a perfect little figure. She got us a couple of Ashai beers and offered me a girl one more time. Then she led my fired up, drunken buddy into a back room.

Ten minutes later, there was a commotion and I heard Dave yelling and swearing and then the hooker screaming back. Suddenly, a small Japanese guy came crashing through the rice paper wall, followed by Devereaux in his skivvies.

"Grab that little bastard," he yelled at me. "He's got my wallet!"

I got the guy by the collar and tried to pry Dave's wallet from his fingers. The whore was on Dave's back, pulling his hair and screaming in Japanese. I grappled for the wallet and got it back and Dave shook off the hooker. She was screaming now in English, "Shore Patrol! Shore Patrol!" She ran out the front door, still screaming.

"Get your blues on! The SPs will be here in a heartbeat!"

Dave went back through the wall he had thrown Kimako's pimp through and I looked out the front door. Our cab was gone and our ten bucks with it. Kimako was in the street talking excitedly to two shore patrolmen and pointing toward me standing in the doorway. She was yelling, "Robbers! Robbers!"

I turned and jumped through the hole in the wall. Dave was tying his shoes. "The bitch told the SPs we robbed her," I shouted. "We gotta get the fuck out of here!"

Just as we cleared the back door, I heard the SP yell, "HALT!"

The neighborhood we were in had small backyards. On three sides were wooden fences about three feet high. Along the fence in each yard was a benjo, or sewage ditch, that ran to the back and emptied into the main sewer underground.

"This way," hollered Dave. He took ten running strides and jumped the fence and cleared the ditch as well. "Come on, Mike! It's easy!" I grabbed my white hat in my fist and took off, sailing over the fence and sewage like a deer running from a mountain lion.

We kept going, yard after yard, fence after fence. I heard the SPs behind us, whistle-blowing, footsteps pounding. We were laughing like schoolgirls. We didn't think they had a prayer of catching us when suddenly, one of the SPs started to close the gap. We were still one full backyard ahead of him when we sailed over the last fence on the block. My right foot landed in the ditch and I would have fallen backward but Dave grabbed my neckerchief and pulled me forward. "Jesus, was that a gunshot?" We turned toward the street and kept on running.

I could still hear the SPs whistle when he came over the last fence and then heard him yell as he went knee-deep into the shit, piss and sewage in that last benjo ditch. We were laughing hysterically as we looked back at that poor son-of-a-bitch floundering in the mess. Dave and I quickly found our way back to Thieves Alley, careful not to be spotted by either the SPs or civilian cops.

We were in Yokosuka for two more weeks and managed to avoid any more near-death situations while still having a great time enjoying the more wholesome attractions of a great city. We bought gifts, drank beer, ate the best chili dogs in the world at the Club Alliance, and saw this terrific new movie, *West Side Story*. The morning we left, Dave and I stood on the sponsor deck and chanted the sailor's motto, "Underway's the only way!" as *Ticonderoga* slipped out of the harbor and turned south toward Australia.

21

Australia

Entering the harbor, every man not on watch lined up, topside. In dazzling dress whites we stood in wide-legged stances at parade rest, hands clasped behind our backs, around the perimeter of the flight deck (called quarters for entering port) while the ship's band played "Waltzing Matilda." There were thousands of people on the pier to witness the first American carrier to visit Brisbane since the Battle of the Coral Sea during the Second World War.

We streamed down the gangway to be welcomed by the wonderful people of Brisbane. They were actually grabbing sailors, kissing them, and hauling the boys away with them to pubs teeming with Aussies wanting to buy a Yank a pint. The pub we eventually made our home was called O'Hara's. Its patrons were uncommonly friendly and we had to fight to buy our drinks, or anyone else's, for that matter. Almost everyone I met wanted to introduce me to his daughter, sister, or cousin. Devereaux, always on the prowl, latched on to a pretty Sheila that first night in port. For the rest of our time in Australia the only time I saw him was on board the ship...and looking fairly worn out, I might add.

I ribbed him about it. "Losing your staying power, cowboy?"

"Staying power, hell, I'm just trying to hang on for eight

seconds and that's plenty tough."

Harry, a fellow who owned a hardware store down the street from O'Hara's, invited me to his home on our first Sunday there. The pubs were closed so I accepted his invitation. He gave me his name and his address and told me to come over Sunday about 1:00 in the afternoon, promising a wonderful meal prepared by his wife Margaret.

I rang the doorbell at exactly 1:00. Harry opened the door, a welcoming smile on his face, and asked me in. He introduced me to a tall, pretty woman with dark hair. She appeared to be somewhere in her early forties. "Mike, this is my wife, Margaret." She started to shake my hand but it somehow ended up a hug. I felt a bit awkward but I couldn't help liking her at once. In from the kitchen came a young man about my age and two strikingly beautiful young women.

"Mike," said Margaret, "these are our children, James, Sally and Ginny. Children, this is Mike. He's from the American aircraft carrier."

Harry wasn't lying about his wife's cooking. The meal was great. After dessert, James excused himself, telling us he had to go to work. He shook my hand, saying we should get together for a pint the next day and that he'd like me to meet some of his mates. After clearing the table, the girls and Margaret went into the kitchen. Harry poured us each a drink and asked me about home and my family. When Margaret came back she was putting on a sweater and said, "Come on, Harry, we'll be late." He tossed back his drink as Margaret called Sally from the kitchen.

"We're going to the movies," said Harry as they started for the door. I was kind of confused.

"You're just going to the movies and leaving me here? Do you want me to leave?"

"Oh, no," laughed Margaret. "You just sit and finish your drink. Ginny will be along in a minute."

They left but I was still mixed up about the whole thing.

Let's see, I thought. *They left me with their teenage daughter while they've gone to the movies. That's nuts.* I picked up my drink and headed for the kitchen. Ginny stood at the sink and turned as I came in. "They're gone?" she asked.

"Yeah, they are. Your mom said they were going to a movie. But I don't get it."

"Well," she said, "Sally and I flipped a coin and I won."

"Won? Won what?"

"You, silly," she laughed.

"I still don't understand. I mean, I'm flattered as hell, but I just can't see why a guy would take his whole family to a movie and leave his daughter with a foreign sailor."

Ginny looked at me for a few seconds and asked, "Are you complaining?"

"No, no, not at all. You're gorgeous. It's just that this is sort of, kind of out of the ordinary, isn't it?"

"Well, I'll explain it for you. My dad is crazy about Yanks, and he really likes you. He has always hoped that either Sally or I would marry a Yank one day."

"Marry!" I yelled. "I just came over for dinner."

"Don't panic," she grinned as she slipped her arms around my neck. "I'm not contemplating marriage either, but I like Yanks, too."

I spent quite a bit of time at their home during the duration of our stay in Brisbane and Ginny and I corresponded for a while until she wrote and told me she had become engaged to a policeman and was moving to Melbourne. So I made it out of Australia still single which was good because I don't think Linda would have understood my bringing home an Aussie wife.

I was glad to be back at sea again. Somehow life made more sense to me when we were underway. The days passed quickly on our return trip to San Diego. Soon we were passing Point Loma and entering San Diego Harbor.

I called Linda when I went ashore and she told me that I should also call my folks. I did as she suggested and learned that my brother Jack had gone to Hollywood to see if he could get himself discovered.

His delusional plan was to travel to Hollywood with three of his nitwit alcoholic pals and then hang out at Schwab's Drugstore until some producer or director saw him and offered him a part in a movie. He figured, hell, it worked for Lana Turner, why not him? As Jack was more than willing to tell you, he was a handsome lad, but he may not have recognized that he wasn't wired quite right.

I went to see my cousin Gail's mother, my aunt Peggy, in Santa Monica and she had the address for my brother's apartment in Hollywood. I took a cab and found the building where Jack was living with five Indian guys, all from Calcutta. The fella who answered the door was called Chuck. I never did find out what his real name was. With a heavy accent, Chuck confirmed that I'd find my brother at Schwab's.

Sure as hell, there he was, perched on a stool at the lunch counter, drinking a Coke. I clapped a hand on his shoulder and asked, "Well, brother, how's the movie star business?"

"Mike! I'm so glad to see you. I haven't eaten anything since yesterday and I just spent my last dime on this Coke." I bought him a couple of burgers and fries and we called our folks. Pop told us Aunt Peggy and Uncle Aale were leaving for Michigan the next week and we should call to see if they might give Jack a ride back to Duluth.

We picked up Jack's things; they easily fit into a taxi for the ride to Peg and Aale's where Jack would stay until they left for Michigan. Aale had said he'd give him a ride but couldn't afford to feed him, too, so I gave Jack fifty dollars spending money for the trip. I took the Greyhound back to San Diego where the *Ticonderoga* got back underway for Bremerton for a month's worth of minor repairs. I put in for leave as soon as we put out to sea.

My dad worked for the DM&IR Railway and in December when my leave started, he had gotten me a pass to ride the train from Seattle to Minnesota. I brought with me a twelve-place-setting set of Noritake china I'd bought for my mother. The china was packed in two large boxes marked FRAGILE. Before boarding, I oversaw the loading and stowing of Mom's dishes. Once satisfied they were safely aboard, I found my assigned car and settled in.

In the next seat was a Marine named Cliff who was bound for St. Paul. There was also a group of college girls on their way home to Fargo for spring break. They had two sleepers in the next car and we all spent a good deal of time traveling between the club car and their sleeping cabins. That trip was an absolute riot. Cliff and I were a little worse for wear when we kissed the co-eds farewell in Fargo. Cliff and I shook hands goodbye in Crookston. He went on to St. Paul and I caught a DM&IR caboose headed for Duluth.

It was early evening and snowing when I dismounted the train at the downtown depot. I got some help from the conductor loading my sea bag and china into a cab and off we sped to my mom and dad's.

As I carried my goods up the front stairs, I heard noise coming from the house. I had come home in the midst of a Christmas party!

I paid the cabbie, straightened my white hat and necker-chief and rang the doorbell. Mom opened the front door and screamed, "Michael! Everybody! Michael's home!"

The house was packed with aunts, uncles, cousins, friends, and neighbors. It was a grand homecoming and that leave, in general, was wonderful. Linda and I became engaged during my time at home and we decided we would be married two months after I was discharged. I hopped a plane back to California to meet the ship just returning from Bremerton.

That next year in the Navy flew by. I was in the Far East when it came time for my enlistment to run out. I should have been elated. Instead, I was full of uncertainty. I had passed the test to become a second-class petty officer. My chief gave me the usual drill about reenlisting, or "shipping over," and it was an appealing option. Except, if I re-upped, my promotion would become official in February, the month I was to get married.

Civilian life seemed like a long line of question marks. But my family and my girl were waiting for me so I took the military air transportation service (MATS) from Manila to San Francisco where I got my travel pay and discharge papers.

Immediately, I wished I could go back. I understood Navy life with my shipmates and the old salts who spoke of "wooden ships and iron men." They had transformed me from a pimply-faced hoodlum into...into what? I figured that was something I'd have to find out.

I exited the plane at the Duluth International Airport and was greeted by Linda, Mom, Dad, Jack, and my sister, Kitty. Pop handed me the keys to the sweet-looking peach and white 1957 Chevy that he and Mom had bought for Linda and me as a wedding gift. It was one week short of four years since I'd been run out of town on that Greyhound bus.

Book
III

22

Family Matters

My dad helped me get a job at the steel plant where the pay was good. I hated every minute I spent in those dismal, gray, depressing surroundings—not to mention the work I had to do. I worked down below in a miserable pit, 120° hot, shoveling slag into buckets for forty-five minutes, then climbing up-top to shovel what was in the buckets into railroad cars for forty-five minutes where the temperature was sometimes below zero. I didn't want to shovel slag for a living, but I knew I had to stick it out. I was about to get married—something I was pretty sure I wanted to do.

Linda and I bought furniture, found an apartment down the street from my parents' house, and finalized our wedding plans. We were married on my mother's birthday, February 20, 1965, an unusually warm winter day in Duluth. Linda made a pretty bride as she walked down the aisle of St. Jean's Church, the sun streaming colors through the big stained glass windows. We celebrated in the customary way for that time and our neighborhood with a buffet of ham, baked beans, and potato salad followed by a good old polka dance at a hall in West Duluth, not far from the 402.

Dave Devereaux, who had taken leave to be a groomsman, spent a good part of the evening dancing with every available girl—including my little sister Kitty. Kitty! What had I been thinking? Devereaux, staying for thirty days under the same roof as my sweet sixteen-year-old sister? Well, by the time I stopped to think about it, my little Kitty had fallen head over heels. But the fast-talking cowboy from Cut and Shoot had met his match in the well-trained Catholic school girl who knew how to say no. He returned to the *Ticonderoga* rebuffed but more than a little smitten. They corresponded for a year before he proposed, but by that time she had met Ben, the man she chose to marry.

In the days and months following the wedding, Linda and I settled into our cozy apartment. I stayed at the steel plant for six months and brought my check home to Linda every two weeks. Then I heard about a big layoff about to hit the plant. In order to get out ahead of the possibility of having no job, I called my old friend, Einar Olson, who was still working at Johnson's Bakery. I asked if I might possibly find work there.

"Maybe,' said Einar. "The boss is opening another shop in the new Shopper's City. Stop in tomorrow morning. I'll put in a good word for ya."

I was hired on the spot and gave a week's notice at the plant. It felt good to be back on familiar ground and I slowly but surely worked my way up to night foreman. The following June, my wife presented me with a ten-pound bouncing baby boy. We named him Robert Michael but decided there were enough Bobs in the world and we would call him Robby. He was a delightful child. People told us all the time they never saw a happier baby. These were very good times for Linda and me.

I moved on from Johnson's looking for more experience and a better situation. I took a job working for a man, Ted Hallila, well-known to be a tough guy to work for but better known for being the most knowledgeable baker in our part of the country. I was a sponge soaking up everything Ted could teach me. A bear of a man to work for, Ted was all business and seldom ever cracked a smile. He liked to listen to Twins base-ball on the radio, but once the game ended, off it went. The two of us worked alone through the rest of the night in complete silence broken only by an occasional snapped order and the hum and bang of the machines. Ted lived up to his tough-guy reputation. My mistakes made him scream. Any time I didn't do something to his satisfaction he'd blow up at me, calling me all kinds of names—stupid, lazy, retarded, you name it. I would have quit a million times except that I was learning a lot from him and hell, I had a wife and baby and I really needed the job. Ted worked me eighty hours a week and paid me a salary based on a fifty-hour work-week. I stayed at that job for eighteen months. That was when my dad died. Even then, my boss was mean-spirited about my taking the necessary time off to deal with our family's loss.

On the Thursday before Mother's Day, 1969, my father collapsed in the kitchen at home. When I was younger, I didn't understand the many demons he had battled through the years but now I recognized that depression and alcoholism were certainly players in the attack on his heart. We buried my dad that Saturday. Grief and guilt nearly knocked me out. I couldn't figure out if it was more grief over his death or guilt for my feelings about him. Most of my life I felt like we never liked each other much. I made myself a promise at his graveside that my children would always know that I loved them and I hoped they would feel the same about me.

Sunday night at 9:00, I returned to the bakery. Ted was loading the proof box with pans of Danish. He looked up at me and remarked, "I hope you had a nice vacation."

"Nice vacation. My father just died, you asshole, and I took two days for his funeral." I changed into my bakers' whites and went to the drawer where he put the paychecks on Sunday nights. Just as I suspected, the son-of-a-bitch had docked me for the two days off. I threw the check onto the workbench and said, "If you think you can get by with not paying me for those two days, you're wrong. Minnesota law and the union both allow for three days' bereavement pay when there's a death in the immediate family so you better fix up that check."

He wrote a new check and when he handed it to me I said, "Ted, I can't work for you anymore. You've got three days' notice."

He snarled at me, saying I could leave right then. I took off my apron, changed back into my street clothes, and walked out the door.

Within two days, I got a phone call from the Karps Bakery Supply representative. He had heard from Ted that I'd quit and he said I should go see George Winthrop at Ideal Bakery and Meat Company. Ideal was one of the last of the old-fashioned mom-and-pop grocery stores. The owners, George and his wife, were partners with their son Harvey and I had heard good things about Ideal from the other bakers around town.

It was a pleasant spring morning when I walked through Ideal's front door. A tall, middle-aged man with black hair graying at the temples and wearing black thick-rimmed glasses smiled and asked if he could help me. I stuck out my hand and said, "I'm Mike Hampston. I'm here about the baker's job."

He took my hand and shook it with a firm grip. "I'm Harvey Winthrop. If you'll come with me, I'll take you to meet my father. He's up in the office." We walked to the back of the building and up a flight of stairs to a loft overlooking the store where we found a small, gray-haired man in his middle seventies sitting at an ancient roll-top desk.

"Dad," said Harvey, "this is Mike Hampston. He's here about the baker's position."

George stood with a wide, friendly smile and shook my hand. "Nice to meetcha."

George was a respected grocer in Duluth and our families knew each other fairly well. The market was a prosperous retail shop that also supplied baked goods for the University of Minnesota, Duluth. We talked for half an hour and then he asked me if I could start that Sunday night.

"Sure I can." We shook hands on the deal.

The Winthrops reminded me that there are a lot of great folks in the world mixed in with a few assholes. I had learned plenty from Ted, including what kind of boss I never wanted to be if I had the chance someday to run my own shop. Baking at Ideal turned out to be a good job. I worked the night shift with two other guys, Glen Schnorr and John Wentland. I'd worked with Glen before, at Johnson's Bakery, and John had good experience as well. They were capable bakers and the night shift ran as smooth as melted butter. We worked six nights a week and would load the freezers throughout the week. On Friday nights, we came in at about 7:00 rather than 9:00 and flew through our work so we could finish ahead of schedule and have some fun.

None of our wives knew that we got done early on those Friday nights. In fact, they believed we worked until two or three in the morning. Instead, on most Friday nights, by eleven we were crossing the street to hit Norman's Bar, a great place where I knew most of the patrons through my brother and father-in-law, both legends in the downtown bar scene. The place was always loaded with characters who loved telling stories and playing jokes on each other, and of course it served plenty of beer—something Glen, John, and I eagerly looked forward to after a long work week.

The owner, Ray Wizner, was a great guy and my father-in-law's best friend. The two of them were often there, talking and drinking while Ronnie Young, the Friday night bartender, handled the rail with ease, despite having only two fingers on his right hand. He had lost the others in an accident while working on the Great Lakes ore boats and answered to the nickname, "Bear Paw."

Ronnie complained about everything. He loved to shout, bitch or just plain yell at anyone who would listen. It was part of the reason patrons went into Norman's, to listen to the ranting of Bear Paw, and that included us. The second the three of us walked through the front door he was complaining that we didn't put enough jelly in our bismarks.

One Friday night, after months of listening to this, I made a bismark, ten inches across, and filled it with a pound or so of jelly, iced it and put it in a cake box. I brought this monster to the bar when we were done work. "Ron," I smiled, before he could start his usual rant, "I've got a present for you." His eyes lit up upon seeing the gargantuan goodie.

"Geez, thanks, Mike," and he held it up to show everyone. "Ya see? The squeaking wheel gets the grease," and he took a huge bite. It was like opening a flood gate. Strawberry goo shot out of the pastry, ran down his shirt and slacks and onto the floor.

"You son-of-a-bitch!" he shouted, murder in his voice as he vaulted the bar. I took off toward the front door on a dead run. I couldn't get any speed because I was laughing so hard but Ron was also having difficulty because he had jelly all over his shoes. Enraged, he lunged for the door but suddenly slipped and fell flat on his ass. My brother Jack and Jim Riley were just crossing the street as I came flying out the door. Jack called, "What's the hurry, little brother?"

"Too much jelly," I laughed as I blew past him.

23

Jack

My Friday nights would remain a secret that I kept from Linda mostly because of the money but also because I thought I deserved some time of my own. Eventually, I added the Paul Bunyan Bar to my after-work destinations. It was a hang-out for bookies, burglars, pool hustlers, and other assorted criminals in the downtown Duluth area. It just happened to be where my brother landed as a co-owner with his boyhood friend, Mickey McClelland. Mickey had been a famous athlete in his high school days, breaking records in track and football within the tri-state area. Mickey was a treat to be around. He could always get something going that was good for a laugh. I learned early on not to put too much trust in him or I could very well end up the butt of one of his practical jokes.

One night at the Bunyan after closing, Mick and Jack were having a bump and telling stories on themselves. Mickey confided to Jack that whenever he peed it was necessary to pull his pants and underwear down around his ankles or he just couldn't go and that he had actually seen a therapist, to no avail. Pants down or no pee!

My brother, never one to be outdone when it came to eccentric behavior, retorted with, "Well, do you know what I do? I like to BBQ in the backyard naked except for my cowboy hat and boots." Jack had one of those Clint Eastwood hats that he wore most of the time along with a little cigar that stuck out of the corner of his mouth. Mickey used to call him "Fist Full of Nickels."

Jack continued to live with my mother when she remarried two years after my dad died. Frank, who had lived just two doors away, was a dear man and a great partner for Mom. He had Jack's number from the get-go. Frank refused to put up with any sort of shenanigans from my goofy brother, such as naked barbecuing. So when Mickey asked how he could get away with this barbecuing in the buff, Jack shrugged and answered, "That's simple. I wait for them to go out of town."

I don't think Jack quite believed Mickey's story about his peculiar pissing preference. But he kept looking for evidence. It happened that Jack and Mick were watching a Twins game at the old Met Stadium in Minneapolis. When "Take Me Out to the Ball Game" blared from the loudspeakers signaling the seventh-inning stretch, Mickey announced that he had to piss and headed for the can. Jack, curiosity nearly killing him, got up and followed, careful not to be detected by his partner. But unknown to my brother, Mickey *had* noticed Jack's stealthy maneuver and determined to carry on his hoax. Resolved to see it through to the end, he walked into the men's room and got in line for the urinal, a long trough that ran along one entire wall. There were about a dozen lines of men waiting for the opportunity to turn into pee the tap beer they'd been consuming for seven innings. Jack positioned himself in a line of six or seven men behind Mick and one line over. He waited. Sure as hell, when Mickey's turn at the trough came, he unbuckled his belt, dropped his pants and underwear around his ankles and pissed. The guys around him backed off, giving him looks like he was a mad man.

Mickey told me this story many years later but made me swear never to tell my brother that he had done this solely for Jack's benefit, just to keep up the gag.

Business was booming at the Paul Bunyan Bar. It had suddenly become very popular with the college kids and every night scores of young people would pour in to drink away their latest test scores.

My brother Jack and Mickey were about halfway through their first year of co-ownership and couldn't stop smiling. Jack was uncommonly good-looking. Girls swooned over him and at any given time he would have a potpourri of young beauties on his trap line. Many girls commented on his resemblance to Elvis Presley. It was around this time that Mickey came up with the remark that would change my brother's life...and mine.

It was a busy night. Mickey was bartending when he noticed the customary large group of attractive young women gathered at Jack's end of the bar.

"Hey, Jack," he called, "you look like Elvis holding court. Soon they will be throwing their underwear. I think I'm gonna start calling you the King."

The girls screamed, "Yes, yes, Jack. You're the King," and chanted, "Long live the King! Long live the King!"

It went to his head. From that moment, he truly believed he was the King and would tell you emphatically, "Get off my back. I'm the King and you're not." He figured this gave him carte blanche to live his life in a style he deemed was suited to royalty.

I missed my brother's coronation but the next morning, after finishing the night shift at Ideal Bakery, I walked into the Bunyan to find James Francis Riley behind the bar. I slipped up on the end barstool, ordered a tap Bud, lit a smoke and asked, "So Jimmy, what's new?"

"Well, for one thing, you're part of the royal family."

"What the hell does that mean?"

Jim told me of the crowning of the King, laughing his huge and hearty Irish laugh.

"Oh, Jesus Christ on a crutch!" I cried. "We have to nip this in the bud or he will become the most insufferable son-of-a-bitch in the world."

"Too late," laughed Jimmy. "The place was packed last night and they were all calling him the King." He paused. "Oh, by the way," he chuckled, "now that your brother is King, I suppose that makes you the Prince." His hefty hand slapped the bar like a clap of thunder and a belly laugh shook him as he laughed hysterically.

"Oh, no, you don't, God damn you, Riley," I protested. "Don't make me a part of this stupid, fucking farce!"

Alas, it was too late. It spread like a virus. Up and down the bar, friends, acquaintances, and people I didn't even know were already calling me the Prince.

Having Jack for a brother came with certain challenges, but now, through no wish of my own, my name had been changed because of him and there wasn't a damn thing I could do about it.

But Jack relished his new moniker. To reinforce his stature as the King in the eyes of his public, he found a woman who could sew him an Elvis jumpsuit, complete with the high collar, belt, and sequins. I've got to admit that when he dyed his hair black, loaded it with Brylcreem and then donned his sparkly black Elvis get-up, he did very much resemble the King himself.

With a twenty-nine-dollar guitar that he had absolutely no idea how to play slung over his shoulder, he would travel the downtown bars greeting his loyal subjects. I think I was a tad jealous that I didn't have his flamboyance. The suit of bakers' whites that everyone saw me wearing when I came into the bar couldn't quite stack up to the King in full regalia busting through the swinging doors.

On one of these Elvis impersonation adventures he called

me at two in the morning. It was my only night off and I didn't much appreciate being wakened out of a deep sleep in the middle of the night. My wife answered the phone and after a brief conversation said, "Mike, it's Jack. It sounds important."

I grabbed the phone. "What's wrong? Is Mom okay?"

"Hell, I don't know," he answered in an alcoholic slur. "I'm at the Rustic Bar and I have to know where to put my fingers on the guitar to make a C-chord. The King should know things like this," he hiccupped.

I slammed down the phone, looked at Linda, and answered her quizzical look with one word. "Drunk!"

Some years later on a very warm October 31, not too long after the real Elvis had gone to his Graceland in the sky, the usurper in Duluth celebrated Halloween in his usual way. Sporting his Elvis jumpsuit, a guitar slung round his shoulder, and a full load of Brylcreem in his jet black hair, he'd been bar-hopping and had a pretty good buzz on when he came into the Mirror Lounge where I was bartending part-time. The bar was busy with people dressed in all kinds of outrageous costumes. I think Jack felt let down that, for once, he wasn't the center of attention. As the night spun forward he drank more than most people could and still remain upright. He became a little melancholy and asked me for cab fare home. I gave him twenty bucks and said, "I've called you a cab. Now go home and get to bed."

As it happened, he gave the cab driver a buck and started walking home, not wanting to waste perfectly good booze money on taxi fare.

He stopped at Curley's Bar in the West End about eight blocks from home for a bracer to shore him up for the last leg of the trek. One drink turned into two and by closing time, two finally ended to be a dozen. Barely able to walk, he was still aware of the fact that if the cops caught him staggering down Superior Street he could be arrested for public drunkenness. He left by the alley door. Jack had grown up in the neighborhood. He knew that only eight blocks down the alley was home and his soft, warm bed. But with a severe stagger, three steps forward, two to the side, one backwards and three more forward, the trip worked out to be considerably longer than he had calculated at the outset of his march.

With his jaw set in determination and guided by a full harvest moon, Jack fought his way onward until he found himself just a block and a half from home. In the distance he could finally see his house under the huge moon that had been leading him like the North Star led the Three Wise Men. The King stopped to rest for a while, sitting on the fender of an old Cadillac convertible parked next to a garage.

Laying his guitar on the hood, he lit a smoke and contemplated the next three hundred yards to his back door. He flipped away his cigarette, put the strap of his guitar around his neck and, strumming to keep cadence with his stagger, set out. Suddenly, from the end of the block, a set of headlights appeared and a car sped down the alley weaving from side to side. Jack stood dazed in the headlights. Just short of hitting the frozen King, the car swung into a driveway and smashed into a garage. The horn stuck, the hood sprung open, and steam came pouring out of the radiator.

Jack lurched his way to the driver's door, took the handle and yanked the door open. A man with bloodshot eyes, and a bloody nose as well, looked up at Jack in amazement. Jack leaned in to the obviously annihilated driver and asked in his best drunken Elvis slur, "Hey, man, you all right?"

Suddenly the man's eyes brightened in recognition. He shrieked, lunged past Jack and ran toward his house while the horn on the smashed car still blared. A woman appeared on the porch to investigate the racket. Jack heard over the din, "Martha, I just saw Elvis! He's out in the alley and he's shit-faced!"

My brother's outrageous behavior knew no limits. He saw Stephanie Powers in the movie *McClintock* and went crazy for her. He desperately wanted to meet this new object of desire and so set about creating a fool-proof scheme to fulfill this dream. It was pretty simple, really.

He went to the courthouse and took out a marriage license application for John P. Hampston, 3059 Chestnut Street in Duluth, Minnesota, and Stephanie Powers of Hollywood, California.

It got some attention, all right. The actress's lawyer called Jack and threatened him with a lawsuit. He also demanded that Mr. Hampston cease and desist with any further public insinuations that he and Miss Powers were in any way connected or, for that matter, even acquainted.

Pop was still alive at the time and he was livid. The guys at Steelton, the DM&IR yard office he supervised, gave him a bucketload of crap about his new daughter-in-law-to-be. Pop demanded that Jack move out of the house and never appear in his doorway again. But Jack had always been his fair-haired boy and before long, it all blew over. I must admit it was kind of fun to see my brother in the middle of a shit-storm for a change.

Another of Jack's bright ideas involved an education program. Since he (in his own vodka-blurred eyes) was cooler than anyone else on the planet, he could make a nice profit teaching less fortunate people how to be cool as well. He placed a bold-print classified ad in the *Duluth News Tribune*:

Do girls swoon over you?
If not, it's probably because you are not cool.
Enroll now in the King's Cool School.
For $50 the King will teach you to be cool.
Call 722-1371 to enroll now.

As ridiculous as it sounds, a dozen or so misfits enrolled in my goofy brother's scam school. The next Monday afternoon Jack went over some text that he had scribbled out for this gullible collection of wannabes and, as he told them, "If you will follow the directions on these sheets, you will immediately become cool. You will no longer have to go through life as hopeless losers."

A couple of these guys wanted to kick the King's ass. Most demanded their money back. One guy threatened to sue. But two of these screwballs actually wanted to know when to show up for the next class!

24

Stork Stories

In January 1970, I was working the night shift at Ideal Bakery with Glen Schnorr, a good baker. A brain aneurism and the break-up of his marriage had thrown Glen out of work for a while. When he returned shortly after New Year's, I was glad he was back to share the load.

Life was not perfect in our little shop on those long winter nights. Bakers and owners did not see eye to eye on lots of issues. For example, the owners didn't want to pay for a phone extension into the upstairs bakery. No phone, no connection with the outside world, even in emergencies.

One night, around 11:00, we heard a car horn blowing insistently outside. It was my father-in-law. I ran down three flights of stairs and opened the passenger-side car door. Linda was huddled inside wrapped in a blanket. She gave me a little half-smile and I leaned in and gave her a kiss. She was clearly in labor.

"She's gonna deliver! I'll get her over to the hospital. You get your ass over there."

I ran back, taking the steps two at a time. "Glen, I gotta go. My wife's having a baby!"

"Go!"

Linda had already gone into the delivery room when I burst

into the expectant father's waiting area and suddenly found there was nothing to do. So I sat down wearily on a hard vinyl chair and got started on waiting. The magazine pile did not interest me and coffee wasn't helping the jitters much. I hoped Linda was holding up OK in one of those rooms back there. A big change was definitely coming to our family—exciting and a little scary—two kids! As the hours wore on, I thought about my mom, the story of my own birth, and the state my dad was in, and concluded, *Well, at least,* I'm *sober!*

As close as I can figure, I was conceived around Memorial Day of 1943. Seven months later, just before Christmas time, my paternal grandmother received a telegram from the war department with the notification that her son Quinlan, who was in the army fighting with the Third Infantry Division near Monte Cassino, Italy, was missing in action. Grandma became hysterical and, according to my dad, my mother was only a bit more composed. The general shock to the family may have caused what followed.

My mother was due to deliver on February 28, 1944 but I had other ideas. In the late afternoon on December 24, I gave an extra hard kick with my wee foot and broke my mother's water to give her a signal that no matter what the doctor had predicted, I wanted to be born at Christmastime.

Mother was home with Claudia and Jack when the flood began. She first called the doctor and he told her to meet him at St. Mary's Hospital. Next she called the 402 where my father was knee deep in Christmas cheer. She let the bartender know that a "He's not here" lie would be unacceptable. After a very long wait, my father finally came to the phone.

"John, my water broke!"

"Well, dammit, call a plumber!" and he hung up.

Mom called her cousin Kay to come take care of the children while she went off to give birth to her Christmas surprise. After that she packed a suitcase and made a third call. This one was to Herb Lien, a neighbor and family friend. Could he drive her to the hospital? Once they arrived at St. Mary's, Dr. Johnson met mom in the delivery room. Together they went to work getting me born.

Eventually my father showed up, a little worse for wear, reeking of Irish whiskey and demanding to know just why the hell I was being born now and screwing up his Christmas celebration when I was supposed to wait until the end of February.

At 12:12 on Christmas morning, Mom and I met face to face for the first time and found that we were instantly crazy about each other. She called me her "dear little angel of the Lord." After he looked me over, Dr. Johnson declared that I was a surprisingly healthy baby considering that I was two months premature and tipped the Toledoes at a mere four pounds, four ounces. In no time, I decided to take a nap.

Mom was tired too. Her day had been almost as rough as mine. Early that Christmas morning we snuggled in for a nice snooze and dreamed of all the things we would do together in the years to come.

Meanwhile, back at the homestead, cousin Kay managed to get my six-year old sister Claudia, my hell-on-wheels brother Jack, and the dog Spot all bedded down. She thought to herself, *Now might be a good time to have a little Christmas cheer.* Didn't she deserve it? Though she was just shy of the legal drinking age, Kay opened a fresh bottle of Jameson whiskey that Dad had put away to pour during the holidays. One drink tasted very good so she had another and the second was tasty enough to suggest a third. Soon she wove her way upstairs and fell asleep on my parents' bed, fully dressed.

Sometime during the night, eighteen-month-old Jack awoke and went to find his mother. She was missing and because Kay was taking a nap on the bed where Mom and Dad usually slept, he and Spot trotted off downstairs where they got down to the business of undoing Christmas.

Jack took charge of opening all the presents and Spot's job was first to knock over the tree and then to assist Jack in the rest of the destruction project. Finding a five-pound box of Whitman Sampler chocolates, the two of them sat down to a Christmas feast.

As daylight streamed in through the bedroom window, Kay pulled the coverlet over her head. Between her ears, a little drummer boy was pounding a big bass drum. She remembered the Jameson and the job she had been assigned to do and dragged her weary self off the bed.

Feeling better after splashing her face with cold water, Kay checked on the kids. Claudia was sleeping peacefully. Jack's crib was empty. She flew down the stairs only to behold the aftermath of the Christmas Eve massacre. Next to the knocked over Christmas tree, Jack and Spot lay asleep on the couch, smeared with chocolate and vomit. Torn Christmas wrappings were strewn everywhere.

Kay sat down and cried for a bit and then, like the good soldier she was, got very busy cleaning up the kid, the dog, and the front room. She had it pretty well finished when my father got home with news of the addition to the family.

Another boy! They had already named me. Fearing the worst, that Uncle Quin had been killed in Italy, I was named after my uncle to plug the empty hole in my generation. Throughout family memory, there had always been a Quinlan Hampston in our lineage. The very thought of these recent events made Pop feel even more tired than he already was after struggling to stay awake all night at the hospital. He decided a little nap would help him get squared around.

Exhausted, Kay started on Christmas dinner. Mom had two capons in the icebox and she'd asked Kay to cook them for Dad and the kids. Kay was game but not much of a cook. She didn't realize that the birds weren't yet cleaned. She turned on the oven to roast the birds—with the guts still in them.

When Kay got around to reading the directions on the empty poultry bag two hours later and realized that she had ruined Christmas dinner, she once again broke down in tears. But when Pop came downstairs he told her, "That's okay, honey, the kids would rather eat pancakes anyway."

So that's what they had for Christmas Day dinner at 3114 Chestnut Street in 1943. Pancakes!

Right after the New Year in 1944, Quin turned up at a hospital in Sicily. He had been severely wounded in the knee.

Sitting slumped in the plastic chair in the waiting room of St. Mary's obstetric wing with my eyes closed, I was thinking about what a blessing Uncle Quin had been to me as a kid, full of fun and kindness, when I was roused from my daydream to learn that after a lengthy labor, our son John David Hampston was born on January 20, 1970.

Right from the start he was a beautiful, cheerful, lovely baby. I was just delighted to have this boy. He had a look that said, *I love you,* that touched my heart when he was a tiny infant. When he was a toddler he'd come over to the couch and crawl up into my arms just to be with me.

Johnny grew to be a kind and affectionate kid. But he also learned to stand up to his big brother. When they were little, Johnny and his older brother Robby got along well much of the time. They also fought a lot, and I worried that my preoccupation with earning a living in the bakery business left me little time to referee their childhood struggles. I felt guilty but I knew we'd have a decent income and security—if I just worked hard enough. I did work my butt off at Ideal and doubled the effort three years later when I bought my own bakery. Then I worked so many hours I would come home with blood in my socks.

I bought the bakery in Lakeside from Ted, my old hard-ass boss—the guy who was a smart baker and a tough taskmaster. I was twenty-nine years old. Robby was seven and Johnny was three. Linda would come down on Saturday mornings and do icing and wrapping. I made two little cots down in the basement and put a TV in there so the kids could watch cartoons. They loved it. Linda had these two little boys to care for and now she had to help her goofy husband make this business go. She did her best, everything she could. Then the sugar crisis hit and there was no money.

In 1974, speculators bought up the entire sugar crop and forced the price of a pound of sugar from thirteen cents to ninety-four cents. Two pails of roll icing now cost one hundred dollars. A hundred dollars was our house payment—two buckets of icing! Small candy companies and bakeries all over the country went under. I laid off all my help and tried to do everything myself. I worked so much that my wife and children hardly ever saw me. When I was home, I was asleep.

The sugar crisis was the death wound to our marriage. No money and no hope. We couldn't make our house or car payments and there was little money for food. My kids were living on day-old bread and scrambled eggs. Linda and I fought all the time. I hated to fight and it was tough on us. We'd been in love since we were kids. I don't know who quit trying first, but we quit.

I gave the bakery away, free of charge, to Peter Lampi, a boy I'd brought along from age fourteen who was still in high school. I sent him to bakers' school but I'd already taught him everything he needed to know. After three months of a two-year course, the school said he didn't need to continue his classes. He already knew everything they would teach him.

Right about that time, Linda and I had a huge fight. There was no money. We couldn't get past the poverty and the pain. I walked away and left my family destitute. I took what money I had and I ran away. I never forgave myself for that.

Shortly after that, we divorced. There were probably things we could have done to head it off if we had been more mature, if I hadn't spent so much time working, but for the record, it was mostly my fault. Not long after our divorce I came to my senses and I sent some money. The court thought I should expand on that desire but I dodged child support as long as I could, acting like the complete asshole that I was. Finally, they caught up with me and for the next fifteen years I worked two jobs to get it paid off.

But now it was 1974 and I was on my own for the first time in my life...except for Charlie.

Book
IV

25

Drinkin' Buddies

I remember the first day I met Charlie Ziegler. At the time, I was still married to Linda. She and I had stopped at the Bunyan after she finished work at a downtown business. Charlie's story was that he had been run out of Boston by gangsters from whom he had lifted some money. He barely got out with his life after a severe ass-kicking. Rumor had it that he escaped Boston with a gangster's high-end hooker on his arm and he hit Duluth and Superior with a half-dozen five-hundred dollar suits, a couple of cashmere overcoats, and diamond rings on every finger of his hands. It was a fact that Charlie could fast talk anyone out of anything.

Charlie introduced himself, mostly to Linda. He flashed a smile, took her hand and kissed it, his eyes looking into hers as he told her that she was absolutely beautiful. I thought to myself, *No woman is safe from this knuckle-sucking son-of-a-bitch.*

Z was a good-looking man with long mutton-chop sideburns and an irresistible twinkle in his eyes. He was one of those rare people you meet in life who have the ability to draw people to them, close and personal. I suppose if he had wanted, he could have been a guru or Bhagwan or started his own religion, but he just liked being a bartender and was a natural whiz at it. He charmed Linda that night but, in the long run, he and I were the ones destined to have a lifelong friendship.

When Linda and I eventually divorced, I took stock and realized that I literally had nothing. I don't only mean things like cars or furniture. I mean I didn't know anything about anything. I had absolutely no social skills whatsoever.

First, my mother had taken care of me when I was a child and then I was cared for by the Navy, Mr. Johnson, Red Dunning, and my wife. Now I was on my own.

I was working at the Bread Board Bakery, half a block from Mr. Pete's Bar in downtown Duluth. I finished work one day and felt a thirst coming on but rather than walk the one and a half blocks to the Bunyan, I turned the other way and headed for Pete's. The day was sticky and hot. Pete's had the air on high and the lights turned low. Red and black candles flickered on the bar and every table in the joint. The carpet was crimson and as I walked through the front door I left a trail of white flour footprints that followed me to my barstool where Charlie and a group of his friends were talking.

He recognized me. "Prince," he smiled. "How ya doin', pard?"

"Fine, Charlie. How 'bout you?"

"Rain, mud, shit, or blood, the Z stays the same," he answered as he slapped me on the back which caused a large cloud of flour dust to rise into the air from my white bakery shirt.

"Jesus Christ," he said, sucking on his Marlboro, "that can't be healthy."

Charlie and I became fast friends and through him I made many more pals. I slid into single life like going down a water slide at Disneyland.

One guy I met at Pete's was Jack LaMar, otherwise known as "the Rev." The Rev was also known as "Slipknot" because, of all the weddings he'd officiated, not one had stood the test of time and sooner or later came untied. He was an ordained minister and I learned that he had been a chaplain on board the *Ticonderoga* about the same time I served on her. Jack LaMar had a colorful vocabulary, mostly the color blue, and it really needed a stretch to wrap your mind around the idea of his being a man of the cloth. The Rev once walked into the Mirror Lounge with a live Canadian goose on a leash and ordered two shots of Guggenheimer whiskey. He tipped one jigger back, wiped his mouth with the back of his hand and proceeded to pour the other shot down the throat of the goose.

Looking down the bar, he spied two girls sitting at the other end. The Rev thought his goose might give him an edge in getting acquainted, so off they went staggering down the bar, Jack with romance in mind, and the goose leading the way. The Rev introduced himself and his pet to the girls. When one of them reached down to pet the goose, it struck out with its beak and nipped her hand. She screamed, frightening the bird. It took off running and flapping and honking back up the bar leaving a trail of goose shit the whole way.

"Now you've done it," observed the Rev. "You've scared the shit out of him." Furious, the bartender demanded that the Rev clean up the mess but the Rev just laughed.

"You're the employee here, not me. Come on, pard, I know when we're not welcome." He grabbed his goose's leash and marched out the door.

The owner of Mr. Pete's, Peter Manolis, at one time or another gave every one in my circle of friends a job. When I came on the scene it was Charlie and Ray Ward behind the bar.

Tony Hoff and Ron Ross would follow sometime later. When I was in between opportunities, it was my turn to have my bacon saved by "the Boss," as everyone called him. He was the nicest and most generous of men and an absolute dream to work for. Bartenders at Mr. Pete's were considered the elite of Duluth mixologists. Beautiful young women would compete to take one of Pete's employees home for the night.

Charlie and I rented neighboring apartments on Park Point, a skinny strip of sand peninsula that extends seven miles out into Superior Bay with the bay on one side and Lake Superior on the other. It was a gorgeous place to live and our beach in the summer was overloaded with eager and willing cocktail waitresses.

Ron Ross and his girlfriend, Mary Ann, moved in upstairs of Charlie and that first summer turned into one continuous party. We worked at all the hot spots: Pete's, the Mirror Lounge, and the Paul Bunyan. But other than as a device to meet more women and make a little whiskey money, work wasn't really that important to us.

Ross had always been an early riser and one warm July morning he shook me out of a drunken stupor. "Get up. I need some help."

"With what?" I asked, rubbing my eyes.

Ross riffled through my closet and threw me my swimming suit, answering in his slow western drawl, "Never mind. I need some help. Put those trunks on. I'll make coffee. You have enough time for one cup and a couple of smokes. Then we have work to do."

Twenty minutes later we were walking down the beach. What a bright, beautiful morning it was. The water was cold but still warm enough to prevent hypothermia from taking hold. I dove into the surf, shocking my system back into sobriety and came out of the water spluttering, "God damn, Ronnie, that water's cold! Now what's this job you need my help with?"

"You'll see in another block or two."

I could never tell what Ron was thinking. He loved covert operations. Secrecy and stealth were his modus operandi. A little farther down the beach Ron announced, "Here we are."

I looked at him. "Yeah, here we are. Now what the hell are you talking about?"

He didn't say anything, wanting to draw out the suspense of his secret plan as long as possible. Smiling and clearly pleased with himself, he pointed to a log that had washed up on shore. "We are going to bring that home." His smile widened.

"Are you nuts? That goddamned thing has got to weigh at least a ton. How do you suggest we get it home and even if we could, why would anyone in his right mind want to?"

"First of all," assured Ron, "we will simply roll it into the water and float it back, and to answer your second question, we are going to plant it on the beach to mark our territory."

"Can't we just go and piss on the sand to mark our territory?"

"Shut up and give me a hand." He moved toward the log.

After an hour of pushing, pulling, dragging, and straining, we had the log floated and were guiding it back toward our own stretch of beach. When we arrived, Ron went to get Charlie to help while I stood in the water trying to keep the log from floating out to sea. Charlie and Ron returned with a shovel and we started digging. Finally, with a six-foot hole in the sand, we rolled the log out of the water and up the beach to the hole. We got the monster upright and quickly packed in sand around it to keep the damn thing straight. Then we stood there triumphantly, admiring our handiwork like Egyptians appreciating the pyramids. It stood twenty feet out of the sand and, to our bloodshot eyes, looked quite majestic. "Now what?" I asked.

"We go get another," answered Ron cheerfully.

I turned and ran for my apartment, locked the door and

pulled the drapes shut.

We did manage to plant four more poles that summer and when a pretty young cocktail waitress would ask what they were, we told her with perfectly straight faces that they were the beginnings of a telephone pole farm that we were starting. One actually believed it. This not-too-bright young beauty remarked, "Oh, THAT's where they come from."

One of the girls that stopped by our beach pad was truly pretty with long brown hair flowing down to her shoulders. She was also smart and gregarious and really fun to be with. Susan and I entered into a whirlwind romance fueled by gallons of brandy. We were inseparable. One night, between the fourth and fifth saloons on a pub crawl, we ducked into the doorway of the Providence Building on Superior Street for a smooch. I asked her to marry me. We had met in July and were married on January 9 at my sister's house with a reception at the Duluth Curling Club. The Reverend "Slipknot" LaMar officiated.

Legend has it that I brought a date to our wedding.

"Not true," said Susan, "but she was there!"

You know me and my wandering eye. We lived together for about five months and terminated our marriage after a year. Our infatuation with each other may have dimmed but we eventually became great pals—and so we stayed.

Neither of us ever drank brandy again.

26

Winging It

For ten years, we rocked Park Point with non-stop partygoers coming and going at all hours of the night and day. One of them was the beautiful Jeanette and we had really good times together. The romance was short-lived, however, when she discovered that I had made advances on a roommate and she gave me the boot. I regretted that for many years. She was a quality woman, but then every time I was lucky enough to be with a quality woman, I screwed it up.

Back on the loose, new temptations were as close as my beach where good-looking women were lying about all summer long. Jeanette recovered nicely too and got married shortly afterward. In a year or so, she started talking to me again and we made the transformation from a broken romance to some-thing better—a lasting friendship.

Even though Jeanette dropped out of the Park Point scene, my other friends made themselves thoroughly at home at my beach pad.

I was taking it easy one summer morning when my sliding glass door opened and three twenty-something girls walked in to find me in my bathrobe reading the Saturday paper and drinking my coffee.

Candy blew me a kiss and hands on hips, squeaked, "Good morning, Princie. May we use the Fun Island?"

The Fun Island was an eight-feet in diameter floating raft that I kept in the garage. It could accommodate a six-pack of sunbathers and was a favorite of the girls who came around.

"Sure." I threw her the garage key and told them to have fun. "I'll be out later."

Summer weather in Duluth is like a big tease. Just when you think everything is perfect, the cold east wind can come up to slap and chill bare skin. But on this particular day, both the water and the air temperature were ideal. On a day like this one, people would show up one or two at a time, check in at the house, use my bathroom as a changing cabana, and run down to the beach to join in the merriment. In a very short time, my driveway was as plugged as a shower drain in a sorority house.

I put on my swim suit and donned my campaign hat like the one Colonel Potter wore on *M*A*S*H*. Then I poured another mug of coffee and strolled down to the beach to ask each person with a car parked in the drive to please unscrew up our parking area. That done, I went into the garage and got my Please Park on the Street sign and placed it at the head of my driveway.

Stopping to wave at a couple of cars that honked at me, I realized I'd better get some more beer. *This*, I thought, *could be the party of the summer.* I threw on a shirt and shoes, grabbed some cash, and drove to the liquor store where I bought two bottles each of vodka and Windsor, a jug of rum, mix, and three cases of beer. And a bunch of ice.

Back at home I loaded all my coolers and went to work setting up a self-serve bar in the garage. I put a metal bucket on the bar and taped a sign to it that hinted, $ Donations, Please $.

Charlie came out of his apartment, coffee cup in hand, dressed in a little towel that he referred to as his "wrappie jabbie." Everything that Charlie couldn't readily put a name to was simply a "jabbie," a word that gained such popularity in the Duluth bar community I wouldn't be surprised if it has now gone viral and is included in *Webster's New Revised Dictionary*.

"They're showing up early today, hey pard?"

"Well, ya know, you can't drink all day unless you start in the morning."

Soon Ron Ross appeared on his porch. "Mornin' boys." He surveyed the crowd of around forty on the beach. "Party today, huh?"

"Well, I didn't plan one, but yeah, it's starting to look that way."

Another car full of girls tried to enter the driveway but serving as parking lot cop, I held my right hand high, signaling them to stop. They backed out and found a place on the street.

The Rev showed up sometime around 1:00 p.m. and immediately got his nose into the bottle of Guggenheimer that he always carried in the trunk of his car. Rev and I checked the donation bucket which happily held enough dough for four more cases of suds and a couple more bottles of booze.

"Wanna come with me, Rev?" I asked. "I'm going to make a booze run." Walking toward the driveway, he suddenly stopped, his hand grabbing my arm.

"Dammit, Prince, I've got an idea! You ever been in a float plane?"

"No. Why?"

"Then it's time, my son. You are going to deliver the beer via float plane. I know a guy down at the airport on the end of Park Point who gives rides," he said, marching in high excitement toward my car.

The Rev called his pilot buddy from the liquor store and he agreed, with me aboard, to buzz our beach, then land offshore and taxi to where I could wade on in.

The plane was tied up to a pier, and we took off from the little land/lake airport at the end of Park Point. We flew down a couple miles of beach until I spotted our telephone pole farm. I laughed out loud and pointed it out to the pilot. He circled once and then buzzed the exuberant crowd. He circled again for his final approach. By this time all of my friends were standing, shading their eyes with their hands, watching and wondering what was this madman in a seaplane doing?

Lake Superior was in a rare state that day. Its surface was like glass with not a hint of breeze or ripple to disturb the waters. The plane floated down to the surface about one hundred yards from the water's edge and taxied toward the shore, coming to a stop where the water was about waist deep.

I climbed out onto the pontoon and stepped into the water, campaign hat still impressive on my head, and a case of Budweiser on each shoulder. A roar rose from the revelers on the beach as I strode through the water with my booty, like General MacArthur wading ashore to reclaim the Philippines.

The Hampston gene pool runs toward the flamboyant. Anyone who might think of this behavior as over the top has only to recall any number of the King's legendary pranks. And I just couldn't help it if I really enjoyed being the center of attention as the crowd gathered around me.

27

Swimming for Dollars

In the 1970s, almost ever bar in town had one thing in common—a shuffleboard-style bowling machine, with a puck that players slid to make the pins rise. The Paul Bunyan was no different except for the amount of cash wagered on the games. High rollers would come from all directions to bet on the high stakes bowling matches.

One game I witnessed had so much money wagered by players and spectators making side bets that all conversation was prohibited. Imagine seventy-five people in a bar and the only sounds to be heard are cheers following a strike and the occasional clink of ice cubes. The machine could handle up to six players at a time but for this particular competition there were four. The buy-in was $5,000 per man. The highest scorer would take home the entire twenty grand.

The King was tending bar and held the dough. His partner Mickey served as referee and rules official.

In this highly illegal contest, the players were all colorful but none more so than Benjamin Harrison George Washington Hutch, III. Hutch had piloted his B17 in twenty-five missions over Germany during the Second World War. In civilian life, he had made plenty of money, first as a stockbroker and then as a first mate on the Great Lakes ore boats. He carried his roll

142

of cash, never less than ten grand, in his pocket, bound by a thick rubber band. Then there was Attorney, a prominent litigator who had an uncommonly large head and hands to match. He was a guy no man would want to have pissed at him—in or out of court. The other two players were Brian, a local entrepreneur who could drink more Petri brandy than most men can lift, and Pilot, a guy who flew for Northwest Orient Airlines.

The game was afoot. Attorney led off and left himself a seven-ten split. The crowd groaned. Mickey raised his hand for silence. Attorney slid the puck back and forth, sprinkled a little more sawdust, moved the puck to and fro, and shot again. He picked up the number ten, but stubbornly, the seven just wiggled and remained upright. Attorney complained that it should have gone down. The machine was at fault! But Mickey assured him that he'd had the amusement company in that morning and the unit had been completely gone over in preparation for the big game that night. Attorney grumbled and shook his massive head back and forth, his great shoulders moving in synchrony. He resembled a great African elephant. Henceforth, that move was called "the elephant shake."

Next went Pilot. Strike!

Then came Brian, Petri water in hand. Strike!

Now Ben Hutch III. Another strike!

Attorney realized that his one open frame might cost him $5,000 and he was in a sour mood. His jaw set, he eyed the board and sent the puck careening toward its target. All the pins fell.

Halfway through the game, both Pilot and Brian had a frame in which they failed to strike although they were able to pick up the spares. It was Hutch, alone out in front, with six strikes in a row. This balance continued, with each man tossing a strike each time his turn came up.

Finally, the game was into its tenth frame. Tension was tight. Attorney spared. He was done unless someone seriously fell apart.

Pilot spared his last frame and left a ten-pin standing in the open. He also was done.

Brian approached the machine and studied it thoughtfully through squinted eyes. He took a breath, held it, positioned the puck carefully and let his shot fly.

"Fuck!" he yelled when only half the pins fell. But determined, he picked up the spare. He had needed a good run to stay close to Ben Hutch but now he offered a heartfelt prayer that Hutch would drop a couple of pins.

Hutch was up and all he had to do was roll two spares to win the whole $20,000. Hands shaking, his face was scrunched like a dog shitting peach pits. "Hang on," he said, giving the time-out sign with his hands. He made his way to the bar.

"Give me a double, King," Hutch told my brother. Jack poured him a steep Old Thompson and Hutch knocked it back in two swallows. "Another."

Jack refilled the glass, and Hutch downed the booze in two quick gulps. He returned the glass to the bar with slow deliberation and stretching out his right hand, pointed out that he had the steady hands of a surgeon. Hutch returned to the bowling machine and demanded, "Where's the puck?"

Mickey said he didn't know. When Hutch had gone to the bar, a stampede of onlookers and side-bettors followed him, and both Jack and Mickey had their hands full serving drinks. With all the side-betting, Hutch wasn't the only guy there who needed a bump. Hutch grabbed anyone who wasn't in the can or holding two drinks to help him search. Exasperated, Hutch returned to the bar.

"Get another puck, will ya Mick?"

"Can't, Hutch. Don't have another one."

Ben Hutch went crazy. A smallish but wiry man, Hutch had a ferocious temper. He threw beer bottles, drinks, ashtrays, all the while screaming, "Call the fucking cops! I want that goddamned puck back!" He ran to the phone booth and we could hear him in there screaming into the telephone to the police, "The puck! The puck! Someone stole the fucking puck!"

Charging out of the booth, he continued his rant until the law arrived. "You cops gotta search these guys, every goddamn one of them. Strip search 'em if you have to. You gotta find that puck."

"What the hell are you talking about, buddy? Just lower your voice, slow down and tell me what this disturbance is all about," the cop ordered.

Hutch somehow gathered himself and did just that. He spelled out the details of the game, the $20,000, and the puck's strange disappearance.

"Wait a second," said the policeman. "Let me get this straight. You say you were involved in an illegal game of chance for $20,000 and now the puck is gone. Is that correct?"

"Correct," answered Hutch, chin out and shoulders squared.

"Who else here was involved in this wager?" asked the cop. Hutch looked around but, alas, his competition had taken flight at the first sight of the law coming through the door.

"Well...well," he stammered, "they're not here right now," beginning to realize that he might have just said the wrong things to the wrong people.

One officer looked at Hutch and began, "You have the right to remain silent," as he cuffed his hands behind his back and marched him out the door. We could hear him screaming at the police out in the street. "You can't do this to me, you pissy-winkle little bastards, you donkey-boy little assholes! I'm Benjamin Harrison George Washington Hutch, III, and I demand some respect!"

Mickey called the game a draw and Jack put each of the principal players' $5,000 in four envelopes with their names on them and locked them in the safe. The next day, when the amusement company brought a new puck, they found the old one lodged in the back of the machine. "They do that every now and then. If it ever happens again, just reach your hand back there and dislodge it."

So no one really tried to rip Hutch off after all. It was only a mechanical malfunction, but Hutch was unconvinced and set out to get his revenge.

The following week, Ben Hutch sat at the bar on Friday afternoon still stewing in his juice over the lost twenty grand and his overnight incarceration. After downing a few drinks, he began to brag that he was the best swimmer in the bar and would bet all comers $20,000 that he could swim farther out into Lake Superior than anyone else in town. This was his challenge. He and his opponent would leave the money with someone trustworthy on the beach and they would begin their swim toward Canada. The first one to turn back would be the loser.

The plan was simple enough. The problem was that it would almost certainly result in the death of one of the swimmers and perhaps both of them would drown. At any rate, it was a pretty safe bet that neither would be wading onto the shore at Marathon, Ontario, about three hundred miles straight across Lake Superior. Still, the discussion persisted among a few people who were willing to wager huge amounts against Hutch in favor of some unknown swimmer—certainly far younger and in better shape than old Benjamin Harrison George Washington Hutch, III.

But in the end, no one was truly willing to put Hutch's life on the line for a twenty-thousand dollar wager so the conversation turned to how to prove or disprove Ben Hutch's claim of being Duluth's greatest swimmer. It was Hutch himself who inadvertently offered a solution. He had been drinking for several hours when he launched into one of his bragging oratories. "Ya know, boys, I'm so goddamn good that I can swim two lengths of a full-length pool, under water, without coming up for air."

"Bullshit!" someone yelled. "Johnny Weissmuller couldn't make that swim."

That's all it took. Hutch raised his glass and shouted, "Put your goddamn money where your mouth is, you pissy-winkle, donkey-boy little shit. I've got twenty Gs that says I can make that swim and fuck Johnny Weissmuller."

Rocky Rockham happened to be in the bar that night. He worked at the Duluth Athletic Club and he had the keys.

Between 5:00 and 9:00, the Athletic Club's closing time, news of the wager ran through just about every bar in town. Local gamblers from all over streamed into the Bunyan, wanting to take advantage of what they figured to be a sure thing. Hutch got scratch paper and a pen from the King and began recording their wagers. At 10:00, the bar emptied out and up the street crawled a block-long centipede of drunks, bookies and gamblers.

I was near the front of the procession and heard Hutch say to Bob, the barber, "I've put out over $60,000 in markers on this bet, kid. Put your dough on me, because I don't have the money to pay off, so if I don't make it, I ain't coming up."

Rocky opened the pool room, flipped on the lights and all the guys crowded in around the edges of the pool. The racket was deafening. Everyone was yelling and side-betting until once more, Mickey, serving as referee and rules official, raised his hands and called for silence.

Hutch stripped down and stood at the edge of the pool. Murmurs rose from the onlookers. He looked kind of pathetic standing there naked with his white ass, nub of a pecker and round little pot belly. Mickey once again called for silence. When it was achieved, he asked, "Are you ready, Ben?"

"As ready as I'm gonna get," and he dove in with nary a splash.

Mickey walked along the side of the pool to make sure

Hutch's head didn't come out of the water. When Hutch made the turn on the first leg, he had been under the water almost two minutes. About this time, I was thinking he didn't have a prayer and I was certain to lose the twenty bucks I'd bet on him. Every now and again that little white ass would surface like a mini white submarine coming up to charge its batteries. Sometimes slow, sometimes fast, he glided along. The yelling and cheering grew to an unbelievable din.

He was now three-fourths of the way and I was starting to think the old bastard was going to do it. I screamed and yelled encouragement, "Come on, Ben! Come on, Hutch. You can do it! Screw Johnny Weissmuller!!" But with six feet left to go, he slowed to a near stop.

"Come on, Ben. Come on, Ben. You can do it!" guys shouted.

About a hundred people were either yelling for him to make it or shouting, "Drown, you old son-of-a-bitch!"

When his right hand hit the end of the pool, Hutch had been under water for almost four minutes. His head came up, with mouth open wide to take a breath, but went right back under, sinking to the bottom. He was drowning. Mickey and two other guys jumped in and dragged him to the surface. Hands were extended to pull him out. He sputtered and coughed and gasped for breath. When Mickey climbed out of the pool, he bent over and checked on Hutch. Mick straightened up. "He's okay. I think he'll live."

Khaki pants and maroon and gold UMD sweatshirt dripping water, Mickey raised his hands and declared that Hutch had indeed swum two lengths of the pool without coming up for air.

A few naysayers complained that his ass had come out of the water but Mickey, fair man that he was, stuck to his decision. Hutch was pronounced the winner—any and all bets in the matter should be paid. There was some grumbling but, since Hutch didn't drown and he collected on most of his bets, it was a satisfying victory for the old sailor.

Andy's Bar

Jack and his partner Mickey were never meant to be businessmen, so they did what they did best. They drank their way through the profits and lost the Bunyan.

Jack got a job on the DM&IR as a gandy dancer, slang for a rail-spike pounder. Mickey went into business with Charlie Ziegler. Their new place was Andy's Bar in Superior, Wisconsin. Andy's had been there forever and I suppose if you went back far enough you would probably find an owner actually named Andy. It was a very busy place doing biz with longshoremen, sailors, railroad and shipyard workers, and there were always a few hookers on hand ready and willing to do their job with anyone that had the price.

Two of the regulars were named Dooley and Muntz. They were almost always together and best friends all their lives. They both were married but both were customers of the working girls around the joint. Their wives were forever chasing them down and if one had a girl upstairs when his wife came in, the bartender would pick up the phone and call upstairs, letting it ring twice before hanging up. This was the signal to exit through the back door and down the stairs to the alley.

One slow Saturday afternoon, Jack and I were sitting at the

bar shooting the breeze with Mickey when in walked Muntz, about half in the mitt. We all greeted him and Mick asked, "Where's Dooley?"

"He had to go to Eau Claire to pick up some parts for the shipyard."

"You must be lonesome," says Mick, putting a drink in front of Muntz. "I thought you two were joined at the hip." Muntz laughed, tossed back his shot and ordered another.

Just then a very pretty woman with red curly hair and a pink and white flowered sundress strolled in the front door. "Hi ya, Muntz. How are you, you big hunk of man?"

"Hi, Mary Lou. You look great," says Muntz. "What are you all dolled up for?"

"A wedding shower. It starts at 4:00 and I thought I'd stop for a beer first." Mary Lou was Dooley's wife but she had gone steady with Muntz in high school before marrying Dooley.

The afternoon wore on with all four of us knocking them back. As the bar filled up, Jack and I were challenged to a game of pool by a couple of college girls. We accepted.

Sometime later, Jack poked me in the ribs, grinning and pointing to the stairs where we could see Mary Lou in her pink dress dragging Muntz by the hand up the stairs and into the room at the top. We went over to the bar where Mickey also wore a knowing grin. Mick said in a very low voice, "It happens every time Dooley goes to Eau Claire. If you want a hoot, go sit at the back table by the stairs and wait for a few minutes."

We got four drinks for ourselves and our pool partners and relocated at the back table. Nothing happened for a few minutes. Then, the screaming started. "Oh, Muntz, oh, Muntz, OH, Muntz, Muntz, Muntz, MUNTZ, OH, MUNTZ!" over and over, louder and louder. Then silence.

I looked at Mickey to share a laugh but instead of smiles, his face looked stricken. In the front door walked Dooley! Mick ran for the phone, left the signal, put his finger on the receiver button and ordered a fake cab. When he turned around, Dooley was laughing, "Boy, I could hear that broad screaming 'Oh, Muntz,' from outside. He must have been doing real good work."

"Yup. He's got a hooker up there."

Then, as if this whole situation wasn't nuts enough, in walked Darlene, Muntz's wife. Mickey ran for the phone, called up the signal again and hung up.

"Hi, Mickey," she smiled. Have you seen Muntz today?"

"Yeah, he was in for a while and said he had a job to do and would be back soon."

Just then, walking back in the front door, looking not quite as organized as she had been earlier, but glowing prettily, was Mary Lou. She and Darlene hugged and went to the ladies' room to freshen their lipstick or whatever it is that women always say they're doing when they go off together. While they were gone, in came Muntz, looking a little wobbly himself. I remember thinking, "This is way too screwy for me."

Muntz greeted Dooley with a "Hey, screwball, I thought you were in Eau Claire."

"Yeah, I was supposed to be, but the parts weren't ready so I'm going Monday."

Dooley bought Muntz a drink and poked him in the ribs, smiling. "You were sure giving her hell up there, partner."

Muntz's face went white and Mickey jumped in and asked where the hooker was? Muntz picked up on it and said, "Oh, ah, out the back."

Just then the girls came out of the ladies' room, kissed their respective husbands and said they had a shower to go to. We watched them walk out the door, arm in arm. Muntz and Dooley slapped backs and ordered another drink.

Jack and I left then, too. Jack gave me the wicked Jack smile and asked, "Where now, Muntz?"

Laughing, I answered, "I don't know. It's up to you, Muntz."

That became our name for each other for the rest of our lives. Simply "Muntz."

Jake and Spinnaker

Big Jake Johnson and Jim Spinnaker were best friends for over fifty years. Jake was a wheelsman on the Great Lakes Fleet. His career stretched from the early 1960s until 2005. Big Jake's size set him apart from every other sailor on the Great Lakes ore boats. With a massive frame and Popeye arms he was a formidable opponent to any man who might want to start trouble with him.

During an afternoon drink fest at the Paul Bunyan, Jake and Spinnaker sat at the bar watching TV when a group of young men strode in, wearing various UMD jerseys that suggested they were athletes. They were boisterous as college boys drinking beer usually are and the racket began to disturb Spinnaker. He yelled down the bar, "Hey, you guys, you wanna hold it down a little? We're trying to watch the ball game."

The largest of the athletes sauntered down to where Jim and Jake sat and sneered, "Which one of you old farts is going to make us?"

Jake turned slowly on his bar stool and reached out with an enormous right hand. He grabbed the young footballer's jersey right below his Adam's apple and twisted it, effectively cutting off his air supply.

Jake's voice was calm, low, and menacing. "Young man, my

friend asked you boys to hold down the noise because we're trying to watch a ball game."

The jock's face turned red and he gasped for breath as he managed to squeak out, "OK...OK...sorry."

Big Jake released his grip on the lad's shirt, freeing him to wobble back up the bar to his buddies. The old sailor turned to Spinnaker and observed, "Ya know, Jim, kids should show a little more respect to their elders."

As the afternoon wore on, the young guys and the old guys got into a more friendly banter. As it turned out, the boys were all members of the UMD football team. The young man who had earlier received a lesson in manners now asked, "Hey, Big Jake, you ever play college ball?"

Jake said no, but he had played some high school football. The conversation progressed and eventually turned into demonstrations of three-point stance blocking. Jake was not as quick as the youngsters but, being half again as powerful as any of the opposition, when he did block one of the boys, the young man went flat on his can.

"Damn strong," remarked one of the kids. "You could move a mountain."

"Not quite," smiled Jake, "but I'll bet I could move that bar an inch or so."

As per usual at the Bunyan, someone said "Bullshit!" and the betting began. After fifteen minutes of preliminaries, wagers and discussion of the rules (there always had to be rules), everything was set.

Jake went into his three-point stance and when the designated quarterback yelled, "HIKE!" Jake charged the bar from six feet away with his arms crossed in a blocking position across his chest and his neck pulled in like a giant sea turtle. There was a crash, a snap, and then a sound like a snowplow dragging its blade across concrete. Sparks flew from busted electric wires. Water was spraying everywhere from the broken water pipes.

When the bartender got the water shut off and the circuit breakers flipped back on, he took out a tape and discovered that Big Jake had moved the Michigan Street end of the Paul Bunyan bar four-and-a-half inches. Jake collected his winnings and gave them to the bartender saying, "If this doesn't cover the damages, let me know and I'll make up the difference." After all was said and done, it cost him $200 to prove himself the most powerful man on Superior Street.

Jim Spinnaker was a Navy vet from World War II. He had seen quite a lot of action during the war and was the most publicly patriotic person I've ever met. After the Navy, Jim got a job at a plywood-producing company on the Duluth waterfront. He spent his entire career there serving as a boilermaker. Jim loved his country ardently and would give a vocal demonstration of devotion at the slightest provocation. A small prompt would launch him into a flag-waving medley including a rendition of "God Bless America" that would have turned Kate Smith green with envy.

The more he drank, the louder he sang, "IT'S A GRAND OLD FLAG...OVER THERE!" Knowing that it would drive the bartenders mad, Big Jake loved to light Jim's patriotic flame. While walking back from the men's room he would yell, "GOD BLESS AMERICA!" Spinnaker's ears would perk up as if he were a schnauzer hearing the doorbell ring and he would blare out another favorite in his wavering warble, "Oh, say can you SEE by the DAWN's early LIGHT..." His tone was penetrating and could reach decibels that the bar's PA system couldn't touch, busting the eardrum of the unfortunate patron sitting on the next barstool.

Whenever either Big Jake or Spinnaker walked into the bar, it was sure the other wouldn't be far behind. They spent nearly every day together visiting their favorite bartenders on Superior Street.

Jake put their friendship on hold when he married a girl named Millie, from Biloxi, Mississippi. She was opportunistic from the outset, being less interested in Jake's sterling qualities than in his considerable fortune. He worked on the boats all his adult life and lived with his mother until her death in the early 1970s. He lived frugally. He didn't even own a car. And he was a whiz at investing. For thirty years he played the stock market like a financial virtuoso, amassing such an impressive portfolio that local stockbrokers frequently sought his investment advice.

When the ice broke up in Lake Superior that year and Big Jake got underway at the start of the Great Lakes shipping season, Millie was left alone in the trailer they shared since they tied the knot. That trailer had belonged to Millie. It was her sole contribution to the marriage but she had finer living arrangements in mind and was determined to move on up, no matter what it took. The marriage soon got rocky and eventually sank entirely.

Their divorce was unfriendly with the gold-digging Millie from Mississippi trying to get her hands on as much of Jake's wealth as a battery of slippery lawyers could convince the court to grant her.

Jake made her an offer. He would give her an undisclosed amount of cash and ship her trailer to Biloxi. She, in return, would have to relinquish all claims on Jake's stock portfolio, bank accounts, retirement funds, and real estate.

Millie turned him down flat and said she was going to take him for half of everything he had.

But then she changed her mind after her trailer

mysteriously burned to the ground one night while she was out dancing at some nightspot. Big Jake was accused of arson. Witnesses testified that on the night in question a very large man wearing a stocking cap got on the bus in downtown Duluth carrying two one-gallon cans and a paper bag stuffed with old clothing. But a dozen witnesses were also available for the defense, ready to testify that Big Jake spent that entire evening at the Paul Bunyan and could not possibly be the large man on the bus who was a suspect in the fire set at Millie's place.

Big Jake was found not guilty and Millie left town with a cashier's check in her pocket. She wasn't heard from until it was proved that Jake was the father of her newborn baby boy. He paid the child support for eighteen years and in the end, proof that unexpected surprises can provide sweet justice, Jake had someone to make his legitimate heir.

New Careers

I made several career changes in my lifetime. As is probably true concerning other people's work histories, mine were life changing.

My first day of bartending since the Crow's Nest in Bremerton came about by accident, on my part at least. It was a little after nine in the morning on a day in 1976 when I came through the doors at the Bunyan. I had just gotten off work at the bakery and wasn't scheduled until the next night so I was ready to have some beers.

Only a couple of customers were sitting on stools watching *The Price Is Right* and Mickey was behind the bar stuffing money into a bank bag. He told me to serve myself a Bud. I started to ring it up when Mickey said, "That's on the house, Mike. You can earn it by watching the bar while I go to the bank. I'll only be a couple of minutes."

I thanked him, checked the two customers' drinks and then sat down, lit a smoke and took a sip of my beer as I began to watch the show and guess the right prices. Twenty-five minutes later, still no Mickey. I began to realize that I'd been had and tried to get hold of my brother. I called Mom's house but she told me Jack had just left with Mickey. "I think they were going to play golf."

So there I was in my bakery whites, tending bar all day long with the absentee owners off having a grand time at my expense. Happy hour hit and the bar was nuts, everyone making comments about the new bartending uniform.

Ben Hutch came in and said, "I'll have a shot of Old Thompson and a glazed doughnut." That got a big laugh. There were plenty more wisecracks. "Hey, doctor, where's your stethoscope?" Ha, ha, ha.

At 5:00, Jack and Mickey came in laughing like hyenas. I was so ticked off I took what I figured my pay should be out of the till, emptied my tip jar and stormed past the two of them, both still doubled up with laughter.

I was still pretty angry when I got home, but then I counted up my tips and discovered that between my pay and tips, I had made over fifty dollars that day, or about twice what I earned at a bakery. And I worked half the hours! That's when I started to rethink my grand plan for a career path. I began to fit in as many bartending shifts as I could to supplement my income.

In 1979 I joined the Army Reserve as a member of the 477th Medical Company (AMB). The US Army Reserve Center was located on Park Point and was very handy. My buddies Charlie Ziegler, Ron Ross, and Tony Hoff were already members. They painted such a great picture of what the Reserves were like that I could hardly wait to join. Having four years of military service under my belt, I was pretty easy to convince. I figured the next sixteen years would pass in a blink of my eye. So I joined up and they were right. We had a ball.

In 1980, when Castro was emptying out his prisons and insane asylums to purge his country of what he considered undesirable elements, Fort McCoy, Wisconsin, was one of many facilities around the United States to receive these exiles.

McCoy housed 15,000 of the dregs of Cuban society. The 477th was assigned as ambulance support to the medical center there. We were sent in separate twelve-soldier increments for two weeks each.

With one exception, every soldier in our increment was either a bartender or a cocktail waitress.

The hospital at Fort McCoy was an antiquated leftover from World War II. The brass assigned our collection of goons an old hospital ward that had private rooms with adjoining bathrooms; at the end of that hall was a larger ward lined with empty hospital beds. We were the second increment so our ambulance dispatch was set up and running when we arrived. We relieved the previous group and got all the pertinent information we could get out of them before they took off back to Duluth.

The day after we arrived, a hospital company from Des Moines—six men, mostly officers, and sixty women, mostly LPNs—moved into the ward next door. It was the end of May and warm in southern Wisconsin for so early in the year. The night the nurses arrived, we went on unofficial patrol to check out the new personnel.

The enlisted men's club was very lame to say the least so Tony Hoff, who was our master of invention, came up with a doozie.

At the end of each ward was a large solarium. Tony designated one of these sunny rooms as the site of our new business. We tipped wall lockers on their sides to serve as a bar, covered them with decorative oil cloth, and then commandeered a couple of refrigerators from other buildings. Thinking a few tables and chairs would be nice, we grabbed some of those, too. A couple of our gals threw together some quick window treatments and the next day, the guys went into town and bought every kind of beer, wine, and booze we needed to open a bar.

The gate guard, who had already been alerted to keep his eye on the crew from Duluth, looked at Tony strangely when he saw the big load of spirits we had in the truck. I believe we had first aroused suspicion as being troublemakers the day we arrived at McCoy in a twelve-passenger black Cadillac limousine with flags sporting sergeants' stripes flying from the front fenders. On each of the front sides of this impressive vehicle were professionally-made magnetic signs that read:

477th Medical Company (AMB) Staff Car

NCOs Only

With Sergeant Stripes from E5 through E8

As we neared the gate, the MP guards automatically snapped to attention and popped off a button line salute that would have made the Old Guard at Arlington look shabby. Needless to say, when they identified the stripes as merely sergeants' rank, they were pissed and unloaded all the shit they could muster on us. After that incident, word on the fools from Duluth spread quickly through the MP Company at McCoy.

Booze was not contraband though, so the guard waved Tony through the gate. He and I got the bar stocked while Bob Burcar, owner of the staff limo, set up field phones in both the ambulance room and the bar. We needed to keep communication lines open between the hospital and the bar in case of any emergency that might arise. Burcar had a girl wearing shorts and on roller skates run phone wire three blocks or so through the maze of passageways in the old hospital, with someone ahead of her putting eye hooks in the ceiling to run the wire through. In no time at all, we were hard-wired and ready for business.

We used IV bottles filled with whiskey, brandy, scotch, rum, gin, and tequila to dispense drinks through IV drip-lines. A cigar box served as the till. We bought cigarettes by the carton and sold them at bar prices by the pack.

Charlie found some people who put a band together with a guitar, banjo, and fiddle, and we paid them in free booze.

A two-dollar cover charge was levied and, for insurance, each customer was required to sign a guest log to ensure we wouldn't get into any legal difficulties. Among the people who signed our log were the post commander, the post inspector general (IG), and the post chaplain. The name for our new saloon was Plasma Pete's in honor of Mr. Pete's in Duluth.

Our new bar got so busy we had to have two bartenders and a waitress on staff every night. We all took turns bartending and making the liquor run into town each day. Every person in our increment developed some sort of romantic attachment during those two weeks. Mine was a pretty little LPN from Des Moines named Colleen. She and I were hot and heavy and spent all our free time together but she told me she was sort of engaged to a hometown guy in Iowa so, at the end of our two week stint, we kissed good-bye and never saw each other again.

By the time we were relieved by the next increment of the 477th, we had made over $2,000 in profits for our unit fund, inspiring the Army to create new rules and regulations pertaining to regular army or reservists engaging in entrepreneurial activities on US Army property. Our relief was left with a closed bar but they did enjoy the remnants of our liquor stock. Later we learned that the management of the enlisted men's club and the officers' club had made formal complaints to the IG concerning lost revenue due to our operation of Plasma Pete's. It seems our business was just too successful.

We left Fort McCoy the Friday before Memorial Day the same way we had arrived—in Bob Burcar's twelve-passenger limo with flags flapping. As we passed through the front gate, two MPs snapped a salute. I recognized both of them from our bar. We returned the salute and headed north toward Duluth and home.

31

Seeing Eye Sergeant

Charlie Z got a full time job as an Army recruiter which was perfect for him. He could charm the birds from the trees or sell bananas to Brazilians so talking a seventeen-year-old kid into joining the reserves seemed effortless. Charlie made his quota every month and helped the other recruiters to make theirs as well. He became the most successful Army recruiter in the state and was treated like the Army's golden boy. But soon he began to complain about all the paperwork and told his station commander that it was too hard to see the fine print.

His commander sent Z to see the eye doctor who found that Charlie had cataracts in both eyes and needed surgery. After surgery he was told to stay out of the sunlight for six weeks. Because the Army felt they needed him on the job, they assigned him a seeing-eye-sergeant who ferried Z, patches over both eyes, wherever he needed to go. This guy's name was Neal Brunmeier.

Brunmeier had served in Vietnam where he had suffered a broken leg when a tree fell on him. He said he would have gotten a purple heart but couldn't prove it was a Communist tree.

Charlie and Neal spent a large amount of their time in Mr.

Pete's which just happened to be right next door to the recruiting station. Every time a young man would come through Pete's door, Z would crook his finger and say, "Hey, kid, ya got a job?" It worked great. Z sweet-talked the kids and Neal did the paperwork. So many boys were signed into the US Army from Mr. Pete's they hung an Army Recruiter's sign on the wall.

These two conscription experts enjoyed a good drink and after a hard day's work of lying to young people about the military, they would both walk next door and hang out at the end of the bar in their dress greens decorated with all their medals and ribbons and get completely sloshed.

My son Robby, who had moved in with me when he was fourteen, was now nineteen and eager to leave the nest. He didn't fly far. He moved out of our apartment on Park Point to a place across the driveway with a friend of his named Brent. Neal became my new roommate and there was a lot of bull slung back and forth about the young guys and the old guys.

Robby, I swear, is part oversized leprechaun. He dearly loves a practical joke. One night, as Neal maneuvered his car into the driveway and staggered into the house, Robby looked at Brent and said, "Come on, let's go screw with Neal," and he picked up the TV remote control. Robby figured that since both apartments had identical television sets and the same cable TV company, he should be able to control the old guys' TV from outside their window by using the young guys' remote.

They crept across the driveway on their covert mission like a couple of Navy Seals. They approached a window and Robby, with two fingers, gave the "eyes" sign to Brent and pointed through the window to where Neal was busy assembling a sandwich in the kitchen. The TV was on in the living room and Robby, mastermind of the Black Ops Mission, pointed his remote through the window at the TV and pushed the power button. The set went black.

Neal's head poked around the corner from the kitchen to look at the darkened screen. He weaved into the living room, picked up the remote and turned the TV back on. He put the remote down and went back to the kitchen. Just as he was adding chips to his sandwich plate, Rob again hit the power button. The set turned off and Neal's head reappeared around the kitchen corner.

Through the open window, Robby and Brent heard a loud "Goddamn it. What the hell's going on?"

The boys, stifling their laughter, sneaked away to the other side of the garage where they could let it out. "OK," says Rob. "We'll wait till he comes back in and sits down. Then we'll really fuck with him."

They made their way back to their post outside the window just in time to watch Neal sit down in the armchair and set his sandwich plate and a glass of milk on the table beside it. Neal grabbed his remote and surfed through the channels until he found something that caught his eye. He adjusted the volume.

Robby was at the ready with his weapon poised. As Neal picked up his sandwich with both hands and raised it to his mouth, preparing to take a bite, Robby fired and off went the TV again.

"What the hell?" Neal put down his sandwich and picked up the remote, inspected it, and then turned the television back on. Once again, he picked up his chow and attempted a bite just as the saboteurs outside changed the channel. Clearly pissed, Neal changed it back. Robby fired off a rapid channel change, pictures flashing for a second apiece before switching again.

Neal, wide-eyed, watched in disbelief as his TV sped off on a wild bacchanalia of functions—OFF, then ON, channel changing at an alarming rate of speed. Then it simply went OFF. Neal sat quietly, sighed, and staring at the blank television screen, took a bite of his sandwich and a drink of milk. It went on again.

Outside the window, Rob and Brent wept with helpless laughter, hands clamped tightly over their mouths so as not be detected by their victim. As Neal settled back into his chair and finished his sandwich, Robby hit the power button one more time and again darkness filled the screen.

"Oh, fuck it," said Neal and he picked up his plate and glass and headed back to the kitchen where he heard giggling coming from outside the open window. He lumbered out the front door, around the side of the house and stood over Robby and Brent lying on the ground, twitching with suppressed laughter.

"I knew it was you, you little bastards," he slurred, which only served to intensify their mirth.

It took Neal a little time to forgive my son for the genius of his practical joke but it had been so well done, he soon saw the humor in it and relations normalized between the two apartments. Neal did give a warning. "Don't worry, kid, everyone gets his turn in the barrel."

32

Making Bread

In 1980, upon returning from the Cuban Relocation at Fort McCoy and during the merry-go-round of bakeries, bars, and bimbos that characterized my experience of that era, I once again found myself out of work. I needed a new job.

I answered an ad for a bakery manager in Bloomington, Minnesota, a suburb of Minneapolis, and nailed the interview dead-on. Two weeks later I was driving a U-Haul van towing my 1974 El Camino, with $500 in my pocket that I borrowed from Ron Ross. I pulled into the parking lot of a duplex I had rented directly across the street from the Holiday Village Bakery, scared to death because frankly, I had lied my way into running this big operation.

I came home to Duluth one of the first weekends with a little jingle and jeans full of beans. My sister Claudia called me to ask for a bit of help. Her son Patrick had graduated from high school. "Mike, Pat has a chance to work for a tree-cutting service down in the Twin Cities near Bloomington. Do you think you could help him get on his feet and, you know, kind of keep an eye on him at first?"

"Sure. I'll pick him up tomorrow afternoon."

Claudia wasn't home when I got there but my eighteen-year-old nephew was more than ready with a packed duffle bag and a "Let's go, Uncle Mike!" look in his eyes. His father, Dick Daly, came out of the kitchen to say goodbye.

"I'm entrusting Patrick to you. He's fiscally irresponsible. Teach him a bit about finance, will you?"

We all shook hands before Pat and I jumped into the El Camino and took off. We headed straight for Mr. Pete's where I introduced Patrick to the Boss. After taking a little ribbing about being the latest Irish version of Pat & Mike, I got serious. "Say, Pete, I need a little favor. Can you hold a $200 check for me? I'll buy it back in two weeks."

With some operating cash and back on the road to Minneapolis—St. Paul, I made my point. "Pat, now you know what I know about finance. When in trouble, pop a jabbie. Have someone hold a check for two weeks. Just be sure to pay him back so you keep your street credibility."

Patrick's education didn't end there. "Buy a drink for a guy who buys you one. But notice the consistent freeloaders. Leave 'em out when it's your turn to get a round. That doesn't apply to a friend who is a little low on cash. In that case, you slip a twenty-dollar bill under his drink glass and quietly say, "When you can, pard."

I mentored my nephew in metro nightlife by bringing him to such 1980s educational institutions in the Twin Cities as the Uptown Bar, Howard Wong's, the Rusty Scupper, and the Ramada Inn bar. Patrick was a good student and picked up on my little hints. I think he carried too many of both the Hampston and Daly genes for bad behavior because he quickly began to show promising talent as a pupil in the uptown ladies' seduction department. In no time, he was fully launched and I could dedicate my entire attention to my work at the bakery.

Holiday Village was the retail center for all the Holiday stores and gas stations in the Midwest. The big gimmick Holiday used to attract customers was to sell one-and-a-half pound loaves of white bread, four-for-a-dollar. The plant employed twenty-one bakers, not counting me, and a half dozen or so women who worked at the retail counter. During the previous few years the bakery had been operating at a substantial loss.

My job was not necessarily to make a large profit but to maintain the four-for-a-buck deal and still bring the operation back to where it could at least break even. Management told me that it wasn't imperative for me to be involved physically in the actual bakery production but to function in more of a supervisory capacity. Still, I knew that if I were to turn this operation around, I would need to win the respect of the bakers who worked for me. I sure as hell couldn't do that sitting at a desk like some big shot.

I came to work my first day dressed in my bakery whites. After talking with each baker, one at a time, I got a feeling for just what the problems were and what strategies I might try to get this outfit running in the black again. I decided to work a couple of days with every baker in the plant to familiarize myself with each one's job. Then I sifted through that information and, after the first two months, eliminated two counter spots and four bakers' positions.

The slimmed-down crew worked hard. We got along well most of the time. On the first Saturday of each month, I bought a couple cases of beer and a bunch of hot dogs; after finishing up the morning shift, we would sit around my backyard and have a little impromptu idea session. It worked. Our bottom line began to improve, and after a year we were fairly close to the company's objective—breaking even.

And then the union contract's expiration date came due. The union was pushing for a dollar-an-hour raise each year for the next two years. Because I was in management, I had taken out a withdrawal card from the union when I took this job so I had no personal interest in the outcome except that I knew, sure as bad yeast won't make dough rise, Holiday Village would not be willing to see everything they had gained in the past year disappear in a union fight or possible strike.

The strike vote loomed and I advised my guys to vote against it. If they did strike, management would certainly close down the whole bakery operation and we would all be out of a job. The business agents and the hotheads kept calling for a strike to force management into a settlement. My advice wasn't taken. The day after the vote passed, I was called into the corporate office and informed that on the first of July, three weeks from that day, Holiday Village, Bakery Division, would close. All bakery employees, including me, were to be laid off.

Holiday gave me a nice severance package with a month's vacation pay and a bonus for the improvements I had made. My last two weeks' pay was also in the check so with almost $3,000 in my pocket, there I was in another U-Haul heading back up north on I-35 and going home.

I was lucky. One of the Richards' Apartments on Park Point was empty. It had been Charlie Z's old place. My hope was that the neighborhood hadn't changed much. I was ready for round two with the Point's singular attractions and I jumped with both feet into my third adolescence.

Charlie had been sent to International Falls, Minnesota, to head up the failing Army recruiting station there. He loaded up his truck with the help of my son Robby and the rest of the Central High School football team. When the military moves a soldier from one duty station to another, it pays shipping costs according to weight. Z felt that he could make a little extra dough if Robby and the two-and-a-half tons of footballers from Central High were in the back of the truck with his goods when it was weighed.

The lieutenant they sent from Fort Snelling remarked that Charlie sure had a lot of heavy furnishings for a staff sergeant.

Z smiled and said, "Family antiques and heirlooms."

I moved in three days after Charlie moved out. My landlord painted and put in new carpeting and here I was again on the Point, only now I had my savings from the last year, my severance package from Holiday Village, and I was collecting full unemployment or, as my old man always called it, my rocking chair dough. I didn't really need the money but I returned to bartending at the Paul Bunyan two nights a week.

My work partner at the Bunyan was a twenty-something named Siggie. She was beautiful and curvaceous—think of Liz Taylor in *Butterfield 8*—and men were crazy for her. When she was bartending they practically threw tip money at her. Lucky for me, bartenders at the Bunyan split tips. I pulled my weight though, with my head down all night and both hands pouring drinks faster than Tom Cruise and Bryan Brown combined could ever hope to do.

I worked furiously on these nights, cranking out drinks to the masses while Siggie, on the other end of the bar, teased, laughed, and joked, driving the movers and shakers wild. She made everyone feel special. Every guy thought that possibly tonight would be his night.

I'd empty my tip jar at the end of the night and Siggie would do the same. Mine usually had an assortment of quarters, nickels and dimes with a few pennies here and there. Siggie would dump out a beer pitcher stuffed to the rim with ones, fives, tens, and an occasional twenty. On a night when she was particularly vivacious, she might find a fifty in there or even a C-note.

Ray Ward was working the full-time day shift at Mr. Pete's and Siggie and I would sometimes meet him for a few bumps after he was done with work. The three of us were kindred spirits, but they were far more clever than I could ever hope to be.

One very hot Saturday in early August, Siggie and I met at Mr. Pete's an hour or so before Raymond finished his shift.

Ray was busy giving out his usual ration of jaunty comeuppance to anyone who didn't measure up to his code of conduct. Siggie and I marveled at Raymond's ability to set any perceived fool back on his heels, rendered speechless. At the end of Ray's shift, I left him a buck and he immediately observed archly that, "In my opinion, you are a cheap prick."

I pointed out that Siggie hadn't left him anything.

In response, Ray pointed out that perhaps she was doing something for him worth far more than the mere one dollar that I had donated to his retirement fund.

We all laughed and after a cocktail or two we came to the decision that it was a perfect day to follow Horace Greeley's advice and "Go west, young man, go west." Except we took a babe along as we sped toward our favorite hotspots in the western part of the city. Siggie was dressed in a yellow sundress, thinly strapped at the shoulders and flared at the hips with a snug belt that accentuated her tiny waist. The combination of that dress, that figure, that long, curly black hair and a Copper Tone tan was more than enough to snap any man's head around; and snap they did. Suddenly Ray and I went from Siggie's drinking buddies to her bodyguards.

At the Amber Flow in the West End, I came very close to going round and round with a massive, drunken goon who wanted to examine some of Siggie's attractions close up. Ray suggested we head farther west to the Rustic Bar where, if there was any fighting to do, the owner Johnny Noark could do it. Johnny was a former heavyweight Golden Gloves champ for the state of Minnesota—for three or four years running. He was also mad for the glamorous young Siggie.

On our way in my El Camino, a group of boys in a convertible next to us started yelling and wolf-whistling at Sig. She turned up the heat for them by taking off her underpants and waving the tiny, lacy things out the window at her admirers. Suddenly, a gust of wind caught and snatched them from her hand. The boys screamed with delight. There went Siggie's skivvies billowing in the breeze down Grand Avenue with a car full of high school boys in hot pursuit. When they stopped to collect their satin-and-lace prize, I jumped on the gas and sped away to avoid her losing any more of her clothing or what was left of her virtue.

The Rustic was packed with semi-upright bodies. We muscled our way up to the bar where I caught Johnny Noark's eye and ordered three drinks. Siggie took off to flirt with a bunch of ballplayers sitting in a booth while Ray and I bellied up to a spot that had just opened up in front of Johnny. "Which one of you two is her date?"

"Neither one," answered Ray. "She's too high maintenance. We're just her drinking buddies."

Johnny's eyes gleamed. "You tell her she can't spend a cent in this place. Anything in this joint is hers for the asking, including the owner!"

Seated next to us at the bar was Ben Hutch III who was in town for just the weekend while his boat was being loaded with iron ore. He couldn't help but notice Siggie who, now playing pool with one of the ballplayers, was bent over the table for her next shot.

"You think she's wearing any underwear?" Hutch wondered aloud.

I glanced at Ray who grinned widely. "No, Ben," I said, straight-faced. "I don't think she is."

"You jerky bastard, little pissy-winkle, I'll bet you she is!"

"How much?"

"I'll bet you $500, donkey-boy," he exclaimed, pulling his wad of rolled up bills from his pocket and knocking his fist on the bar. "Let's see the color of your money!"

I was sure that Hutch figured I was the last little jerky

bastard in the world who'd be walking around with $500 in his pocket. I slapped down five one-hundred dollar bills on the bar. Hutch's face went white. He knew that I had him but in order to maintain his reputation he was honor bound to go through with the bet. He slipped the rubber band off a fat roll of bills and added five to mine.

Siggie was standing at the far end of the pool table near the right corner pocket. Her opponent was lining up a shot at the opposite corner pocket.

"Hey, Sig," I hollered. "You wearing any underwear?"

She laughed out loud. As the bar went silent she reached down, grabbed the hem of her pretty yellow dress and pulled it over her head revealing to everyone in the bar what the girls in Catholic school called her Holy of Holies. Noark's chin dropped along with the bottle of vodka he was holding which shattered onto the floor. The pool cue shot out of the ballplayer's hand and flew across the table, clattering to another section of tile.

I reached over and scooped up the wager money and shoved it into my pocket.

"Ray," I yelled as some of the men began to cluster closer to Siggie. "Grab that crazy broad and let's get the hell out of here!"

We ran out the back door and across the parking lot, each of us dragging Siggie by a hand. The three of us piled into the El Camino and sped out of the lot and down the street like bank robbers.

"Jesus Christ, Siggie! You could have just said, 'No, I'm not.'"

Siggie simply smiled.

33

Z's Childhood

In those carefree days, on Sundays, you couldn't buy a drink in Minnesota so if you wanted to light your alcoholic flame, you either drank at home or went across the bridge to Superior, Wisconsin. Our Sundays would start at Charlie Z's mother's restaurant. She was in her sixties or seventies and owned a small hotel and café. Mrs. Ziegler would make us all bacon, eggs, hash browns, toast, and lots and lots of black coffee to wake us up and lay a base for the day's drinking about to begin. On these Sundays, Z's mom would tell us stories of Charlie as a child. All of them were memorable, but four stood out for the vivid way she told them.

I. THE CATTLE BARON

The summer following first grade, Charlie and his friends were playing one afternoon in his back yard. They had been at the movies and seen *The Cattle Baron* and were now inspired to reenact the plot.

Z, always the desperado at heart, volunteered to be head of the rustler gang and he appointed Charlie McCuffy as head of the cattlemen's association.

McCuffy's crew chased Charlie Z and his gang all over the neighborhood trying to recapture their stolen cattle. Finally surrounded and abandoned by his gang, Z was captured by the ranchers in his own backyard. Now an angry mob, they tied the rustler kingpin's hands behind his back and mounted him on his horse—in this case an old kitchen chair. A rope was thrown over the limb of the apple tree and a hastily fashioned noose was slipped over Charlie's head.

The original plan was all right. At this point, the Ziegler gang was to reappear to save their rustler leader. But as it happened, it was suppertime. The door across the alley opened and Mrs. McCuffy called for her son to come in for supper. He dropped what he was doing and hot-footed it home. And so it went, mothers called from up and down the alley.

"Oh, Butch! Supper!"

"Jim-mie! Come home. It's time to eat."

The Z gang, instead of showing up in the nick of time to save their boss, all headed home for dinner.

Suddenly, the King of the Rustlers found himself alone, standing on a rickety old kitchen chair with his hands bound behind his back and a noose around his neck. After waiting for what seemed like a very long time, Charlie did what any self-respecting rustler would do in a tough situation. He yelled for his mother.

Z's mom heard him calling for her and went to the kitchen window where she saw her six-year-old boy standing on a chair with a rope around his neck. She screamed. This had the effect of causing Charlie to wobble and rock back and forth on the chair. Desperately, Mrs. Z charged down the back stairs and reached her son just as the chair gave way, catching him in her arms as she cried for help. A neighbor heard her cries and came to the rescue.

Once untied and back on the ground with his mother kneeling in front of him, still shaking with fear, Charlie gulped, "You're not my rustler gang, Ma, but you'll do."

II. WAR

This day's game included the kids on the next block. The rules were explained by Charlie Z. "Homemade bows and arrows, sling shots, or BB guns are allowed, but only body shots—no aiming at the head. My ma says we got too many kids around here with eye patches."

Ziegler's Raiders were to be the attacking forces. They knelt in a circle and Charlie, as general naturally, drew the battle plan in the dirt with a stick, assigning captains, lieutenants, and sergeants. His men spread out up and down the alley, at the ready, waiting for their general's order to charge. The opposing forces were dug in behind garages, garbage cans, and junk cars, waiting for the attack to begin. All were armed with an assortment of approved weapons except for one young private (a five-year-old) who had found what he believed to be his brother's Red Ryder BB gun. It was actually a loaded .22 rifle.

Charlie looked down the alley and admired his line of brave soldiers. He raised his hand, paused, then let it fall and shouted, "CHARGE!"

They moved out, up and down the line, boys shouting and shooting their BB guns. The din of the battle was everywhere. People poked their heads out of windows and doors to see what the racket was all about, including Z's mother who came out just in time to see Charlie catch a .22 slug in the shoulder. He crashed to the ground, grabbing his right arm, blood running between his fingers. Mrs. Z stopped the bleeding with the dish towel she had in her hand and looked around for a neighbor to drive them to the hospital. The doctor said that it must have been a very old round because it lodged into the meat of his shoulder. A new one would have shattered the bone.

Mrs. Z told Charlie when they got home, "Lord, boy, I swear you are going to make an old woman of me."

III. THE GERMAN HELMET

Charlie Ziegler's uncle served in the Second World War and came home (when Charlie was around eight years old) with a gift for his favorite nephew—a German helmet. It had a bullet crease in its side and Charlie told all his buddies, "See this is good German steel, the finest in the world? Bullets bounce right off of it."

"Bullshit," said Z's best friend, Charlie McCuffy.

"I'll prove it to you," bragged Z. "You go up on the roof and drop a brick on my head and it'll bounce right off because of this here good German steel helmet."

McCuffy agreed and he and two cohorts climbed the three floors to the roof where they found some loose bricks from the chimney. Ordnance in hand, they went to the edge of the building. Looking over the edge, McCuffy called to Z down on the sidewalk. "You ready, Charlie?"

Z replied, "Yup," he was, and called back up to McCuffy. "Take dead aim, Charlie."

Charlie McCuffy eyed the shot, stuck his forefinger in his mouth and held it up to check the wind and shouted, "BOMB'S AWAY!"

The brick whizzed past Ziegler's ear, just missing his left shoulder that, had it been hit, would have been smashed to smithereens. Z looked up at Charlie McCuffy, his hand shading his eyes from the sun.

"What the hell's wrong with you, Charlie? You missed me altogether! You couldn't hit a bull in the ass with a hand full of rice. Move a little to your right and try again."

Although this helmet was an authentic German trench helmet, and did in fact have a bullet crease, the helmet liner that might cushion any blow in combat was missing.

"All right," hollered Charlie Z to his bombardier, "take aim and don't miss this time."

Charlie McCuffy again wetted his finger, gauged the wind,

took aim and let her fly. This time the brick hit its mark directly on the center of Charlie Z's German helmet.

He went down like a shot, out cold as a watermelon. Someone yelled, "He's dead!" and everyone scattered.

McCuffy came down from the roof and checked to see if Z was still alive and went in to get his mother. They brought Charlie to the hospital where he was diagnosed with a severe concussion and kept for the next couple of days for observation. His mother said he was never quite the same after that. Later that summer when Z's head injury had healed and the lesson learned had faded in his memory, a new adventure formed in Charlie's addled brain.

IV. THE PARACHUTE

In addition to the helmet, Charlie's uncle brought a silk parachute as a gift for Charlie's mother. Such luxuries had been hard to get during the war and a big piece of silk would make some nice drapes or a bedspread, but Charlie's imagination saw it for what it was—a parachute. Our little daredevil wasn't about to stand by and let a useful implement of war be so dishonored. So he and his band of assistant knuckleheads hatched a plan, assigned roles, and climbed to the top of his grandmother's barn lugging the 82nd Airborne parachute.

They made their calculations down to the last detail knowing that the jumper (Charlie Z, of course) wouldn't have enough time to free fall and open the parachute before he hit the ground. The plan went like this. Four army aides, two on each side, would spread and hold the parachute taut while Charlie, wearing a leather football helmet on his head to protect his previous injury, would strap himself in, making sure that all the straps and buckles were drawn up tight. On a countdown of three, two men on each side, spreading the parachute as wide as possible with Charlie straining to keep the shroud lines tight, would run as fast as they could from the far end of the barn. When they reached the opposite end of the roof, Charlie was to jump just as the Four Horsemen threw the silk over the brink. Z would float gently to the ground under the billowed silk parachute. But as the poet Robert Burns said, "The best laid schemes o' mice and men…"

Everything was at the ready. Charlie barked out the order like a cavalry sergeant about to make a charge. His soldiers responded with "Roger, Sir! Wilco!" As the thrilling moment of truth approached, Sergeant Ziegler began his countdown.

"Three! Two!" He paused slightly and then shouted, "ONE!" Together, they careened down the length of the barn. Charlie reached the edge and fearlessly flung his little body into space.

Now if anyone had taken the time to measure the lengths of the shroud lines and parachute silk, they would have discovered that when those two numbers were added together and that sum was subtracted from the height of the barn, it would have been clear that the mad parachutist would hit the ground just about the time the last of the silk left the top of the roof.

Charlie broke his leg. His mother was not pleased with Charlie or her brother, who was made to promise—no more gifts of hand grenades, Lugers, Mauser machine pistols, or any other battlefield souvenirs with which her son might kill himself.

Tubby

Dennis McDonald came into my life like a charging bull elephant. I was at the Paul Bunyan watching a Twins game when from down the bar came a laugh—loud, wall-shaking, and unforgettable. It came with such force I thought it might loosen the fillings in my teeth. It was also infectious. Even though I had no idea who in the hell was laughing or what in the hell he was laughing at, I starting laughing too.

Dennis is half Scot and half Ojibwe. He earned the nickname "Tubby" when he was a little boy and never lost it. Often though, he introduces himself as "the Big Indian," and with a wide grin immediately launches into irreverent observations about your girlfriend, your big ears, or your ethnicity.

Tubby worked for a large cracker company as a traveling salesman and did quite well for himself; in the early 1980s, he tended bar on the side to earn a little extra walking-around dough.

Tubby enjoyed nothing more than making me the butt of a joke. I always said that if I ever really wanted to get even, I'd have to kill him. We became great buddies.

The friendly mischief began when we worked weekends together at the Amber Flow in the West End. There was live music and it got very busy on those rock 'n' roll nights. I relieved the day bartender at 5:00 one Saturday afternoon. It was the first of the month and there was a set of buns on every barstool and two more waiting for each one to empty. Candy, the girl I relieved, wore her blonde hair long and flashed her big green eyes and sparkling smile liberally. She was better at flirting than bartending. A two-drink order would throw her into a panic and God forbid anyone should ever say, "Get 'em all one," for Candy would lock up completely and we'd have to look around for any customers with paramedic experience.

I swung around behind the end rail and there was Candy, elbows on the bar and chin in her hands, flashing those big green eyes at a young buck. He was wearing a stupid grin and close to slobbering into her cleavage. She must have been holding this pose for a while as there was not an ice cube to be found in either bin. The sinks were empty and every glass in the place was either in use or dirty and lined up on the bar rail. Customers were yelling at me for drinks.

With the promise of a free beer, I got one of the regulars to run for ice while I filled the sinks and delivered as many beer orders as I could. My full-tilt was interrupted when I saw Candy grab her overflowing tip jar and head for the door. I stopped her escape with, "Where the hell are you going?"

She pouted her lips and murmured, "Well, I'm done at five," and walked out from behind the bar.

She would have been in my way anyhow so I dug in and went after the job of catching up. For the next three hours I ran at breakneck speed pouring drinks, drawing beer and restocking coolers, fruit, straws, and napkins.

At about 7:30, I glanced up at the clock and remember thinking that if I could only hang on for thirty more minutes, Tubby would arrive. With two bartenders we should be able to keep up. But the next time I looked, the clock read 8:10. The son-of-a-bitch was late. I was very, very pissed, and wondered as I flew up and down the bar how I could best murder him. The joint was getting busier and I was getting angrier. The band came in and began to set up their equipment.

It was now 8:45. Customers were three-deep at the bar. The phone was ringing. I wiped the sweat that ran off the tip of my nose on my shirtsleeve. I got farther and farther behind and that goddamn phone continued to ring. After ten minutes of continuous racket, I'd had it. Grabbing the receiver, I screamed, "AMBER FLOW!" The voice on the other end of the phone asked, "Is Tubby McDonald there?"

Livid, I shouted into the phone, "No, goddamn it, the son-of-a-bitch was supposed to be here an hour ago and he's not here yet!"

Then I heard that laugh, starting in a low rumble from far away and getting louder and louder. "AND HE'S NOT GOING TO BE EITHER, YOU LITTLE ASSHOLE!" he bellowed, his laugh erupting like a full volcano before he hung up.

What I didn't know was that Tubby had been swilling liquor downtown at the Mirror Lounge and his work schedule had become irrelevant. Ten minutes later, I heard him coming in the door. You always heard Tubby before you saw him. The roar of his laughter boomed through the bar. He waved at me as he hung up his jacket and hollered, "You're not mad at me are ya, buddy?" The jocularity didn't stop there. Every time he looked at me for the rest of the night, it busted out again.

I took my time getting over being burned up at Tubby's obvious delight in my discomfort but by the time the night was over, I was seduced by his hilarious crowing and was able to appreciate the big man's latest practical joke. There were many more to come.

When I got back from Minneapolis, I got a job tending bar at the Chinatown Restaurant, an outfit that Mickey was involved in, along with two other fellas, one named Lee. They were hooligans who had never made it in any of their businesses through complete fault of their own.

I was working during the honeymoon period of the new ownership. Jeanette was the hostess and an assortment of Duluth bartenders was on hand, including Ray Ward. One Friday night I was working by myself and business was very, very brisk. My unnerving friend Tubby came in, announcing himself to me as, "Your worst nightmare, pal!" He ordered a stinger.

I poured it and he directed me to run him a tab. "My girl-friend's going to join me and we're going to have dinner." After three or four more stingers, "brown loudmouths" as he called them, the girlfriend showed up. He ordered one for her as well. Then they went back into the dining room to have dinner.

They ordered all the most expensive items on the menu and I thought, *Boy, Tubby must have won the lottery.* More heavy-duty drinks were added to the tab as they plowed through a feast of Asian delicacies. And then they finished up with cherries jubilee. I lit the flambé for them at their table. Not yet plumb full, they toddled back into the bar area for some lovely after-dinner stingers. How much longer could they keep going?

"Tubby, you want your bill?"

"Yeah." He looked at it for a long, long time before he took a pull out of his stinger and then he ripped up the bill into a hundred little pieces and threw them in my face. "Well, I'm not gonna pay it! How do you like THAT, ya little asshole!?"

Laughing, he and his girlfriend headed out the door as the other patrons gaped in astonishment at the sheer power of that booming roar.

I didn't sleep a wink that night wondering how in the hell I was going to present this expensive situation to the owners. The next afternoon, I came in to work with a rock in my gut, only to learn that Tubby had been in earlier, laughing uproariously, as he squared away his debt.

Tubby was on the road selling crackers. He was traveling on familiar ground—the White Earth Indian Reservation in west central Minnesota—calling on one of his accounts, a grocery store. He knew there was a little bar close by and he thought, *After work, I'll stop in for refreshments since my motel is right around the corner.*

Tub walked into the bar wearing his usual work attire, a suit and tie, and got into a friendly game of pool with his native brothers who were not so elegantly dressed. A white guy came in, also wearing a suit and tie, and gravitated to where Tubby was now seated at the bar. This fellow sat down and introduced himself to Tubby, telling him he was on a new sales route. They got to talking shop.

After an hour or so, the new guy loosened up a little with his newfound pal. He looked around and leaned toward Tubby, saying in a low voice, "Say, have you noticed that we're the only white guys in here?"

That slow, deep roll of laughter came rumbling out of Tubby as he slapped one hand on the bar and laid another firm hand on the man's shoulder. "No, Kemo Sabe—YOU ARE!"

Through the many years of our friendship, no matter how bad things got for me (or any of our buddies), Tubby could find something hilarious to lift my spirits—sometimes focusing on one of my own character flaws or dumb mistakes. He taught me that there is humor in life at every turn. A lost sweetheart, a lost job—even in times of death, as delicate as that situation is—Tubby can always put a smile on my face. Just as often, he's the butt of his own jokes and that's the best lesson of all—don't take yourself so damn seriously.

35

The Military Ball and
St. Patrick's Day Parade

The military ball in April was a yearly event in Duluth. Organized by Army Reservist Tony Hoff, it was our most important social event of the year. The venue was the Greysolon Ballroom of the majestic Hotel Duluth. A large orchestra played and hundreds of people attended. For this particular occasion in 1984, I bought a set of Army dress blues and I must admit that I looked quite dapper all decked out in gold stripes and ribbons. The local servicemen competed with each other to see who could show up with the most beautiful date. I don't like to beat my own tom-tom but I usually placed pretty high in these competitions.

Gwen Johnson was one of these beauties. She was given the name "Gone Johnson" by one of the guys because when we were out partying she had a great way of ditching us when she felt it was time to go home. Instead of simply saying goodnight, she would leave a half pack of cigarettes on the bar and a smoke burning in the ashtray next to a full drink. She would excuse herself by saying something about the ladies' room, and then she'd disappear in a puff of smoke. When someone asked, "Where's Gwen?" someone else would answer, "Oh, she's gone."

Hence, Gone Johnson.

Early in the evening of the military ball, it was customary for the men and women of the 477th to meet at Mr. Pete's for a bump to steel ourselves for the patriotic formalities of the party. I picked up Gwen for our date, much to the chagrin of her father who was only year older than I was. Charlie was already at Pete's bar when we got there. Two or three other stag noncommissioned officers filtered in to get "tuned up" in anticipation of going to a ball without a woman on their arms. Triumphantly, I noted that Gwen was a knockout. She was also a great gal to pal around with and we were soon properly fortified at Pete's before heading over to the Hotel Duluth.

At the Greysolon, I noticed that three of my former military ball dates happened to be in attendance, escorted by three military comrades. One of these was my pal, Neal Brunmeier.

Neal had a noticeably large nose and he took no end of flak about this feature. He put up with many clever comparisons invented by his pals. Neal's handsome nose had a talent for sniffing out young women who just happened to be in-between boyfriends. Sometimes these ladies weren't exactly out of one relationship before he made the move to pry them a little looser from a would-be "ex," earning him the pet name of "Bushwhacker" by watchful buddies. Whenever Neal came through a pair of swinging doors, his entrance would spark a laugh and a chorus of "Hide your women! Here comes Bushwhacker!"

I kept losing Gone Johnson in the crowd that night as she had already begun to wander. I knew I'd have to keep a diligent lookout to prevent her from going AWOL. My diligence must have slipped because suddenly there was a puff of smoke and... she was gone.

What could I do? I certainly didn't want to spend the rest of the evening up against the wall with the noncom stags.

I turned on my sonar. A broad sonic sweep soon turned up a beep from across the room where Neal sat with an ex-girlfriend of mine. I waited for him to head up to the bar for liquid reinforcements and then I deftly whistled her out the back door, leaving a bewildered Neal with his nose in a glass of good scotch.

It was a great satisfaction to bushwhack the Bushwhacker.

The St. Patrick's Day Parade was another big springtime event in downtown Duluth. The route annually wound down Superior Street from Fifth Avenue West through the heart of the business district and ended at Third Avenue East. Grand Marshal of the parade was traditionally none other than our very own Irishman, James Francis Riley, who held this position for many years. Jimmy would dress up in a Kelly green tuxedo with tails and an emerald green top hat. James Francis held St. Patrick in very high regard. He would drink many, many toasts along the route to his patron saint and get so tipsy by the time the float arrived at the finish line he would have to be helped down from his place of honor.

For that year's St. Pat's Day parade, I had been asked by the organizers to find an appropriate queen. They wanted someone beautiful with a bright smile, someone with a winning personality who would interview well. In a heartbeat, I knew that someone was Gone Johnson. I called and begged her to help us, pointing out that it was not only her civic duty but a good way to get herself into the public eye where many other opportunities might present themselves. "And who knows, Gwenie, this might make you a star!" That did it. She caved right there, agreeing to be the 1985 St. Patrick's Day queen.

The day of the parade arrived and we all gathered at Mr. Pete's, just half a block from where the parade would begin. March 17 is usually cool or even cold in Duluth, but as the day began, the sun shone brightly and thousands of people lined the street to see our wild-eyed Irishman, the pretty raven-haired queen, and our members of the National Guard parade past them.

Riley was one of the first to arrive—at 10:30 a.m. The parade was scheduled to start at 2:00 p.m., but Jimmy insisted that he would need that much time to "brace himself."

Gwen arrived at noon, dressed in a green strapless evening gown, her beautiful black hair cascading down her perfect white shoulders. The crowning effect was a sparkling tiara that had been loaned to her by a local jewelry store. She truly did look like a queen and the guys were all trying to buy her drinks, including Riley who was about half in the mitt by this time.

Gwen accepted a couple too many of these generous offers and soon found herself feeling a little weary. One of the parade officials came in and shouted, "Okay, folks, let's saddle up!" Riley and Queen Gwen got to their feet and headed out the door and down to the corner where they were helped up onto their float.

The parade began with marching bands, clowns, and drill teams leading it off. When the royal float passed by us lowly spectators, Riley tipped his green top hat, nose crimson with whiskey. Gwen, in all her loveliness, waved to her loyal subjects. She mouthed to me, "I'm freezing!"

Just five minutes before, the wind had switched and now blew in off Lake Superior, lowering the temperature from forty-five to twenty degrees in the wink of an Irishman's eye. I was very concerned about Gwen and ran back to the bar and grabbed her coat. I found a cop who agreed to help me save the queen from freezing to death and he got me to the end of the parade route as quickly as possible. I could see the grand float coming two blocks away and went at a trot to Gwen's rescue. Breathing hard, I pulled up alongside it, and gasped. She wasn't on the float! And neither was Riley! Both of them had mysteriously disappeared.

I made my way through the crowd, asking the guy pulling the float, "Where are they?"

He turned around and looked very surprised to not see them there. He shrugged his shoulders and said, "Beats me. They were there a while ago. They're just gone."

Gone Johnson! I thought. *She's done it again. She's ditched me again!*

I was very grumpy and marched down Superior Street carrying Gwen's coat over my arm, stepping into every bar on the way, searching for the wayward queen and the drunken Irishman. Finally, after checking a half dozen or so bars, I found her majesty and the nearly passed-out grand marshal in the Paul Bunyan surrounded by a throng of merrymakers. Gwen's tiara was cocked sideways on her head and she ran to me crying, "Oh, Princie, I'm so sorry! I was awfully cold and Jimmy said I should find somewhere to get warm and he helped me down from my throne and, well, here we are. Sorry."

She looked up at me gratefully as I draped the coat around her cold-as-marble shoulders. She smiled and managed to slur. "I'm a little drunk."

I couldn't stay mad long. She was just too darn cute.

As it turned out, that was Duluth's last St. Patrick's Day parade. I guess the promoters figured that if they couldn't keep their grand marshal and their queen sober, they should maybe get out of the parade business.

36

Telling Tales

That same spring, following the demise of the St. Patrick's Day Parade, the 477th Medical Ambulance Company had its annual training at Fort Sam Houston, Texas where the medics worked at Brooks Army Medical Center. I had recently been assigned as food service administrator (that's mess sergeant with a lot of class). The Army does that from time to time just to keep us on our toes—and to provide a job for some guy at the Pentagon who sits around thinking up new names for army cooks.

There were two mess halls at Fort Sam; I dispersed my seven cooks, three at each hall and one in the food-issue warehouse. I assigned myself the role of liaison among the three locations and our company headquarters. In other words, I did nothing other than drive my guys to work in the morning and then pick them up in the afternoon. In the meantime, I played golf with Lieutenant J. Hall, Executive Officer of the 477th. The daily grind was overwhelming.

In the evenings, some of us would carpool into San Antonio where we lost no time in hitting the shit-kicker bars looking for cowgirls. Others would head to the River Walk for dinner. It was a great annual training. I remember the feeling of disbelief that I was getting paid for my efforts. That's what Lieutenant Hall and I would chant in a limerick, sing-song way as we

191

were choosing an iron or a wedge. "The most amazing thing to me, is we get paid for doing this!"

When we didn't go into San Antonio we would sit around the barracks playing cards, drinking, and telling stories. Two of the best storytellers I've ever known were on the President's 100, the Army Shooting Team, an elite group made up of the top 100 marksmen in the entire US Army. These two sharp-shooters from the 477th were Dale Sandstrom and Jim Dombrowski.

We were sitting around drinking beer one afternoon telling tales. Naturally, each guy tried to one-up the previous narra-tive with his own true life experience. I volunteered to stick in a true story about my first rodeo.

I

In the days before television, or at least before anyone in our neighborhood even owned a TV, boys had to use their imaginations to find ways to entertain themselves. Daytime was filled with baseball, swimming, constructing homemade bows and arrows, rubber guns, and slingshots. In a lot of ways it was a boy's ideal life. I had the good company of bad compan-ions in the days when parents were working too hard to find time to organize and supervise their kids. Mostly seven-and eight-year-olds, we wandered in packs of ten to twelve boys, taking lots of risks like riding trains heading down the hillside to the DM&IR docks near our house or jumping through narrow spaces between rocks into the deep pool at the Lincoln Park Fifth Street Bridge.

Returning from West Duluth where we had seen a Saturday matinee of *Mighty Joe Young* at the Doric Theater, we were taking our favorite mode of transportation, a slow moving freight that we'd hopped, the easiest way to reach the ore docks, three blocks from where we lived. Fueled by the heroics in the movie, we each took a diving roll off the car, landing on the withered grass along the track.

We lingered near the tracks where we had a grand time placing nickels and pennies on the rails and letting the train wheels flatten them when they rolled by. They made great arrowheads.

From there we could see the railroad siding for Elliott's Meat Packing Company and noticed three cattle cars pulling up to deliver their live cargo. Elliott's employees unloaded the cattle down a ramp and guided them through chutes into a holding pasture about three times the size of a football field.

We all ran to the pasture at top speed. A dozen kids climbed the fences as the cows, happy to be free of the hot and crowded confines of the boxcars, ran bucking and kicking up their heels. Someone laughed, "Boy, how would ya like to try riding one of those guys?"

Eleven heads turned slowly in unison toward the speaker to consider this interesting possibility.

"Let's do it!" exclaimed Dean Blomberg, our self-appointed leader. "Let's come down here tonight, climb over the fence and ride some of these cows! It'll be a hoot!"

We all nodded in agreement. A plan quickly took shape. After dark, we'd each sneak out of the house and meet at midnight behind Wade Stadium, our local ballpark, to reconnoiter our spying mission and scout the lay of the land.

Every one of us managed to meet there at the stroke of midnight. From the back of the stadium it was just a short distance to the animal pens. We crawled through grass up to the fence around the pasture. Figuring the coast was clear, a couple of us were just beginning to climb over when someone spotted a light and whispered, "Jiggers, it's the night watchman!"

We lay low as he passed and for most of the night, timed his rounds on Dean's Roy Rogers watch. The watchman came by every hour, on the hour, and it took him ten minutes to complete his inspection. It was almost morning and too late to ride on this night, but by our calculations, we'd have fifty minutes of cow riding time when we returned. We sneaked back home, disappointed but not defeated.

We hadn't planned on a five-day rain delay, but finally the weather was nice enough to try again. With the same plan in mind, we met behind the ballpark at midnight and checked the time carefully before making the final approach. We'd get our fifty minutes of ride-'em-rodeo time before the watchman made his next round.

As we crept through the grass, somebody complained, "Wow, this grass is really wet."

"Shhhh!" came from along the line of boys.

We were at the fence. Quickly, everyone clambered over and dropped to the other side into three inches of mud. Undeterred by a little mud, we advanced on the herd of cattle dragging our cowboy equipment; a piece of rope to use as a lasso and more guts than a government mule. We managed to get the loop over the head of a cow and led it to the fence where A.D. Royall grabbed the rope and slid his slim eight-year-old body onto its back.

Spooked, the cow took off like a bullet with A.D. hanging on for dear life.

We were all hollering and yelling, "Jump, A.D., JUMP!" But he continued to hang on, frozen with fear on top of the rearing and plunging beast.

A.D. and the cow disappeared into the rest of the herd which by this time had been stirred up and had begun to stampede around the pasture. Five, then ten minutes passed without a sighting of A.D. We decided that he was probably dead. Once the cattle settled down, we would have to retrieve his body for his mother.

As we moved toward the center of the pasture, the mud got deeper and thick...and smelly. I lost a tennis shoe, as did at least three other guys. Eddie Mackenzie lost both of his. But we found A.D., still alive although pretty used up. He was covered from head to toe with cow shit. His mother would be mad but it was just cow crap. He was still alive. She ought to be grateful.

Just then we heard a shrill whistle, the kind football coaches use, and a guy was yelling at us. It was the watchman hollering, "Stay where you are or I'll shoot!"

"Kiss my ass," someone yelled back.

We took off back over the fence and dashed wildly across the lot, as fast and as far from the Elliott's Meat Packing Company as our partially shod feet could take us.

A short sprint brought us to St. Louis Bay, just past the railroad yards, where we washed off the mud and cow crap and then hit for home. Luckily, we all made it back to our bedrooms before the sun lit the eastern sky. I got back into my bedroom the same way I'd gotten out, up the tree, over the limb, along the roof and in through the open window. In the morning, we told our parents that some kids from another neighborhood stole our shoes while we were swimming. Seeing as how that misfortune happened to a lot of us, our folks bought it.

For the next year or so, every time A.D. showed up at the ball field or swimming hole, sure as hell, someone would wrinkle his nose and comment, "Jesus, A.D., you smell just like cow shit." That always brought a roar of laughter from the whole gang and A.D. was the kid who laughed the loudest.

Dale Sandstrom was laughing too at this tale and slapped his knee, sloshing his beer on his shoe. "Whoops! Hey, Jimmy, you go next. I'm saving my stuff for last."

"Oh, all right. You just wanna see how much you have to lie to out-B.S. me, Sandstrom. Well, I do have a story to tell about my grandfather Glen and an old hound dog named Duke."

II

For fifteen years, Grandpa Glen and Duke would head through the back pasture looking for whatever game they might bring home for supper. Glen toted his shotgun on his shoulder and Duke trotted by his side. Gramps had a sort of limp or hobble, kind of like old Walter Brennan from the movies. He had been wounded in World War II. The surgery they did on his hip never healed quite right and he was left with a strange gait. He claimed it didn't hurt at all, just looked kind of irregular.

As they hit the tree line, Duke would race ahead, excited to be out hunting again. At the end of the day, Glen and Duke could be seen from the house heading back through the pasture and past the barn, Duke wagging his tail and Glen bouncing along, carrying a future dinner if they had been successful. Glen would put his shotgun in the house on hooks above the mantle and Duke would head for his place under the back porch where he had slept since he was a pup.

The years passed all too quickly and Duke began to slow down until one day, coming home from hunting, it seemed to Glen that his old dog was barely keeping up even with the slow pace he set. He brought him to the vet the next day and was told that Duke had cancer and would very soon be in a great deal of pain. The veterinarian advised that Duke should be put down before he got to that point and offered to do it himself, right then and there. Glen didn't hesitate. "No. No thanks, Doc. He's my dog. I'll do it myself."

The following morning Glen fed Duke a steak for breakfast, which the dog barely touched. The old man took down his rifle and walked out the back door. Just as they had done hundreds of times over the last fifteen years, the pair moved at their slow, jerky pace past the barn and through the pasture to the forest. Glen had asked his son to go out earlier and dig a grave for Duke. They reached the grave where there was a shovel stuck into the mound of dirt next to the hole. Glen knelt beside his old dog and took the dear head into his hands and said, "Well, my old friend, I guess this is it. I'm sorry I have to do this but you're very sick and this is the only thing to do. Goodbye, Duke. I'll see you on the other side."

Glen stood and gave Duke the command to sit. Duke obeyed and Glen raised his rifle and took aim. Tears streamed down his cheeks and his hands were shaking. Duke looked up at him with the unwavering trust a dog gives only to his master. Glen dried his eyes and tried again, but no dice. He just couldn't do it.

They headed back home, where Glen told his wife what had happened. She held him and said, "You'll figure something out. There must be another way."

In anguish, Glen tried to think of some method he could use to effect his dog's demise in such a quick and sure stroke that there would be no chance of Old Duke's feeling any pain whatsoever. That's when he had his brainstorm. Glen remembered hearing a story about a dog and some explosives. Out in the barn he had some dynamite that he kept for blowing up tree stumps. His plan was to take Duke out into the woods, tie him to a tree, tie some dynamite around his neck, leave a long fuse, light it, go home, and wait for the boom. He wouldn't see it. Duke wouldn't feel anything and the job would get done. They wouldn't even need the grave. It was a perfect plan.

The next morning, he went to the barn and got two sticks of dynamite. He calculated how much fuse he would need and measured it by stretching it out with his arms and looping it around his hands. When he had enough, he found a length of rope, went back to the house, and called Duke out from underneath the porch. His old pal came out, looking a little ragtag, but tail still wagging, happy to be with his master.

They walked together for their last trip to the woods. Glen was feeling very melancholy. He looked down at his dog and tears welled up in his eyes. When they reached the spot that

Glen had chosen, he tied Duke to the tree, fastened the dynamite around his neck, and attached the fuse.

"Well, Duke, this time I've got to do it." He said goodbye to his dog, scratched him behind the ear one last time and gave him a command to stay. Then he ran out his fuse, lit it, and turned and walked away. He figured he should be just about to the barn when he'd hear the explosion.

Three-quarters of the way through the pasture, he heard a dog bark. Panic stricken, he turned to see, just at the tree line, Duke bobbing after him dragging the rope and burning fuse behind him, the bundle of dynamite bouncing at his neck.

"Christ, I'll be killed! I've got to outrun him!"

He picked up his pace and got up to what was as close to a run as his old, crippled body could manage. He could hear Duke's barking getting closer. Choked with terror he prayed the explosion would come before the dog could reach him and send them both to their great reward. At the house he grabbed his rifle just as Duke ducked under the back porch.

The explosion blew the porch off, and knocked the house off the foundation.

"Thankfully, no one was hurt. Well, no one other than Duke, of course," said Jim as he paused in his narrative. It cost $3,000 to put the house back on the foundation, a lot of money in those days. The porch was completely gone and neither hide nor hair of poor old Duke was ever found."

Dale Sandstrom's competitive juices were running. He drank deeply from his beer, put it down with a flourish and spoke. "Now, I've got a story for you boys."

III

Dale came from a family of four brothers. His father owned a place outside of town with a herd of about a hundred cows. To make extra money they also boarded horses. Dale's father, Al Sandstrom, was a rugged guy. He'd lost an arm in World War II but he remained strong and fully capable of running the farm and rearing four growing sons.

One day in late October, fourteen-year-old Dale hopped off the school bus and looked up at the sky. It was cool and a storm was on its way. You could feel it in the air. Just as Dale got some milk from the fridge and sat down at the kitchen table to do his homework, the phone rang. It was his dad calling from the feed store.

"Dale," he said, "those three horses of the Swanson's are in the north pasture and there's a big thunderstorm coming. You'd better get out there and bring them in. We don't want any of our stock getting hit by lightning."

"Aw Dad," Dale whined. "I don't want to go way out there and have a storm hit. Geez, I could get hit by lightning too and I think I'm more important than a horse."

"Dale, what did I just tell you? Get your butt out there and bring those horses in or I'll kick your ass when I get home."

Dale knuckled under and agreed to do what his father had told him. He put on a hat and jacket and walked out to the barn, opening the big gate to the horse corral and looking out across the pasture. He shouted as loud as he could but the horses were three hundred yards away and didn't hear a thing.

He got some rope and was heading out across the corral when two of the horses started coming toward him. The closer they got the more speed they picked up. He opened the corral gate and they ran past him into the barn.

Clouds gathered quickly now and the storm rumbled in the distance. The last horse was still out there, standing as if he didn't care how bad the weather was. He wasn't coming in.

But young Dale was resourceful and he had an idea. He went back to the house and got his Match Grade M14, a rifle he used in shooting meets, and went back out to the corral. His plan was to whistle a round or two past the horse's ear to scare him back to the barn.

Just then he heard his little brother calling his name.

"Tim! I'm out here in the corral."

Timmy, his ten-year-old brother, thought the idea was nuts and offered to bring the horse in himself but Dale said, "Naw, I'm sticking to my original plan. Besides, this will be the shot of a lifetime and someday you can tell this story at the hunting shack and the whole family will laugh till they pee their pants."

He raised his rifle, resting it on the fence rail and took aim. It was a 300-yard shot and if done right, this truly would be the shot of his young life. Checking and estimating the velocity of the wind, he took dead aim, held his breath and squeezed off the shot.

A millisecond after he pulled the trigger, the horse picked up his head just a bit and then dropped in a heap. Timmy looked at Dale, eyes like saucers, and said very quietly.

"Oh, boy, are you in trouble. My God, Dale, you just shot that poor horse."

Dale just stood there, staring across the pasture, his brain not wanting to believe what his eyes just saw.

"Yeah, Timmy," said Dale softly. "I think you're right. Sure as shit, I just shot that horse. Pop is gonna shoot me with this same gun when he finds out."

Together the two brothers ran across the pasture to where the horse lay, obviously dead. Dale knelt by its side to inspect the horse and found a hole in the left temple, so small you could miss it. It was a misguided shot he wished he could take back. But he couldn't. He looked at Timmy.

"Tim, run back to the house and get a scissors, the glue pot, and a curry comb from the shed. I've got an idea and if it works, Pop will never know what happened."

Timmy shot for the house and was back in ten minutes with the supplies. Dale cut some hair from the dead horse's tail, chopped it up fine, and mixed it with glue. He wiped the little bit of blood from around the wound and applied the horsehair and glue mixture to cover the small hole. The glue dried quickly in the wind. Finally, he gently arranged the hair so that it would blend in nicely. He stood back and appraised his handiwork.

"It worked! Holy shit, it worked. Tim, you can't see the hole at all!"

They went back to the house and, very quickly, Dale cleaned his rifle. Then he called his dad at Evenson's Feed Bin.

"Pop," he said, "there's something wrong with one of the horses. I think he might be dead."

Al was home in a flash. With Dale and Timmy at his heels, he trudged out into the rainstorm to inspect the dead horse. He looked the horse over carefully and said, "Yeah, he's dead, all right. Probably had a heart attack, what with all this lightning. I'll call Swanson and find out what he wants us to do with him."

The next day Al got out the backhoe, dug a grave for the horse, and buried him right where he lay. He charged Mr. Swanson fifty dollars for the job.

Twenty years later at their deer-hunting shack, Timmy was with two of his brothers and their father. Everyone was drinking, laughing, and telling stories. Dale wasn't due in for another hour or so. He was driving north from Minneapolis. As the evening progressed, Tim got pretty loaded and decided this would be the perfect time to tell the horse story. In great detail, Tim told his dad and brothers the story of Dale and the shot of a lifetime. The brothers broke out into uncontrollable laughter. Their dad did not even crack a smile. He just sat there, a shot of Jack Daniels in his hand, his face darkening.

A short time later, in walked Dale, sporting a giant smile and loaded with gear. He put down his burdens and greeted his brothers, then went to hug his dad.

Al stood with a roar like a grizzly bear and yelled, "You son-of-a-bitch! You shot that goddamned horse!" Dale ducked but did not entirely deflect the blow. His one-armed father could still throw a hell of a punch. And he knew he deserved it for shooting that poor horse. It was almost a relief, something he figured he'd had coming for a long time.

Well. I was there at the riding of the cows and know it to be true. Whether these other two stories were entirely on the level, I couldn't say, and they may carry at least a whiff of bullshit. Doesn't matter.

37

Games

Bartending isn't always action-packed. One dreary Monday afternoon in the early 1980s, a lonely barman was becalmed in a sea of boredom while working at the Mirror Lounge. Business was terribly slow from 1:00 to 3:00, except for Fridays when things picked up to medium—slow. On this particular day, a guy from the vending machine company dropped off a new cue ball to replace one that had gone missing over the weekend. The barkeep put the ball in an ashtray intending to bring it down a short staircase to the game room the next time he had a reason to go there.

TV couldn't break the monotony. In his opinion, game shows were always stupid and even the soap operas were uneventful this day. He had cleaned the entire back bar and polished the sinks and fixtures. There was nothing else to do so he wiped down the bottles again. Not one customer had come in for the last hour and a half and he was bored to stupefaction.

Joe, the bartender, set down his coffee cup and picked up the cue ball from the ashtray, giving it a little spin on the bar as he lit a cigarette. The ball spiraled slowly. Joe picked it back up and set it gently into the long slot between the bar and the wooden arm rest where it nestled perfectly, looking comfortable in its new resting spot. Joe gave it a little push and the ball rolled down the bar along the chute as if, instead of being whacked around in a silly game of pool, it had discovered a new calling. Joe imagined the little cue ball enjoying the ride and giving forth in a wee voice, "This is so amusing, rolling down the bar on this track that a knowing someone has built especially for me."

Joe rolled it over and over again and made a little game out of trying to see how far he could roll it without the ball falling off the end of the trough.

He took three pieces of masking tape and marked them with numbers one, two and three and placed them at six-inch intervals approaching the end of the bar. The object was to roll the cue ball to the number three, but not go over the edge. That feat would earn three points. If the ball only got to one, he awarded himself a single point. If it got to two, it was two points.

He practiced for an hour and was getting quite good at his new game. Then he decided that a player should have three shots with not more than four players participating in each inning.

I happened to stroll in the door just then and Joe showed me his game. "What do you call it?" I asked.

Joe thought a bit and declared, "Watch-um-Ball-Rolla."

We played a game. He won, of course. I paid my quarter purse and he dropped it into his pocket. It was getting on toward 3:00. More people came in and got involved. Soon Watch-um-Ball-Rolla was the talk of the bar. Business began to pick up and customers from other bars dropped by, wanting to learn the rules.

In the days following, we organized tournaments and it was only a matter of time before leagues began. It was fun while it lasted, but in the long run, the game became a deterrent to business. It's hard to drink your beer with a bunch of drunken fools rolling a cue ball past you yelling, "Get the hell out of the way. Can't you see we're playing Watch-um-Ball-Rolla!?"

Of the men who gathered in the bars of downtown Duluth, surprisingly, many were athletically inclined. Mickey McLelland, my brother Jack, James Francis Riley, and Alan Nisius (our local investment broker) were, in their own times, terrific athletes, and they worked to stay in the game well past their prime.

Each year, usually in early summer, the talk started flying. Who could field the best softball team—the Paul Bunyan or Lofdahl's Corner Bar? It never took long before word spread, the gauntlet was thrown down, and the contest of clowns was scheduled.

I remember one year when we arranged to reserve the ball field at the Buffalo House, a restaurant and watering hole just outside Duluth that boasted two ball fields plus a full-service bar strategically located not thirty yards behind the center field fence. The business featured an unusual attraction on the premises—a live buffalo herd. The big mythic animals stood quietly contemplating the action on the field as they munched their own favorite concessions treat—green grassy cuds.

Our game between the mighty Bunyan team and Lofdahl's fighting nine was scheduled to begin at 1:00 in the afternoon, but due to problems prying loose eighteen already over-served ballplayers from their barstools, the action didn't get started until closer to 2:00.

A steady stream of wives and girlfriends got their teams warmed up by running back and forth to the spigots behind center field, enthusiastically replenishing a liquid lifeline to their favored combatants. Fortified, the team captains called the coin toss and then took their designated places either on the field or in the dugout.

The Bunyan got on the board early in the first inning with

what should have been a single, but with three errors and Lofdahl's second baseman, Len Peters, finishing his cocktail before throwing the ball into home, the hit turned out to be an inside-the-park homer.

During the second inning, the game was turning into a real knuckle-biter with a tight score of twenty-one to three, as Paul Bunyan's crew of Lumberjacks took the lead. This seemed like a perfect opportunity to break the tension—and some idiot opened the pasture gate where a dozen buffalo were grazing. These buffalo must have been very athletic themselves because three of them decided to come over to the ball field and join the game.

Two teams of Duluth's finest ballplayers-turned-cowboys got to the job at hand and began what later came to be known as the First Annual Bunyan—Lofdahl's Summer Round-up.

It took eighteen guys and half again as many girlfriends, wives, and spectators about an hour to get the wayward bovines back to their pasture, luckily with only minor injuries to the herders. The beasts appeared unscathed.

The game resumed with slightly less vigor but with yet enough drama to keep everyone on the edge of the bleacher seats during the fourth inning. The Bunyan increased its lead over Lofdahl's to a scant thirty points. The score was now thirty-six to six.

Suddenly, as if he had been hit by a gunshot, James Francis Riley went down at third base. He was obviously in some sort of terrible trouble. No one had a clue what it was, but everyone was scared. Heart attack? Stroke?

In hardly any time at all, an ambulance came screeching onto the field. Out jumped the paramedics who loaded up Riley. Sirens blazing, they bounced back out to the highway and raced toward St. Mary's Hospital in downtown Duluth. They were followed by a dozen or so cars loaded with equally loaded ballplayers. Len Peters was hanging out of a passenger window yelling, "We're right behind ya, Riles!"

When the ambulance reached the ER, Riley was immediately spirited away to a treatment room somewhere down a back hallway. Meanwhile, the boozy entourage, in hot pursuit, poured itself into St. Mary's emergency waiting room.

This was long before hospitals employed armed security guards and a good thing, too. Considering the shenanigans that followed, those guards would likely have felt justified in shooting at several in our crew.

No matter where we were, a competitive spirit forever simmered in our gamester hearts, so when boredom began to set in, mischief was not far behind. The first game, a leg wrestling tourney for a buck a throw, didn't get us kicked out. But when we became fully engaged in the First Annual St. Mary's Wheelchair Races, that was it!

From every direction, we heard, "Out! Out! Out!" Doctors, nurses, orderlies, and assorted hospital staff members swarmed down, ushering us out the door with clear orders not to return, bleeding or not.

As for our pal Riley, he had suffered a brain aneurism that called for immediate surgery. We heard that his doctors gave us credit for doing something right. They said it was a good thing we got him help quickly because fifteen more minutes and he wouldn't have made it.

We never did finish the ballgame. Much to the chagrin of the high-scoring Bunyan Lumberjacks, it was declared a tie since we didn't get to the fifth inning at which point the ten-run-rule would have been implemented and the Paul Bunyan declared the winner. Over a post-game glass of beer, I think I overheard one of Lofdahl's outfielders promise to find a two-headed buffalo nickel for next year's coin toss.

Jack on the Job

In 1980, Jack, my gandy dancer brother, bid on a DM&IR crane operator's job in Two Harbors. After three interviews, he was hired. The project was on a big crane down at the ore docks and it turned out Jack had a knack for the work and was quite happy on the job. It came with a substantial raise, but he still was unable to save a cent. Poor judgment, drinking, and gambling would cause Jack to make mistake after mistake through his life but if he did nothing else, he provided plenty of opportunities for people to look at him, shake their heads, and say, "What on earth could he possibly have been thinking?"

On a fairly regular basis the King would lose his entire paycheck when he played gin rummy with a crook named Darby Jones. Jack would come through the front door of the Paul Bunyan and Darby Jones would start rubbing his hands together, murmuring, "Railroad payday, I believe."

Darby had spent most of his adult life in prison. He was known in the Federal Penitentiary at Stillwater as "the Shark" because of his almost supernatural card playing talents. Jack was a pretty good gin player himself, but he was often delusional, and he just couldn't bring himself to admit that he would never beat this guy.

Paycheck after paycheck went from the DM&IR paymaster

to Jack who, six or seven hours later, would endorse it over to Darby Jones. For some reason, Jack was never happy unless he was dead broke. It somehow got his creative juices flowing and fiscal necessity would help him to come up with another King get-rich-quick scheme.

In one instance, I was finishing a shift at Perrault's Bakery in the Miller Hill Mall, just scraping the work bench at the end of a long day's work, when the phone rang. It was Jack's foreman in Two Harbors. He told me Jack had taken a fall and was on his way in an ambulance to St. Mary's Hospital. I punched out and ran for my car.

When I got to the hospital, Jack was just being rolled in on a gurney. But I didn't get a chance to talk to him until after he came back from x-ray when he told me that he had slipped on an oil spill on the stairway going up to his crane. He'd fallen about twelve feet onto a steel platform. The x-rays were inconclusive. They did show a spinal abnormality but it wasn't clear if it was because of the fall or a pre-existing condition.

Jack spent three days in the hospital for tests and the next six months on workers' compensation. He initiated a lawsuit against the railroad after his ambulance-chasing lawyer hired a doctor who would testify in court. In the doctor's professional opinion, the abnormality in the King's back was not a pre-existing condition but a direct result of the fall on the crane stairs. The lawyer argued that the oil slick had been called to the foreman's attention by none other than the plaintiff himself, not once, but on three separate occasions. Therefore he argued that the plaintiff, through no fault of his own, was now unable to work and had experienced an enormous amount of pain and suffering. Furthermore, he was no longer able to engage in the two sports he dearly loved, golf and softball. In closing, the King's mouthpiece demanded that $150,000 be awarded his client, "to be paid within one month of these proceedings."

He won! In December of that year, after giving the lawyer

his cut, the King walked away with a check for $88,000. The railroad had made him an offer of a guaranteed sit-down job for the rest of his life with no lay-offs and a promise to pay any medical expenses he might accrue in relation to his back injury—this in lieu of the one hundred and fifty grand.

Perrault's Bakery was for sale at a great price and I tried to convince my brother to buy it. I had been working there long enough to know what a gold mine it was. I told him I'd do all the baking to begin with and train him and my two sons.

"Just think, Jack, your own profitable business! Jobs for all four of us and you'll make your investment back in two years."

"I'll think about it," said the newly well-heeled ex-crane operator.

Maybe he did think about it as he boarded a plane bound for Honolulu, his arm around a blonde bimbo he'd picked up in a bar and carrying a suitcase full of hundred dollar bills.

Jack called me from the airplane (which at that time was very expensive), then from the condo he rented on the island of Hawaii, and again from the other condo he rented on Maui. He hired a full-time helicopter pilot to fly him from one condo to the other. Finally, life was giving Jack the full benefits of his imagined status. He was living like a king.

He called one day and told us to watch the *Don Ho Show*, telecast from a hotel on Waikiki Beach. We tuned in that Saturday night and there was my brother in his Elvis sunglasses and a red silk scarf draped around his neck being interviewed by Don Ho himself. As usual, Jack made a complete fool of himself, telling Don Ho, "I'm the King and you're not." They didn't actually show the King being thrown out the door, but he said they whistled him out so fast he didn't have time to pay his dinner bill.

The King lived this lavish life for about two months. After returning to Duluth from Hawaii, he continued to spend like a pixilated sailor. One afternoon, while I was working at the Paul Bunyan, the King walked through the door.

"Mike, hold on to this dough for me." He handed me a roll of bills wrapped in a rubber band. "I'm going to the YMCA to take a steam bath and I don't want to leave this much in my locker." I counted it after he left—all $13,000 of it. That's what he was carrying around in his pocket. Thirteen thousand dollars! I made a mental note to give him hell about it later.

On March 15 of that year, just three short months after receiving his cashier's check for $88,000, the King asked me for bus fare.

I could have given him a lecture but he probably would have said, "Get off my back. I'm the King, and you're not." I just shook my head and handed him five bucks.

He smiled back at me as he walked out the door, "Easy come, easy go, Muntzie."

Swinging Bottles

I was working fourteen hours a day at my two jobs, baking bread and pouring booze. In my spare time I was still a cook in the Army Reserves, 477th Ambulance Company. Reserve weekends were brutal. I went from Thursday night at 11:00 until Sunday afternoon with almost no sleep. The schedule took a toll on both my easy-going attitude and my health. I lost a lot of weight during that time and told myself, *Michael, my boy, you have got to find a way off this merry-go-round or you'll work yourself into the grave.*

I bartended occasionally for a Chinese restaurant and bar that was about to go out of business. I approached the owner and offered him $10,000 for his liquor license which was a little less than 25 percent of its real value. Liquor licenses were worth real dough in Duluth at that time. I didn't think there was a chance in hell that he would go for this lowball offer, but to my surprise he accepted the proposal and three days later the City of Duluth Liquor Board transferred the Chinese joint's liquor license into my name. I had two years to put the license into use before it would revert back to the city and be resold to the next person applying for the license.

I had already spent almost everything I had on this venture and set about finding further financing. Everyone turned me down.

Then one day a guy named KJ called me with a proposition. His parents had just sold their grocery store to a developer with plans to gut it and put in an office complex. KJ said, "With your liquor license and my parents' money, we can go into a three-way partnership on a new bar. All we have to do is find a suitable building for our new enterprise." It didn't take long before we settled on a building to lease. The remodeling would be up to me and whatever work party I could assemble. I was to work the day shifts, order supplies, and manage employees for all other shifts. KJ was to walk around on his parents' dime, playing the role of suave bar owner.

A good space was found on First Street. We rented all three floors for peanuts. The bar was to be on the first floor. The second floor would remain empty. The business office and my living quarters would take up the third floor. I gave our new joint its name—Malarky's—before saw or hammer was ever put to work. And we started some clever advertising on all the radio stations and in area newspapers.

Coming Soon ~ Let Malarky's rock your summer!!

My usual work crew, my sons John and Robby, and the entire Central High School football team, came in that first day with Saws-Alls and sledge hammers and in one eighteen-hour day they had knocked down all the inner walls and carried them out to a dumpster on the street. The next Monday, with blueprints spread out on the cloverleaf bar that I had bought cheap, we met with the carpenter, electrician and plumber. I split Rob and his guys into two groups, one that had some technical knowledge and the other with bull labor talents.

One month from that first day, Malarky's opened its doors to crowds beyond our expectations. Business boomed. I worked the bar seven day-shifts a week and my former girlfriend Jeanette ran our mini-kitchen featuring a soup and sandwich menu. The summer of 1985 was a blur of energy and effort.

Not being a very smart businessman, I hadn't read the fine

print on the contract with KJ and learned after six or seven months that I was legally the *junior* partner. Then money began to disappear. KJ suggested that my bartending staff was light-fingered, but that staff was made of Rob, me, and four hand-picked guys that I would trust with all I owned. The final straw came on a Monday morning when my phone rang. It was KJ's mom Betty who came into the bar mornings to get the bank deposits ready. She was crying as she told me that upon coming to work that morning, she discovered that the door to the safe was wide open and it was empty except for a few rolls of quarters.

"Mike," she cried, "did you take the money home for some reason?"

"No, Betty, I didn't. Call KJ. I'll be right there."

I threw on a pair of jeans and a T-shirt, slipped into my shoes, and hurried down the hall to the office where I found Betty on the phone with KJ. She sobbed as she told him about the missing money. After Betty got off the phone, I called the police. They were there in ten minutes and questioned Betty and me and then waited for KJ so they could talk to him, too.

KJ suggested that a safecracker had "cracked" the combination. The cops told him that only happens in the movies and that it was more likely that one of us had forgotten to lock the office door and left the safe open. I was positive that when I had gone to my apartment the previous night, the safe door was locked and so was the office door.

I figured the best move I could make at this point was to ask Betty if she wanted to buy me out of the business. She thought that it might be a good idea and I walked away with all the money I had invested and a bit more in consideration of all the time and effort I had put into the venture.

Whatever did happen to that dough, I was just glad to get out. I'd had my fill of Malarky's.

Starting over wasn't a new thing for me but it was becoming more difficult. Every time I had to find a new job and place to live it seemed like I was paying for it with a piece of my life I could never get back.

I was forty-four years old and beginning to worry about my future. I made myself a promise that if I ever got into a business again I would take a lot more care and time to learn what sort of situation I was getting into.

I landed a job at Super One Bakery with a crew of guys that I had worked with in several shops in the past. It was a pretty good job, but now that I was older, the work was harder, and for the first time in my life I began to really dislike what I did for a living.

One morning, just before I was done work, one of the girls answered the bakery phone and yelled back into the shop, "Mike, it's for you!"

It was the new owner of the Mirror Lounge. He had just bought the place from his dad and was offering me a full-time bartender's job with my pick of any shifts I preferred. I gave notice at the bakery and two weeks later started at the Mirror where, as it turned out, I made more money than at Super One, and I was working thirty fewer hours a week!

The new boss was delighted to own a bar and often kept the place running after the doors were locked, supplying himself and his friends with free booze. You can't make money doing that. Eventually, the boss's wife put her foot down and it wasn't long before the place was on the market.

They approached Ray T. Ward and me, suggesting we go in together to buy the bar from them. They offered us a great deal and we jumped at it. The next two weeks were spent figuring out the finances and kicking around ideas for what to call our new place. I asked Ray, "What's the name of the bar you always imagined owning someday?"

"R. Tease," he answered. He had always enjoyed the bar banter that goes on between bartender and customer. "What's yours?"

"I always thought I would own an Irish pub and call it Quin's." After many different combinations, Siggie, proving that she was more than a good bartender and a pretty face, came up with one we both liked, R.T. Quinlan's.

"That's it!" we exclaimed in unison. We had agreed on the first big decision, our name.

Ray and I were both forty-six years old and pretty sure an opportunity like this one would never come again. We made a promise that each partner would carry an even load in doing everything possible to make the place fly.

On the fifteenth of September, 1990, we turned a brand new key and unlocked the back door to let ourselves and the soon-to-be-former owners into R.T. Quinlan's Saloon. That first day was both terrific and terrifying.

Ray and the owner's wife went down into the basement storeroom and walk-in cooler to take an inventory. Back upstairs, they also listed items on the back bar and in the coolers. With the inventory completed, we all three signed the transfer papers, shook hands, and opened both front and back doors. It was official. We owned a saloon and R.T. Quinlan's was open for business.

As customers streamed in both doors, I sprang into action and took my very first drink order—a bottle of Bud, a vodka diet, and a rum and Coke. Ray stood at the end of the bar grinning while I, sporting the exact same grin, punched the transaction into the till. I stood with the twenty-dollar bill in my hand and looked into the cash register. "Dammit, Ray!"

"What's wrong, pard?"

"We forgot about a bank for the till. We haven't got any change."

Ray went up and down the bar borrowing money from customers. We made a list of who was owed how much, but as business picked up we realized this wouldn't work for long. I told Ray to watch the bar so I could go home for my piggy bank. I figured she'd have about a hundred bucks in her belly.

"I've got some, too. I'll go for mine when you get back."

That first day we were back and forth to the bank for change at least a dozen times. We made it to closing time and when I rang out the tills, I looked at my partner and beamed, "Ya know, pard, I think we're going to make it all right."

"We'd better, or we'll be jumping off the Blatnik Bridge tied together with a white flag wrapped around a bowling ball."

Word on the street was that a couple of well-known shit-heads were new management and they'd never last. The bookies had the over-and-under at six months before we drank ourselves out of business.

From the first day, business was brisk and Ray and I worked like a team of plow horses either tending bar or taking care of the business end—banking, ordering, and organizing the cleaning helpers and staff. We alternated work schedules, each partner on the day shift for a week and then on nights for the next. Our bank account began to build, and it was beginning to look as if we would prove the bookies and naysayers wrong after all.

Then Saddam Hussein and his army invaded Kuwait.

Book
V

Drumming Up a War

Saddam Hussein's Iraqi army attacked the State of Kuwait on August 2, 1990, and suddenly, all hell broke loose. President George H.W. Bush and other world leaders demanded that the Iraqis withdraw their troops from this defenseless, oil-rich country. The Iraqi dictator thumbed his nose at the Free World, claiming ownership of Kuwait for himself and his government. He vowed total destruction of any army that any nation or group of nations might send in an attempt to remove his troops. He now claimed Kuwait as Iraqi soil.

Despite Saddam's grandiose threats, a group of allied forces came together with the United States, sending troops to the Middle East, mostly to Saudi Arabia. There they set up staging areas that in three short months would accommodate over a half million allied troops.

I had been a member of the 477th Army Reserve Unit based in Duluth for seven years. Rumors ran rampant through the unit, and every day or two I would hear from one person or another that we would be called up any day now. I was at R.T. Quinlan's working the day shift the Saturday before Thanksgiving when the bar phone rang around 2:00. The 477th company clerk gave the code word verifying that this was legit and then alerted me that the unit would be sent to Fort McCoy in Wisconsin to begin mobilization training in one week. I was ordered to report to the unit on Monday morning to begin readying my mess section for deployment.

We stood in formation at 0700 hours that Monday and listened to half a dozen or so speeches regarding how the men and women of the 477th were about to embark on a great and noble mission to aid a helpless nation in its fight for freedom. At forty-seven, I was a little old for a pep talk, but standing in formation with my fellow soldiers that morning, I felt like Teddy Roosevelt about to charge up San Juan Hill.

My mess section was staffed with three women and four men. We would work in two groups. I was to be section leader of one group and Sergeant Duane Nelson would head up the other. All through the week we cleaned, packed, and loaded mess equipment, made out our wills, filled out mountains of paperwork, and in general made ready to begin our convoy to Fort McCoy.

My older son Robby had been working construction in Minneapolis, but when he got the call that I needed him back in Duluth to assume my responsibilities at the bar, he immediately came home. My younger son John worked for us as well, but he was still too young to tend bar so he became our swamper and cleaned the bar every morning. John took on that thankless job with a good spirit. For a guy his age, it had a couple of advantages; it didn't require a great deal of thought and the boss wouldn't be on his tail all the time.

The media was all abuzz about the coming war in Iraq. An NBC affiliate called and asked if they might interview me at Quinlan's. I agreed, mainly because I felt it would be good and free advertising for our fledgling business. When the reporter asked how I felt about being activated so soon after opening our enterprise, I explained that I felt like a new father being drafted two months after the birth of his baby.

On the morning we convoyed out of town, I didn't want an emotional goodbye so I got up early at 0300h. Formation was

221

scheduled for 0500h and departure was set for 0700h. I wrote a short note and quietly left the house being careful not to wake Robby. My brother Jack brought my mother to the Reserve Center to see me off. She was very sentimental about the whole thing, reminding me that it was nearly thirty years ago that I had kissed her goodbye and gone off to the Navy.

Our adrenalin was pumping as we lined up the vehicles in front of the building. First was the skipper in his command vehicle and then an office truck carrying the company clerks with assorted records. Following them was supply with its two trucks and the next was my mess vehicle, a Korean War vintage deuce-and-a-half. Behind me were the medics and nurses in twenty-one ambulances and finally, the motor pool and its chase vehicle. It was still dark when we pulled away from headquarters precisely at 0700 hours.

A minute or two before sunrise, as our convoy passed by my apartment, I saw that the lights were on but Robby's car was gone. "The little shit's laying in wait for me," I told Duane Nelson who was riding shotgun with me.

Moments later, there he was, standing with a group of our friends gathered just past the Aerial Lift Bridge, waving us goodbye. I could tell Rob was crying.

"He's always been such a goosh," I choked, wiping tears from my eyes.

Fort McCoy was bursting at the seams with deploying troops. I heard from one old sarge that 50,000 guard and reserve soldiers would deploy from McCoy by the first of the year. No United States post had processed that many troops so quickly since the start of World War II.

A couple of two-level barracks buildings were assigned to us, one for men and one for women, with the mess hall between.

I signed for the mess building and for all the equipment in it before we could get our first ration delivery. Every mess hall got the same amount of food every three days per one hundred soldiers, but it was up to the individual unit to decide what they actually did with the food they received. That's where we could shine. We always bragged that we had the best mess in the Army and could make candy out of horseshit if necessary. Now was our chance to prove it. Nelson and I talked it over and came up with a plan for making sure our operations ran smoothly while allowing us time for our own military training.

We would work long days. Each twenty-four-hour shift prepared the lunch and evening meals and did cleanup afterward. They would also rise at 0400h and put breakfast out, afterward doing the cleanup before the next twenty-four-hour shift came to relieve them. The incoming crew did an inspection of the dining facility to ensure that the previous team had properly cleaned and stowed all gear before the outgoing shift was relieved.

A competition soon began between Nelson's shift and mine. My crew consisted of Adam Kruchoski and Monty Lyons, both spec-fours and both pretty good army cooks. Nelson's crew was made up of three women—also spec-fours.

We gauged our success in this culinary combat not only by the compliments we received from the troops but by the number and rank of visiting dignitaries. We figured the more brass that opted to dine at our mess hall, the more likely word had gotten around about the quality of chow we served.

We attracted so many officers from other units I found it necessary to request additional rations in order to feed the twenty or thirty extra soldiers that came through our chow line three times a day. Gary Lindgren, a well-known professional wrestler, about six feet seven in height and wide as an army footlocker, was the first hungry soldier in line every single day. His appetite didn't faze us, but about a week into our training, the 477th was augmented by forty more medics and ambulance drivers from Milwaukee. That brought the number we were feeding to 170 officers and enlisted personnel. The addition to our ranks put a tremendous strain on our mess section but, with what I think was a persuasive sales job on my part, I was able to convince the first sergeant to assign two KPs per shift to ease the workload on my cooks. So every other morning, while the duty shift rose early and served breakfast, the off-duty shift got a couple extra hours of well-deserved sleep.

At 0600h, the chow line opened and the lights came on in the barracks. Early risers who awoke before reveille were greeted by ten-to twenty-below-zero weather as they trudged out across the coal-blackened snow fifty yards to the mess hall, the frigid stuff squeaking beneath their boots.

SFC Tony Hoff, Third Platoon Sergeant and go-to guy for creative ideas, took care of any company needs that didn't fall under the authorized military equipment category. He procured us a television for the mess hall to help us keep current on the war buildup in the Middle East. During meals, troops gathered around the TV, eyes glued and hanging onto every word of information regarding the latest developments of the coming war.

We in the mess section were required, in addition to our mess duties, to undergo every bit of training that was required of the medics in the 477th. This left us little time for any sort of recreation. Because being resourceful is part of being a US soldier, somehow we found a way to squeak out some time to relax at the NCO Club (the same NCO Club that we almost put out of business during the 1980 Cuban relocation).

There was a three-day period when Monty and Adam had to take over for me when I came down with the flu. They dug in, shoulder to shoulder, and fed nearly two hundred soldiers by themselves until I was back on my feet. When the chips were *not* down though, Monty was a genius at finding ways out of any sort of work or responsibility, and that was how he earned the all-purpose nickname "Shithead." Every night he found a way to sneak off to the club and get himself totally crocked. Mornings were a trial for me. My first duty was to find Monty. Our own Beetle Bailey was a master at ferreting out places to sleep and then camouflaging his nest to make it appear as if a soldier couldn't possibly be hiding in there.

If and when I did find him, he was nearly impossible to rouse out of bed. On very cold winter mornings, a PT instructor inside each barracks would lead us in calisthenics that included jumping jacks, sit-ups, push-ups, and running in a circle around the barracks. Monty had devised a plan whereby he took extra blankets and tucked them under the upper bunk mattress so they hung down like curtains around his lower bunk. The blankets hid him from the physical training going on at the foot of his bed. We all, including our superiors, knew he was in there. And you might expect that one of us would have hollered, "Hey, Shithead, get your ass out of the rack." But for some weird reason, no one ever did. The physical training proceeded while Monty could be heard snoring in his hide-out oblivious to the thunder of boots on the tiled floor as the rest of his company did their jumping jacks.

We spent a total of six weeks at Fort McCoy learning not only basic soldiering skills but also how to deal with cultural differences once we got to our destination, Saudi Arabia. Units scheduled to leave McCoy in the morning could be found at the spacious NCO Club the night before, enjoying their last buzz before leaving the country, and singing along with Lee Greenwood's "God Bless the USA" as it blared from the public address system.

When our turn came to ship out, on the night before our deployment, Tony Hoff stood on the stage at the NCO Club and led the 477th, women on one side of the floor and men on the other, in an impromptu rendition of "Paradise by the Dashboard Light." I will never forget that scene—women singing at the very tops of their voices, asking for eternal love, and men lunging forward in response, louder and louder, back and forth, asking for time to think about it.

It brought the house down. At least a thousand voices joined in throbbing sound that night. Somehow it seemed every bit as patriotic as the Lee Greenwood song or any of the other flag waving that went on during that time.

The next morning we got out of bed at "O-dark-30," long before dawn. After a breakfast of steak and eggs that, for once, my cooks didn't have to cook, we boarded a plane at Volk Field, Wisconsin, and took off into the cold January sky, heading east. The sun was just beginning to rise.

41

Looking for an Oasis

We stopped for fuel in Bangor, Maine where we were permitted to deplane and have our last cocktail before leaving the country. Naturally, Monty "Shithead" Lyons got loaded in a short half hour and had to be practically carried aboard the airplane. I shored him up with a soldier on each side to hold him upright and get him into a seat before the skipper could notice his inebriation.

Twenty-four hours later, he woke up with the rest of us in Dhahran, Saudi Arabia. It was January 10, 1991.

We waited on the tarmac for the buses to take us to our billets in Dhahran. We were assigned an empty complex that had been built for Bedouins by the Saudi government in the hope that they could integrate this nomadic people into an urban society. The lavish, modern neighborhood with fifty three-story apartment buildings didn't seem to have worked for the tribal people, but it could have worked well for us if we'd had half the troops or twice the space.

The transport arrived and we were driven to temporary housing where we would live until our vehicles and equipment arrived at the Dhahran port. There were 25,000 troops billeted there. At the time, this was nearly twice as many as the complex could accommodate. The overflow lived in underground garages located between the apartment buildings.

The 477th soldiers, being the new kids on the block, watched a deployed unit file out of one of the buildings and mount trucks to begin their motor march out the front gate. In turn, another unit moved out of the parking garage and into the building. We were then ordered by Dick Sturvich, our commanding officer, to shoulder our gear and take possession of the cavernous garage that would be our home for the next week.

We were permitted to use the indoor bathrooms once every other day—men on odd numbered days and women on even. Other bathroom needs would be handled by Porta-Pottys located in the commons area across the street. The Porta-Pottys were almost always overflowing and we all prayed that nature would not call until we got our turn at the facilities inside the building. There was also an outside spigot that delivered non-drinkable water that was only good for shaving and hand washing.

Then the rains came. The temperature dropped to a high of forty degrees and the rain continued for the next four days. Even though the garage was covered, light ports let in rain-water, making it next to impossible to keep our gear dry. With little rivers running in every direction, our best trick was to keep everything up and off the floor.

Adam found a couple of pallets outside which we quickly confiscated; Lieutenant Hughes, our executive officer (XO) appointed the first platoon to bring in as many more as they could find. They returned with about three dozen. We covered the wet area and stowed our gear high and dry.

My mess section had little to do since the Saudi nationals ran the mess halls at Dhahran where we ate breakfast and supper. Our noon meals were meals-ready-to-eat (MREs). I picked these packages up every third day and doled them out to the troops at 1130h each morning. To keep my section busy, officers assigned my soldiers to pose as litter patients for the medics to use in their training classes every morning at 0900h and again at 1400 hours.

After a week in the parking garage, one of the buildings was vacated and we moved in as another incoming unit took over our subterranean dwelling. Finally, we could take a shower every day and when a trip to the bathroom was really compelling, we didn't have to search all over the compound for a Porta-Potty that wasn't full.

On the second night in our new digs, Scud missile attacks began. We were all pretty nervous about this because we heard that Saddam Hussein had chemical warheads in his Scud missiles, the same ones he'd used in his war against the Iranians. He had killed thousands of people. When the loudspeaker sounded, "Scud alert, mop level three," we scrambled into our gas masks and "mop gear" (mesh vests from which we hung all our paraphernalia, canteens, and other survival stuff). We stood out on the verandas of our building staring into the starlit night and watched as a Scud streaked across the sky. Out of nowhere, a Patriot missile responded like the cavalry coming to the rescue and exploded with a direct hit into the Scud, making a flash that would bring an "ooh" or "aah" as if we were sitting on a blanket at a Fourth of July celebration. Fortunately, there were no chemicals; still, these attacks kept up four or five times a night, making sleep impossible at first.

Unintentionally, Monty found a way to serve the unit. As everyone else was close to panic during the first Scud attack, he put on his mop gear and gas mask and went right back to sleep as if he had merely wakened for a piss call. Someone noticed, and said, "Get a look at Shithead." There he lay on his cot, snoring peacefully away. It seemed to have a calming effect on the rest of the troops and soon most everyone would don their chemical gear when the attacks came and do "the Monty," as his relaxation technique came to be known.

One week after dragging all our gear over to the barracks, the ship carrying our vehicles arrived in port. After an inventory and some work got done to repair damages received in the crossing, we hopped into our assigned wheels and pulled out of Dhahran, heading northwest for King Khalid Military Compound. The convoy to KKMC took seventeen hours, with only one stop at a refueling depot where there was a tent set up for soldiers to get food, coffee, and water. The food was either MREs or a choice of canned Beef-a-Roni or Ravioli they had bobbing around in large pots of hot water. After living on MREs, the new rations were welcome. I had no idea that canned ravioli could have such flavor and went back through the line again and again until my pockets bulged with the hot little tins of culinary delight.

Fed and filled, we boarded our trucks and continued on the last leg of our motor march. At 0500, three hours before dawn, we entered through the main gates of King Khalid Military Compound. It was January 20, 1991, my son John's twenty-first birthday. No doubt, everyone would raise a toast to him at R.T. Quinlan's. Not me. I would have to send my best wishes from a dry country, a world away.

The MPs led us to our new home, a large field in the middle of nowhere. It was about six square city blocks in size, bordered on each side by a paved road marked on one end by a fire hall and on the other by a huge water tower.

During the night, the weather was miserable. It was so cold that when it started to rain, I muttered, "Geez, it just might snow." We slept in our vehicles that first night as best we could until the sun rose.

The next week was a blur of sixteen-to eighteen-hour days with a staggering amount of work to do. My cooks, Monty and Adam, went to the wall for me. They worked with barely enough sleep to keep their legs moving and offered few complaints throughout the process of setting up our compound.

Everyone was under constant pressure. A lieutenant was sent on loan to us from another unit to beef up the inadequate number of officers. Lieutenant Angelo Monetti assumed a figurehead assignment as supervisor of the mess office but he performed his actual duties elsewhere; the mess continued to be operated and managed by me and Sergeant Nelson.

At first, the cooking was done outside under the front flap of our big tent in every type of weather imaginable. We were issued a sixty-foot refrigerator truck, called a reefer, and given an authorized account at the host nation warehouse (HNW) where we were issued fresh food, called A-rations. Our days started at 0400h. Using the same method we had at Fort McCoy, the shifts changed hands after the breakfast cleanup. The off-shift had the responsibility of hauling garbage to the dump after breakfast and then cleaning out the mess unit's five-ton truck. On the truck doors, we had painted an emblem of a skull with crossed spoons above lettering that read:

477th AMB. CO. MESS
-Death from Within-

Lieutenant Monetti, walking past the truck, paused and growled, "Jesus Christ, Hampston, it's supposed to be a mess truck, not a pirate ship!"

Three times a week, after the truck was cleaned, we picked up rations. Nelson and I along with Adam and Monty (if I could find him), would drive to the host nation warehouse and submit my ration request. I became friendly with the chief warrant officer who ran the warehouse. We'd sit in his office drinking coffee and playing cribbage or talking golf while Nelson and the boys loaded our order. Nelson was as light-fingered as seemed prudent and when necessary, was able to produce a look of innocent surprise when he discovered that a half dozen or so cases of steaks had accidentally fallen out of the sky into the back of our truck.

Our unit ate better than any other in the field of operations, largely due to the piracy of our larcenous Sergeant Nelson. While other units ate dehydrated potatoes and scrambled eggs burned in an aluminum square-head cover, called an army pot, we dined on eggs to order, "everything" omelets, and blueberry pancakes prepared on a cast iron grill top that I'd bought from a defunct restaurant in Duluth. It had handles welded to each side to fit the grill base. I also had a support rack of angle iron built that would accommodate M2 burner units, one to heat the grill and the other to cook SOS (shit-on-a-shingle, the army classic), coffee, or whatever we might desire.

Our breakfasts became legendary, and once again the 477th mess earned a reputation as the mess every officer in the area chose to get a good start on the day. A typical menu would be SOS, a choice of ham, bacon, eggs to order, or a loaded omelet jammed with everything imaginable except cheese which was, even for an accomplished thief, almost impossible to find. Other items on our breakfast menu were fresh American fries made from potatoes Nelson had dug up from somewhere, toast grilled to a handsome brown, fresh fruit, orange juice, and all this accompanied by gallons and gallons of hot coffee.

My head count numbers shot up to 225 soldiers and officers. With the extra appetites to feed, we were pushed almost beyond our abilities and supplies. I found it necessary to have our CO step in and limit the number of officers to only those from our battalion headquarters located five hundred yards up the hill from us. With that limit established and with a couple of extra KPs, we were once again back to a more manageable work load.

Now that we had more help, all of us cooks were required to help fortify our compound by filling sandbags and stacking them five feet high around our entire enclave, which meant that any time we weren't physically engaged with our mess duties, we worked on the "Great Wall" as we called it. Mind you, we knew that this structure would not stop an attacking force. In the first place, if it did happen that the enemy got through the infantry and marines on the front lines, the war was lost. Although we were prepared to fight, if necessary, you couldn't really expect a bunch of medics and cooks to win a battle that the foot soldiers couldn't win. But our wall looked good anyway, and one thing it did accomplish was that it got us all into great shape. Everyone who was overweight dropped pounds and those who were too thin gained muscle mass. At night we listened to the war's progress on Armed Forces Radio. We read or wrote letters. That first month we didn't have to concern ourselves with boredom. Work consumed almost every waking moment.

Eventually, the rains stopped and the weather warmed— and how it warmed! The Saudi sun can cook a soldier's brain in short order. Staying hydrated was the most important thing, especially for cooks working inside the mess tent with M2 burner units operating at full capacity.

Monty had been deep-frying chicken, working behind the chow line on a day that the thermostat read well over 100°F. I came into the mess tent through the back door and looked around. "Goddamn it, Shithead's disappeared again!" I couldn't turn my back on that kid for a second without his taking it on the lam. I stormed out the front of the tent and scanned the area. No Monty!

"SHITHEAD!" I hollered. "If I have to come looking for you there's going to be trouble!"

I figured he was dogging off in one of the medic's tents. I turned in disgust and went back to attend to the chicken he had left bubbling away. To my complete surprise, there was Monty, lying spread-eagled behind the line, passed out from the heat.

I called in the medics who revived our down-for-the-count soldier. We got water into him and put him in our reefer truck to bring his body temperature back down. He fully revived after his ordeal but we learned a valuable lesson. Stay hydrated and the hotter it gets, the more water you need to drink.

The ground war started in early spring. I was at the airport picking up a truckload of water when the ground began to shake, followed by a deafening roar. Someone pointed to the sky and a flight of a hundred or so Cobra and Blackhawk helicopters flew over our heads, blackening the sky.

"Holy crap!" I said to Adam. "How'd you like to have those guys coming at ya?"

"Yeah, they're in a world of shit, all right."

The horde of choppers routed out starving, weary Iraqis who had been hiding in rabbit hole bunkers. They'd been lying low for months during the taking of Kuwait, while receiving very little food or aid from Saddam. Now, they came scurrying out to join the throng of terrified people fleeing Kuwait City, heading back to Baghdad.

Three of our guys were driving an ambulance back to camp when the vehicle got stuck in the sand. Their mad efforts to scoop away the shifty sands were going nowhere and they were in a precarious position. One of the medics looked up and saw five Iraqi soldiers come over the rise of a dune.

"This is it, guys. We're gonna have to fight our way out of this hole."

But the enemy guys came running, waving, and yelling. They helped free the ambulance, piled in, and made it known they wanted a ride to our camp so they could surrender.

Soon the Iraqis were surrendering to anyone they could, not only to our medics in Kuwait, but even to foreign correspondents and their camera crews. They probably would have thrown their hands up in the air at the sight of my cooks armed with large serving spoons.

As our tanks chased Saddam Hussein's army back toward Baghdad, the level of readiness decreased and the decision was made that we could now (probably a make-work project to keep us busy) take down the Great Wall we had labored so hard to erect.

SFC Tony Hoff was sent to Riyadh, the capital, to shop for some creature comforts. Armed with a big stack of Uncle Sam's dough and a wish list from every department head, mine included, he set off on his spending spree. Three five-ton trucks rolled out of KKMC, headed for Riyadh. They returned three days later, loaded to the top with goodies that would make our lives more livable.

The whole company, including the truck drivers and medics that had been assigned to us, pitched in and went to work transforming our bivouac area into a tent city, complete with outhouses and an enclosed laundry that boasted a wringer washer and a clothesline area outside. The most amazing new installation was a six-stool john that Tony Hoff designed and constructed—an outhouse on a hill. To create urinals for the guys, six large plastic funnels were tightly fastened to the wall inside our outhouse. Their small ends were connected to six plastic hoses that ran to the outside. Gravity delivered urine down the hill and emptied it into a leaching field of rock and gravel.

The women of the 477th designed their own outbuilding to deal with Mother Nature's whispers. I never saw the inside of this facility but our female contingent bragged it was the finest in all of Saudi Arabia.

For the more solid results produced in these two buildings, fifty-five gallon barrels were cut in half and handles were welded onto the sides. In the back of each building, in cubbies just below the toilets above, there were spaces behind doors that housed the half barrels. Each day, they were removed, carried down the hill, and burned with fuel oil until everything that had been in them vaporized. Each platoon was required to take its turn with this not-so-desirable task, with the exception of the mess section because of the sanitary aspects required in cooking. But there is an exception to every rule.

One morning, just as we secured the chow line, I looked for Monty and Adam to attend morning formation. Adam was hard at work carrying pots and pans out to the wash line.

"Come on, kid, get your battle rattle on (helmet, gas mask, web gear and rifle). It's time for formation. Where's Shithead?"

Strapping on his web gear, he shot me a grin. "I didn't know I was supposed to be watching him."

"Don't start with me, Adam. Where is he?"

"He was working on the grill when the chow line closed. That's the last time I saw him."

Ten minutes later, the rest of the mess section stood in formation along with the other two hundred members of the 477th Medical Ambulance Company. The captain stood in front of the company with two platoons facing him and one platoon on each end, forming a three-sided box to make it easier to be heard. Captain Sturvich was reading our company the riot act about going around the compound out of uniform; in other words, with an unstrapped helmet and without a gas mask and rifle.

"You people are getting too damn slack and I'm going to tighten your asses up starting NOW! The next person I see out of uniform will be burning shit for the next week!"

Just as those words came flying out of his mouth, in my peripheral vision, I caught sight of Monty approaching. He lumbered right past the commander wearing, not a helmet, but a doo-rag on his head, a Guns N' Roses T-shirt with the sleeves cut off, civilian high-top tennis shoes, and mirrored sunglasses. A cigarette dangled from the corner of his mouth. No web gear, no gas mask, no rifle. It would have been impossible for the casual observer to determine that he was in the army at all.

As he sauntered by Captain Sturvich, he slightly lifted his sunglasses, looked at the commander, said, "Hi, Boss. How's it goin'?" and went on his merry way, puffing on his Marlboro and heading toward the motor pool.

Nobody said a word. Dead silence. And then Captain Sturvich shouted, "SERGEANT HAMPSTON!"

"Yes, sir," I answered weakly, looking just to the right of his beet red face.

"Immediately after this formation, you and Specialist Lyons report to my tent!"

"Yes, sir, Captain."

He gave the order to dismiss the company and I went looking for Shithead.

Cook or not, Monty burned shit for a week. It was like throwing Br'er Rabbit into the briar patch. Monty was never happier in his life. The job was easier than short division—pour on fuel oil, light match, add more fuel every now and then, and sit down on an old bus bench to read smuggled girlie magazines and smoke cigarettes.

Adam and I were left one man short on our shift. While Br'er Rabbit smoked and joked in his briar patch, we shouldered a work load heavier by one third.

I asked the commander, "The next time Specialist Lyons screws up, instead of burning shit, can I just shoot him?"

The captain said he'd consider it.

Blast Furnace

We were outgrowing our tiny World War II mess tent. I went through the chain of command and requested a GP Medium, twenty-four person, garrison tent to accommodate the additional troops our section had inherited—a company of bus drivers brought in to transport casualties once the ground war started. My request was denied.

Headquarters deemed the mess tent, issued to the 477th in 1954, to be perfectly sound and adequate. Barring some unforeseen damage that might occur to said tent, I would not be requisitioned a bigger better one.

The following week, while biscuits were baking in the mess, the M2 burner oven, which had been inadvertently placed too close to the back wall of our decrepit canvas kitchen, started a fire that wasn't noticed until the sad old WWII tent was almost destroyed. Thank God, I was able to save my personal belongings only because I had taken them out for cleaning and reorganizing that morning.

The next day, thanks to Lieutenant Jeff Hall, I took possession of not one, but two brand new GP Mediums, one to serve as the mess facility and the other for supply and bottled water and my personal living quarters. A light bulb snapped on in my head as I remembered what a little home decorating had done for my apartment on Park Point in Duluth!

With the help of Tony Hoff who provided two-by-fours and plywood, I had wooden floors installed in my new digs. The walls were seven-foot-high stacked boxes of water jugs that I decorated with a cheap roll of wallpaper held up with thumbtacks. Next I used plywood and two-by-fours to construct a coffee table, end tables, and a nightstand, all of which I painted a cheerful yellow. It was no problem to commandeer benches from the back of a couple of school buses that had been stripped to serve as ambulances. They were my new couches.

I stored my clothing in an army fifty-gallon ice chest that had been punctured during the trip across the Atlantic and was useless for storing food. This kept my duds dust free...very important in the desert. For the final touches, I made a trip into Hafr Al-Batin, a small town twenty miles north of KKMC, and bought two lamps for my end tables and a couple of throw rugs. The lamps were powered by a generator thirty feet from my tent and were hooked up by the 477th mechanics. Mosquito netting that I'd purchased back at Fort McCoy hung over my bunk. It proved to be a lifesaver. The flies were murder and anyone without netting suffered terribly.

Lieutenant Monetti came into my tent one afternoon while I sat on my couch doing mess paperwork that I had spread out on my coffee table. He looked slowly around, not saying anything at first. Finally, he cleared his throat and inquired, "Hampston, why is it that everyone else lives in a crowded tent out of their duffle bags and you live in a fucking apartment?"

I explained that I had signed for two GP Mediums. One was my mess tent and this one stored our bottled water and dry goods and also served as my living quarters. I pulled out a few thumbtacks and peeled back the wallpaper to show him the cases of bottled water. I pointed out that I deemed it advisable to live with the supplies to prevent any pilfering. And I further explained that my furniture was made from scraps that were left over from tent flooring that every other tent had.

The benches had been discarded when the buses were modified.

"How about these lamps and rugs?" he demanded, a dark scowl creeping over his face.

"Personal property bought off the local economy, sir."

"Well," he snarled, "it's legal, I guess, but I don't like it."

There wasn't a goddamn thing he could do. Not one of my things was contraband and he couldn't take my personal belongings away without confiscating everyone else's ghetto blasters, guitars, and homemade book shelves.

As he stomped out, he turned and pointed a finger at me. "I've got my eyes on you, Hampston. Slip up once and your ass is grass."

I wasn't very worried. I knew I had him over a barrel. We had the best mess in the war theater and made the commander look good. He sure as hell wasn't going to screw with that. In total disregard for the lieutenant's feelings, I continued to make improvements to my living quarters by adding all the creature comforts I could devise. And my co-cook Nelson and I continued taking turns having a nice tray of breakfast-in-bed delivered to each other on our days off.

Sherrie Mitchell, one of the cooks on Nelson's shift, asked permission to use our mess vehicle to travel to the other end of KKMC to visit the optical technician bivouacked there. She needed to replace her broken glasses. I gave her the keys and told her, "This isn't carte blanche to go joy riding all over the desert."

She grinned. "Thanks, Dad. I'll be home early."

A couple of hours later, I was stooped over my desk making out ration requests for the HNW when I heard someone open the tent flap. Turning, I could see a soldier standing in full battle gear. His back to the sun shining in the doorway made it difficult to make out his face. Then he spoke.

"What's a soldier hafta do to get a drink in this joint?" It was Neal Brunmeier!

"Jesus Christ, what the hell are you doing here?"

I threw my arms around him and we thumped each other's backs, laughing the laugh of old friends.

"I'm running the optical lab on the other side of the post. One of your cooks came in for glasses. I was doing the paperwork and asked her, 'What's your unit designation?' She said, '477th Medical Ambulance Company,' and here I am!"

He dug into his cargo pockets and took out a dozen little airline bottles of Canadian Windsor whiskey. "Can you find some Coke?"

I found the mix and ice in my reefer truck and we drank heartily into the night. This wasn't legal by Saudi law, but we enjoyed remembering old stories and telling the new ones we'd collected since our transport. Neal's unit had been in-country since September, shortly after the invasion of Kuwait, and they were scheduled to rotate back to the States the first of April, only a few weeks off. Though we saw each other just a couple more times before he left, each visit brought a wonderful taste of home, family, and friends.

With the ground war over and the weather heating up, someone was bound to come up with the next great idea. "Let's use the leftover sandbags from the Great Wall to build a swimming pool!" We'd found a huge ruptured water bladder on the side of the road. When filled, these bladders required an entire semi-tractor trailer to transport the load. Sand bags were stacked up four-deep and twelve-high to form the pool frame. The water bladder was then cut and shaped to fit the pool and a drain was built into the bottom that brought the emptied water downhill to a rock leaching field. Next we acquired a Saudi tanker truck that we could fill at the water tower.

Draining the pool every other day and refilling it with the

tanker kept things clean and the chlorine we added kept it sanitary. The water came out of the tanker at about seventy-five degrees which felt grand compared to the air temperature of 115 degrees. It really did seem a little like Park Point with cute little bikini-clad medics splashing around in the water right next to my apartment. Another six months in the desert and I'm sure the collective ingenuity of the 477th would have found a way to reopen a Plasma Pete's speakeasy.

Eid, the three-day Muslim holiday following Ramadan, is a holy celebration. During this sacred time, Saudi nationals, almost all of whom embrace the Islamic faith, fast and pray in accordance with directives laid out in the Koran. The allied command decided, in keeping with the host nation's wishes, that all allied Jewish soldiers, sailors, and airmen would be sent to Bahrain for a little timeout from their bases. They were to spend the holiday week housed on a cruise ship that was leased from the Princess Cruise line.

I had another run-in with Lieutenant Monetti about a meal I had served that provided no hot food. The menu included cold cut sandwiches, cold beans, potato salad, fruit, and ice cream.

"God damn it, Hampston, my soldiers get hot meals! Is that clear?"

I argued with the lieutenant that it was 121 degrees and the troops loved the cold meal I had provided. It also gave a necessary break for my cooks who had to work inside the mess tent cooking those hot meals that he wanted us to serve three times a day regardless of the weather.

"Furthermore," I informed him, "the menu selection is the mess sergeant's responsibility to determine and not the mess officer's."

A shouting match quickly developed. Given that sergeants

don't normally win arguments with company officers, you can imagine that this whole situation didn't go well for me. The only reason I didn't have to stand in front of a summary court martial was that our XO, Dennis Hughes, explained to Captain Sturvich that if he court-martialed his mess sergeant (irreplaceable, according to the company), the commander could end up with a mutiny on his hands.

"I think Sergeant Hampston is just overworked. Why don't we send him to the cruise ship in Bahrain with Sergeant Jerry Goldberg for the duration of Eid?"

They gave Nelson and Adam a couple more KPs to help out in my absence, and the next day Goldberg and I boarded a C-130 transport plane for our three-day R & R on the Canard Princess. I felt a little déjà vu walking up the gangway and found myself wanting to salute the ensign and OD to request permission to come aboard. We were assigned private cabins and after a shower and a change into civilian clothes, we made a beeline for the bar.

I was the only Irish Catholic among nine hundred Jews. Jerry said, "No problem. When you raise a glass of beer with someone, just say, 'L'chai-im!' and you'll be fine."

Of the nine hundred troops on board, only about a hundred were female. They mostly got scooped up by the pilots and other assorted officers so Jerry and I just said, "To hell with it. We'll get drunk for three days."

And that's just what we did. We ate gourmet meals, drank our fill, and soon I began to feel a little less like an overwhelmed mess sergeant and more like a damned lucky civilian.

Three days later I walked back into the mess tent, rested and ready to get back to work. While I was gone, Adam and Nelson had got blasted on some of Monty's homemade wine that he kept hidden in plain sight. The stuff was stored in water jugs that had been marked and stashed behind the mess tent among the twenty or thirty other water jugs stored there.

Nelson augmented Monty's fermented Welch's grape juice with a bottle of French wine he bartered for with a couple of French soldiers he'd met. Not having had anything to drink since Fort McCoy, the boys got totally wrecked. Nelson was still sick when I got back. I gave him the day off to recuperate in his bunk and he was cured by the next day.

The old wringer washer that Tony Hoff had bought for twenty bucks in Riyadh was a godsend. Our mechanics got power to it and used the same funnel and hose technique to drain it down into the leaching field behind the latrine. No more did we have to scrub our clothes in a bucket of water and wring them out by hand. Clotheslines were placed next to the washer and we used little pieces of rope called clothes stops, like those I used when I was in Navy boot camp, to fasten our duds to the line.

I was working in the mess tent one afternoon getting the evening meal started when Lieutenant Monetti stormed in, crimson-faced, holding up a couple of pink T-shirts in one hand and a bunch of matching socks in the other.

"What the fuck is this?" he bellowed.

A huge smile broke out on my face. "Gee, I don't know, lieutenant, but I think you'd better be careful the skipper doesn't find out."

He didn't think that was at all funny and threw them at me.

"I want to know who's responsible for this!" he screamed.

As it turned out, he had taken two water bottles from the back of the mess tent and poured them on top of a load of clothes, not realizing he had grabbed two of Monty's wine jugs for his rinse cycle. I don't know to this day how any knucklehead in the world could not notice that he had just poured not one, but two jugs of red wine over his white clothing. But somehow this character managed to do just that.

For another week, Br'er Rabbit went back to his briar patch and burned shit. I think he had figured out that if he screwed up just enough he could get through the entire deployment doing the job it seemed he was born for.

43

Home Again

The ground war was over. By March 17, military command started moving companies out on a first in, first out basis.

When our turn came, we got busy dismantling our company compound. The last week of KKMC was a rude awakening for the soldiers of the 477th. Our creature comforts began to disappear at an alarming rate. The floors and shelving from all the tents, even my coffee and end tables, were burned and went up in smoke. My mess gear was loaded into our five-ton truck and we left KKMC in convoy, headed southeast back to Dhahran.

For a week, we lived in the same building we had stayed in after first arriving in Saudi Arabia. During that time we cleaned gear and brought our vehicles to the wash racks to scrub and power-wash every grain of Saudi sand from every ambulance and truck we owned. It was a huge job. The whole 477th worked from daylight to dark for six days before we passed inspection. Only then were our vehicles permitted to be loaded onto a cargo ship bound for New York. On arrival in the States, they would get shipped by rail back to Duluth, a trip that would take over two months.

We departed Dhahran as we had arrived five months earlier, transported to the airport in school buses. At the airport, we waited on the tarmac in 120 degree heat for four hours before boarding a 747 along with another company of men and women that was bound for Detroit. The plane made a stop in Germany for refueling and another in Bangor, Maine.

Twenty-three hours after flying out of Dhahran, we landed at Volk Field in Wisconsin. Vietnam vets were deplaned first—Dennis Hughes, Gary Lindgren, Rick Moss, and me.

I marveled at how green Wisconsin was. The trees and grass exploded with color so intense it was blinding. As we marched single file from the aircraft, a Duluth soldier from the 367th Combat Engineers, Mike Anderson, waited for us to pass by while handing out airline bottles of brandy and vodka to his hometown buddies.

We stayed for three endless days at Fort McCoy while we out-processed. Out-processing stations were set up in familiar surroundings, the same old World War II hospital we used during the two weeks of the Cuban relocation. But being there now, returned from active duty overseas, the goofy days of Plasma Pete's seemed to have happened in another lifetime.

On Memorial Day, May 26, 1991, we boarded two chartered Greyhound buses heading north and struck out for Duluth, Minnesota. As we passed Rice Lake, Wisconsin, there was a gigantic sign hanging from a freeway overpass.

 WELCOME HOME 477th !!!

Soon we began to see people standing along the highway, holding similar signs and flags. The closer we got to home, the more people there were waving hearty welcomes.

We had a rest stop in Trego, a small town sixty-five miles out of Superior. We picked up fast food and were getting ready to re-board the buses when we were met by 477th soldiers who had been left behind to man the Army Reserve headquarters in Duluth. They alerted us to the fact that thousands of people were lining the route through Superior and Duluth to welcome us back.

Some of us hopped into the backs of two pick-up trucks equipped with large American flags flying from twelve-foot poles. The trucks were also loaded with individual-sized flags that were passed out to every soldier in our convoy. Meanwhile, the hatch on top of the bus was popped open and soldiers scrambled up to the roof. I couldn't imagine that Greyhound's fleet insurance would have approved of this method of transporting its passengers. But unquestionably, this was a very unusual event—maybe the bus drivers decided it was worth the risk. Anyway, off we went—at a substantially reduced rate of speed.

Now every overpass was loaded with enthusiastic citizens waving flags and shouting, "Welcome home! Thank you! We love you, 477th!"

By the time we reached the Superior, Wisconsin, city limits, we began to realize just how big this thing was. Thousands and thousands of people were cheering. A brass band waited for us at the Superior Courthouse. We dismounted the trucks and buses and listened to the governor of Wisconsin and the mayor of Superior give speeches, telling us how they appreciated our going off to war for our country and what fine young Americans we all were. It was great to be appreciated, but most of us just wanted the pomp and circumstance to be over so we could find ourselves a cold beer.

Re-boarding our vehicles, we finished our trek through Superior and across the Bong Bridge that straddles St. Louis Bay and into West Duluth. Once again, many thousands of people greeted us. We rolled very slowly down Grand Avenue, passing just two blocks from my mom's house, the house where I grew up and where, so long ago, I said goodbye and headed off to the military instead of jail.

As we came into Duluth's downtown City Center, I spotted my mother and some neighbors. I handed my flag to the man next to me and jumped from the back of the moving truck. Nearly losing my feet in a reckless leap, I ran to my mother, threw my arms around her and gave her a mighty kiss.

"I love you, Mom! I'm so happy to be home, but I've gotta go. I'll see you later!"

I turned and ran for my truck, now half a block ahead of me. I was totally winded when I overtook it. A couple of guys reached out and dragged me back into the pick-up. Someone restored my flag to my hand and we continued on our parade route.

I heard later that, from Rice Lake to Superior and Duluth, over 200,000 people from all parts of the region turned out to welcome home the 477th.

At Bayfront Park, we all climbed up on a stage and stood at parade rest in front of an ocean of smiling, cheering supporters. After speeches by the governor of Minnesota, the mayor of Duluth, and a couple of Army generals, we were called to attention. Captain Sturvich dismissed us.

Robby and a couple of our friends found me as I descended from the stage and after finding my gear, we made the six-block walk back to R.T. Quinlan's where my son John was waiting and keeping up with yet another celebration in full swing. The place was jammed with grinning faces. My sons at each elbow and my mother now seated at a table, I was just about as happy as a man can be.

Monty and Adam came in shortly after me and received warm welcomes, too. Full of excitement, Adam's mom, grand-parents, and aunt Sally were waiting impatiently for their soldier. Adam introduced us and for the first time, I met his mother, Sharon Rose. She was an absolute knockout. I told Adam's entire family what a great kid they had and how he had been a big help to me during our deployment. His mother stayed in my mind as I moved on to mingle with others at the reception, thinking to myself, *Sharon Rose. Too bad she's married.*

All my pals were crowded into the bar and it seems every female I had ever been associated with in the previous ten years had turned out, willing to prove her affection by offering up whatever chastity she had left. I was greeted as a conquering hero and I thought of my just rewards...but Robby offered a wiser course, advising me that to pluck one luscious plum off the tree on this very special day might limit my choices in the future. Maybe I should just get loaded and go home with him? I could get back to my bevy of beauties one at a time at some later date. I took his advice. I got totally hammered and went home with Robby.

Book
VI

Vrooom!

I went back to work after a week's vacation during which I bought an 1100-CC Yamaha Virago. You might think that a forty-seven-year-old bartender who drinks more than he should is a fool for putting himself in harm's way riding a crotch rocket capable of speeds up to 140 mph. You would be right. But throughout my life I had never been one to choose the smooth road. Even though buying that scooter wasn't smart, I had one hell of a time riding my new bike that summer after the Gulf War. For a guy like me, motorcycles were good for only two things—attracting women and going from one bar to another. I did far too much of both.

One night, while riding my bike home, a considerable amount of Budweiser sloshing behind my belt, I turned into our parking lot on Park Point and discovered that, in my absence, the wind had picked up half the beach and deposited it smack dab into the middle of our driveway. My front wheel hit the knee-high sand and I went over the handlebars, landing flat on my back and accidentally kicking the gear shift lever into neutral.

The bike lay on its side idling away like a calico cat purring on a window sill. Well, if the bike could take a nap, so could I. After a short period of reflection, I shook off that temptation, lifted myself up from the ground and staggered over to my bike's side where I placed one hand on each handlebar.

The 1100 Virago was a really heavy bike, and was now heavier covered with sand, but I lifted it. In doing so, my hand twisted the throttle, producing a tremendous growl from the machine. I gave it a dozen more tries. Each try produced the same result—the beast roared—and equally pissed, I swore back. After my last effort, I sat down in the sand and lit a cigarette, listening to the "put, put, put" of my Virago in the dark. I wondered just what in the hell I was going to do.

In answer, the outside house light went on. The door opened. Robby stepped out.

I looked up at him from my sitting position. "Hi, Son."

"Goddamn it, Pop. How many times do I have to tell you not to ride that motorcycle drunk? You're going to get yourself killed some day. Now get your old drunk ass into the house. I'll put your bike in the garage."

He lifted my bike with ease and guided it through the sand to the garage while I swerved my way into the house and to my room before I got a further butt-chewing from my son.

I never did get loaded and ride after that incident. I limited my alcohol intake to just two beers before swinging my leg over the saddle of that scooter. I'd made it back from Saudi Arabia alive—there was a lot of living I wanted to do.

I got rid of the Virago after a woman, who will be grateful for remaining anonymous, ran it through the back wall of my garage.

45

Bar Maniacs

Every bar in every town in the world has patrons that we in the business refer to as "bartenders' nightmares." They include regular customers who can be so annoying that when they come through the swinging doors they are sure to raise an, "Oh, God, no!" out of the long-suffering barkeep. One of these characters was Richard T. Urbanski, a retired civil servant who had served valiantly in the US Army during World War II. He was a sergeant in the 101st Airborne who parachuted into France the night before D-Day.

He had a regular routine. He would scream out in a high-pitched screech, "I'm Richard T. Urbanski, a screaming eagle from the 101st Airborne and I'm the toughest man in this bar, but I'm not as tough as Margaret Mary. That's my wife, Maggie! She's tough. She kicks the hell out of poor old Richard all the time."

When Richard was drunk he always referred to himself in the third person. "Richard wants another brandy charge," or "Richard wants a beer!" and the command we all loved to hear, "Call Richard a cab!"

When Richard left in his taxi, the bartender would blow a long sigh of relief, get on the phone, and call the next bar on Richard's trap line. The bartender on the other end of the wire would hear those riveting words, "Urbanski alert! Headed your way in a yellow cab!"

Some bartenders would lock the door and shut off the lights to try to fool him into thinking the joint was closed. Mostly we just put up with him until we couldn't anymore. When he started crashing into people and spilling drinks, bartenders cut him off and dialed for a cab. Why we served him, I don't know. I suppose it was because he was pretty comical and deep down he was a very nice guy.

Once when Al Nisius cut him off at the Paul Bunyan, Richard demanded another cocktail. When he got nowhere with Al, Richard began to beg, "Bartender, please give me a brandy charge."

"No. No more brandy. You're cut off. GO HOME!"

"Well, give Richard a beer then," insisted Dick.

"No," answered Al.

"Well, then, how about a cup of coffee?" Dick pleaded.

"No, dammit. Dick, you're all done. Now get the hell out of here. Go home."

Richard narrowed his eyes, set his jaw and commanded, "Well, then give Richard a new bartender!"

To his credit, when Richard drove downtown and got loaded, he would never drive his car. Once he ran out of bartenders who would serve him, he'd take a cab home. But if he got started early enough in the day he would often taxi home for a nap and then take either his wife's or daughter's car and return downtown. The next day's problem would be how to get two vehicles back home.

One pleasant June day—a good day to sit in a bar with the doors open—Richard entered the Bunyan with a look that signaled he had played by Margaret Mary's rules for too long and, "I'm going to give 'er hell today."

"Bartender!" he shrieked. Not getting any response, he tried again, only louder. "Bartender, give me a drink and step on it! I have to be to work in September."

By 10:00 that morning, Richard had been cut off and was headed home via the Yellow Cab Company. Rejuvenated by an hour-long nap, he reappeared, this time at Norman's Bar with his thirst as severe as it had been in the morning. Once again, an hour and a half later, Richard was making the trip back to Vernon Street in a taxi, leaving the second family vehicle behind. Refreshed by a short power nap, he drove his daughter's car downtown and for the third time that day, the bartender's nightmare appeared in yet another doorway, this time Mr. Pete's, just in time for happy hour.

He was smart enough to know that if he ordered a drink in any of the bars he'd already been thrown out of that day, he would go dry. Before long, the accumulation of the day's brandy imbibing got the better of him and his head hit the bar with a thud.

Cut off again, Richard T. made his third and final cab ride home about 6:00 in the evening. But he wasn't about to have the bartenders and cab drivers of Duluth get the better of him. Oh, no! After another little siesta, Richard was back in the driver's seat, heading down Grand Avenue for the fourth time that day. He got as far as 21st Avenue West before the police forced him over to the side of the road. Richard T. Urbanski was driving his John Deere riding lawn mower.

Richard went to jail, the John Deere went to the impound lot, and the cars belonging to himself, his wife and his daughter gathered tickets all over downtown Duluth.

One of our new regulars was Ed, also known as "Boobie." He called everyone else Boobie because he could never remember anyone's name. I am sure that, given a royal audience, he would address even Queen Elizabeth as "Boobie." Ed first came to Duluth in 1960. He was with the Air Force and was stationed at the Duluth Air Force Base. After a three-year tour, he had developed an attachment to our city and opted not to return to his native Philadelphia. Boobie landed a job in sales with KDAL, the local CBS affiliate, where he discovered that he was a natural born salesman.

Ed had also developed an attachment during these early days at KDAL to alcohol. Driven by an unquenchable thirst, Eddie, or "Fast Eddie" as he liked to call himself, had mastered the art of the three-martini lunch that seldom ended with three. Sometimes he could suck down six or seven before returning to work. Still, he did quite well and sales for the radio station skyrocketed.

This went on until the policy changed and management stopped looking the other way while alcohol abusers got loaded on company time. After a few warnings that he totally disregarded, KDAL and Ed, alias "Boobie," parted company

Eddie met and married a pretty girl named Rita and together they went into the life insurance business. They prospered for some years. But Ed's drinking habit continued and a total of three trips through rehab didn't seem to affect his drinking in the least. Over fifteen years, Ed and Rita divorced and remarried three times. Some thought it unusual that a couple would even consider the marriage hat-trick with the same partner but, as I said, Bobbie really was one hell of a salesman.

As the years marched along, Boobie provided us all with more entertainment than a troop of circus clowns. He was obsessed with women, especially large-sized women, but he was usually not able to keep a woman of any dimensions on the line for more than a month.

Patsy comes to mind. She had a figure like a keg of beer, but along with this barrel-shaped body came a very pretty face. Like Eddie, she loved the sauce. Unlike Ed's easy going alcoholic demeanor, she had a flair for drama. After a whirlwind romance and a messy break-up, Patsy filed a restraining order against him. Eddie was heartbroken but not beaten.

A week after the restraining order was filed, Boobie was arrested for climbing a large Norway pine tree next to Patsy's house, hoping to catch a glimpse of her. His friends at the bar were reminded of the Frank Sinatra tune, "My Way." When Eddie was let out of jail and reappeared in R.T. Quinlan's doorway, a dozen guys joined in singing, "I did it NOR-WAY!"

It wasn't just women that got him into trouble. He took another trip to the clink in the wee hours of the morning when police picked him up at an all-night convenience store, dead drunk. He had cleared off a shelf that held toilet paper rolls, stretched out and gone to sleep. When the cashier informed him that this was unacceptable behavior, he retorted, "Well, if they didn't want people to sleep on these shelves, why did they make them so long?"

Karaoke was made with our Ed in mind. Any bar in town with one of the music machines could expect to see Boobie glide through the door dressed in one of his pastel sport jackets, the sides of his hair—all he had to work with—slicked back and a carefully chosen handkerchief or boutonniere brightening his ensemble. Every fourth song found Eddie on stage crooning out his initially pleasing and later painful renditions of forties and fifties standards.

My business partner Ray always invited Boobie to Thanksgiving dinner, an addition to a guest list that included Ray's father, brothers and their wives. On every one of these holidays, Eddie showed up totally plastered and he would either pass out face-first into the mashed potatoes or infuriate Raymond with some other outrageous behavior. One year, while the bird was still roasting, Ed decided to be helpful and took it upon himself to adjust the temperature on the oven. Inadvertently, he turned the thing completely off.

Dinnertime came and Ray opened the oven door, expecting to find a golden, perfectly roasted turkey. He discovered instead a pale half-cooked bird. He went so crazy with anger that the offended guest stormed out, slurring over his shoulder, "There is no need to ever invite me back, for I shall never darken your door again!"

But crusty Ray softened over the course of twelve months, and the next year he did invite Boobie to attend the Thanksgiving feast. Ray also called to invite his father, of course, to join the rest of the family for the traditional meal.

After a short silence, Mr. Ward questioned cautiously, "Is the tall, bald guy who drinks too much going to be there?"

Another infamous regular in the Duluth bars was a musician, Bunny Waterhouse. Bunny was a product of Chetek, Wisconsin, and had migrated to Duluth to attend the University of Minnesota—Duluth. While attending classes, he made a living playing bass guitar and singing with a band called Green Apple Quickstep. After seven years of college that weren't really successful enough to justify continuing, he dropped out of school.

Bunny said many times, "I'm only one hit away from becoming a star." He sincerely believed that he would one day make a hit record that would bring him the fame that he thought he deserved. He truly was a gifted guitarist and singer, but as was the case with many rock 'n' rollers, life was one big party and fame and fortune remained just beyond his grasp. In later years, he DJ'd the karaoke machine, coaxing vocalists up to the stage in his raspy Wolfman Jack voice and interspersing his own classic renditions.

Bunny always drove a vehicle that was one short step from the scrap yard. When weather permitted, his transport was an old Vespa motor scooter that he had fitted with an extra wide seat covered in sheepskin to accommodate his extra wide ass. As Bunny drove away from our back door on his scooter one summer day, wearing a pair of black and white checked shorts,

Ray Ward drove up behind and parked. As he pulled up to a barstool, Ray commented to the bartender that Bunny looked like a Checkered Cab going down Michigan Street with the doors open.

Although he never became famous on a national level, he did achieve notoriety in and around Duluth. Aside from his musical abilities, Bunny's chief claim to fame was that he would frequently fall off the stage. He must have made the nose-dive fifty times in his career and each time that old "Parachute Waterhouse" bailed off a stage, the news would travel like wildfire through town, the buzz every bit as entertaining to his fans as his music.

On New Year's Eve in 1985, Bunny was playing at the Amber Flow in the West End. At close to 2:00 in the morning, when the rest of the world was trying desperately to get a cab with little or no success, they were disgruntled to learn that Bunny had been clever enough to call up the pizza joint next door to the Amber Flow and pre-arrange a pizza to be delivered around closing time to his home, eight miles away in Lakeside. "Just let me know when the driver's about to leave." He simply got in the car and rode with the delivery guy to his house. He saved cab fare and had a late night supper to boot.

Bunny worked on Friday and Saturday nights and in his entire life he never had a real job but he lived pretty cheaply and drank only tap beer...unless someone offered to buy him a drink. In that case, he would move right up to a Johnny Walker Red. He always said that money didn't really mean much to him but, by God, if he had a chance he would go to the ends of the earth to beat you out of a nickel. He could nurse a glass of beer forever, waiting for happy hour to start. But if someone else was buying, then he kicked into high gear, drinking at breakneck speed.

After a couple of drinks his speech would become slurred, and two drinks after that, no one could understand one damned word he said. One day I was working the dayshift at the Mirror

Lounge when, precisely at 4:00, the beginning of happy hour, Bunny raised his hand and pointed to his beer glass with a crooked smile. I knew he wasn't capable of ordering a drink but I thought it might be fun to make him try.

"Well, "Mattress-Face," what's it gonna be?" I asked. Another character, Tubby McDonald, came up with this name for Bunny because of his long, thick black beard.

He looked at me and blurted out a string of words with lots of *s*'s, *sh*'s and *z*'s, not one word in any way resembling English. Still, Bunny wasn't as drunk as he sounded. His motor skills were quite good. He could walk and even run if necessary. He simply could not talk without sounding like he had a mouth full of marbles.

At the end of the bar, standing near the door to the basement stairway, Bunny spotted Vic Martinson, the lead guitar player from his band. I regarded Vic as the most talented musician I'd ever met and also a very funny fellow who could do spot-on impressions of dozens of Hollywood stars.

Bunny picked up his beer and made his way to where Vic was chatting with a gorgeous blonde girl and proceeded to slur his way into their conversation. She looked at him, then at Vic, and asked, "What did he just say?"

Vic smiled and said, "He thinks you're beautiful."

Bunny nodded his head in agreement. Vic played music with Bunny for so long that he had learned to understand Bunny's gibberish.

With one hand holding his glass of beer and the other outstretched, leaning against the closed basement door, Bunny continued to put the mumbles on this pretty young girl, with Vic translating.

Meanwhile, I asked one of my regulars—a guy who was willing to stock coolers and replenish ice for me in exchange for a beer—to go down and get me a few buckets of ice to prepare for the shift change. He dodged by Vic and the girl and excused himself to Bunny, explaining he had to get past him.

Bunny moved aside, and my "bar dog" opened the door and went down the stairs.

Bunny returned to his attack on the English language while romancing the blonde. I was filling the sinks with fresh hot water at the other end of the bar when I glanced up just in time to see Bunny raise his arm to resume his leaning position on the door that now stood wide open.

I choked out in warning, "Bun!" That's as far as I got when I saw him disappear down the stairway.

It sounded like someone had just rolled a keg of beer down those basement stairs. I was sure that he had been killed and ran to the door where Vic and the blonde stared down in disbelief.

There was Parachute Waterhouse standing on the bottom of the stairs, beer held high, and a big stupid smile on his face. He pointed to his beer as he garbled out, "I dinna shpill a dopp!"

46

Norman's Bar

Norman's Bar became my home away from home. When I needed to get away from problems at R.T. Quinlan's, I would spend time bellied up to the bar at Norman's where drinks were dispensed by three of my favorite bartenders of all time— Steve Hake, John "Mouse" Montera, and Ron Korkki.

Swinging open the door of Norman's I was always sure to be entertained by at least two in this cast of over-the-top characters. It didn't really matter who was walking the bar rail. At least one of the others was sure to be perched on a barstool giving the guy working an oversized load of grief.

Mouse was a sports fanatic and a die-hard Viking fan. He was far more informed about football than most sportscasters. Mondays were great fun, especially after a Viking—Packer game. As much as Mouse loved the Vikings, he hated the Packers with an even greater fervor. He especially hated their quarterback, Brett Favre. With an enthusiasm that bordered on fanaticism, he would charge up and down in front of the bottles, recounting play-by-play, throughout the entire football game. He'd work himself into such a frenzy he would spit as he screamed out his dissatisfaction with either the officiating or the outcome, or sometimes both.

"That goddamn Favre is a prima donna sissy-pants asshole!"

he would shout to anyone who would listen, waving his arms wildly. Good-natured shouting matches would break out between Korkki and Mouse. Ron loved to pull Mouse's chain, although everyone's chain was vulnerable when Ron Korkki was around.

Mouse was short and a little round. Nonetheless, he was admired for his excellent taste in clothes. He spent money at exclusive shops as liberally as the King did on booze. Every time I saw Mouse, he was sporting some new extravagant garb he had purchased. Ron usually came on duty at 5:00 to relieve Mouse for the evening shift. One late Saturday afternoon, noticing Mouse's new pair of pants, Ronnie purred, "Mousey, nice slacks. Did you have a tailor make them for you?"

"No," beamed Mouse, pleased that Korkki had noticed his new threads. "I got them at Allenfalls."

"Unbelievable," laughed Ron. "You can buy a size forty-four, extra short, right off the rack?"

At every opportunity, Ron pushed Mousey's buttons until he broke out into a shouting, spitting, stammering fit, giving the delighted Ron material for the telling and retelling of his latest barb to everyone who walked into the bar.

Norman's Bar, operated at the time by Ray Wizner's son, Gary, had a clientele that began to dwindle over time as the regulars aged. Gary's father's customers were now in their seventies or older, and few young drinkers chose to make Norman's their watering hole. But there was still a pretty good supply of people in my generation who would decorate Gary's barstools on a regular basis.

Wiz got some money from the city when Duluth was involved in a project to revitalize the downtown area. With this cash, he remodeled eight apartments upstairs of the bar. In three of these lived Ron Korkki, Steve Hake with his girlfriend Tiny, and our old friend James Francis Riley who by then had retired from bartending.

On a humid summer afternoon, Steve and Tiny decided to

barbecue out on the upper back porch rather than heat up an already-warm upstairs apartment by using their oven. While Tiny sipped her vodka Diet Coke downstairs in the bar, Steve made a trip across the street to Fichtner's Meat Market where he bought four gigantic generously-stuffed pork chops.

Returning, he carefully folded back the white butcher's paper and showed Tiny what she could look forward to dining on that night.

"Be careful cooking those chops," she advised. "Just brown them, then move them to the cooler side of the Weber, and cook them indirectly for an hour."

Steve did as Tiny instructed, then returned to join her at the bar to enjoy a cocktail or two while the chops slow-cooked upstairs on the residents' community grill.

The hour passed in what seemed to Tiny and Steve like a mere flicker of a butterfly wing. Korkki, who was behind the bar that day, reminded them of their supper upstairs, but by now they were well into their cups and were sure that their repast would be just fine. They raised their empty glasses, gesturing to Korkki that they would have just one more before ascending the stairway to their perfectly browned feast in the upper garret.

Meanwhile, Riley, having just risen from an alcohol-induced nap and suffering from an acute case of the hangover hungries, caught a whiff of roasted pork through his open window. He followed his nose to the unguarded Weber. Lifting the lid of the grill, Riley's eyes must have lit with the delight of a boy discovering that Santa had dumped his whole bag of goodies under the Christmas tree.

He picked off a small piece of meat and popped it into his mouth. "Gosh. These are barely warm. Someone must have forgotten them here and I'd sure hate to see them go totally to waste. I'll just take one." He returned to his apartment to fetch a plate.

After devouring the pork chop with great appreciation, he

considered seconds, reasoning that whoever had left them there must have already eaten the ones that had been cooked in the middle of the grill. Surely these on the side were simply leftovers—left for anyone who might want them. He returned to the crime scene with his fork, knife and plate. Twice.

On finishing the third chop, Riley was almost, but not quite, full. Back at the grill, he looked down at the last lonely chop and he muttered, "Oh hell, even if someone does come back for them, one won't do them much good. I might as well polish off this one, too." He stabbed the chop, dropped it on his plate and returned to his apartment.

Meanwhile, Steve and Tiny were just polishing off their seventh "one more and we gotta go" cocktails. They were saying their extended good-byes to Korkki and the crew with whom they had spent the better portion of the afternoon drinking. Unsteadily, Steve and Tiny made the climb up the stairs to their apartment. While Steve made a salad, Tiny warmed some beans and set the table.

"We'll probably have to microwave those pork chops," suggested Tiny.

"You're right," agreed Steve as he started out the door with a platter and tongs. Placing the platter carefully on the porch table, he lifted the Weber lid.

Tiny heard a shout and ran to her man's aid, fearing he had fallen or burned himself. There he stood, Weber lid in one hand, tongs in the other, his face horrified.

"They're gone! They're gone! Someone has stolen our dinner. Call the cops. When thieves come right onto your porch and steal your food, something needs to be done, by God! Let's ask Riley if he's seen anyone snooping around the back porch."

Steve knocked just as Riley was pushing himself away from the table, barely able to move after consuming over two and a half pounds of stuffed pork chops. He opened the door and smiled at Steve and Tiny, wiping grease from his mouth with the back of his hand. "What's up, guys?"

Looking past Riley, Steve spotted the pile of pork chops bones on the plate in the middle of the table, let out a yell and lunged for him. Tiny stepped between them, subduing the situation, and calmed Steve by convincing him that pork rustling was not a hanging offense in Minnesota.

The storm settled. Riley paid Steve for the chops, and as Tiny and Steve headed for their own apartment to order from Sammy's Pizza next door, Riley called after them.

"Steve, I'll get some more chops next week if you want to cook them. They were great."

Steve slammed his door shut in disgust.

Wynona with a "Y"

In August of 1991, Duluth, Minnesota held its first Bayfront Blues Festival. It was expected to attract thousands of blues fans from all over the tri-state area and I saw this event as a tremendous business opportunity for R.T. Quinlan's. For the bachelors in town, including me, the prospect of untold numbers of lovely young women coming to town was enticing, and I intended to take full advantage of the opportunity.

On Friday afternoon, the second day of the Blues Fest, I parked my bike outside the back door of the bar. Inside, the band had already set up their equipment and was doing sound checks. I sat at the end bar stool and ordered up a Budweiser, checking with the bartender to make sure we had plenty of change and were thoroughly stocked and ready for what I believed would be a banner night.

Satisfied that everything was in order, I was sitting back and sipping on my beer when I looked up and noticed a redhead coming down the front stairs. She was leading a parade of a dozen or so other girls, all singing "Mustang Sally." They weren't singing very well, but at least they knew the words.

The front gal looked like a country western singer with big, curly red hair. She was wearing very tight designer jeans and a white cropped tee top that revealed a sensational pair of headlights on high beam. As she got closer, a flash of recognition lit her face.

"Prince?" she squealed, throwing her arms around my neck and planting a kiss on my lips.

Now I remembered her. Wynona with a "Y," as I called her, had joined the 477th Reserves unit ten years earlier, right out of high school. At the time, it was hard not to notice her, but because she was just seventeen years old, and my subordinate, even a self-indulging womanizer had to say, "Whoa!" I knew better than to attempt dipping my pen into government ink. By now, Y was twenty-seven and out of the Reserves.

I thought to myself with a smile, *Fair game,* and did what has always come naturally to me. I applied the full court press. Her defensive game crumbled. Slam dunk.

On the Saturday after Labor Day, I hosted the first R.T. Quinlan's Golf Classic at Proctor Municipal Golf Course. There were six teams that first year, each made up of five golfers. I cooked a breakfast at home and brought it to the bar in food containers I borrowed from the 477th. The chow included the famous army SOS spooned over my homemade baking powdered biscuits, scrambled eggs, hash browns, and fruit. After the tourney, I had Sammy's Pizza deliver an assortment of their best pies, and I awarded trophies and door prizes. The whole day was a complete gas. The participants all agreed I should do it every year.

"Well, I'm not sure if I really want to go through all this work every year, but I'll think about it." Wynona assured me that she was more than happy to give me all the help and support I would need to recreate this event the following year. I told her, "If you're still around next September, I'll consider it."

Wynona was living in Minneapolis and came to town every other week to visit her mother. This worked perfectly. Every other Friday she would breeze into town and stay with me until Sunday night. That left me free to carouse with my pals every other weekend.

This arrangement went very well until Thanksgiving when she informed me that she was moving back to Duluth. She planned to live with her divorced mom until she could find a job and a place to live. I had mixed emotions about her moving back to town. The sailor in me knew I was diving into dangerous waters.

Y moved in with her mother but that only lasted about two weeks. One afternoon she showed up at my Park Point door, suitcase in hand. With tears in her eyes, she pleaded with me to let her stay until she could make other arrangements.

I never did learn the trick of how to deal with a crying woman, so I caved right away and consented to this new cohabitation agreement. It went quite smoothly at first. I enjoyed having her around and began to imagine that she might be the girl for me. But the sailor's warning I felt when she decided to move to Duluth loomed large when I learned that Wynona had a fiery Irish temper. I was now swimming in waters over my head.

I continued to swim because, by this time, she had me hooked. The initial blowup passed and she begged me to forgive her. I did. We settled into a romance that was marred with occasional noisy arguments, followed by tears and then a return to shaky romance.

In 1994, Wynona and I were married in a civil ceremony performed by a district court judge and attended by Tony Hoff and his wife, Susan—yes, my good friend and my second ex-wife. After the ceremony, the Hoffs joined us for dinner and drinks to celebrate our taking the plunge. A legally married couple, Wynona and I then returned to our small Park Point apartment to resume housekeeping—and our pattern of bursts of happiness interrupted by bouts of quarreling—exciting, if you like that sort of thing.

Wynona's father had been suffering from advanced emphysema and shortly after the wedding, he lost his battle with the disease and died. We were there and watched him take his last breath. Losing a parent is never easy, as I knew, and Wynona took it very hard.

Her dad had set her up pretty well and when all the legal dust settled, Y realized that not only would her inheritance clean up all her many debts but would also provide a nice down payment on a home of our own. A solid and attractive three-bedroom home in a good neighborhood caught our eye. We made an offer.

On April 22, 1994, with the help of no fewer than seventeen family members, friends, and bar patrons, we moved into our house. Watching this effort, our new neighbor Willie sat on his front porch with his four-year-old son on his lap, taking it all in. Counting the parade of movers filing up the front walk, little Joey asked, "Daddy, how many people are moving in next door?"

With my young bride and our own house, I asked myself, "What more could we possibly want?" The answer to that question was Molly, an English springer spaniel needing, as the newspaper ad said, a loving home. Molly had a sweet personality and was pretty as could be with her liver-colored coat, four white socks, and brown freckles on her white snout. I went head over heels for this dog and she fell just as much in love with me.

Wynona used her inheritance money to furnish all three floors of our new home in beautiful fashion. It became her showcase. The house looked great but, frankly, I could be content living in a cardboard box under the freeway and wasn't all that interested in furniture arrangements. It soon became clear that we had mismatched interests and temperaments. I do admit she was justified in her major objection—my hanging out with the guys at the bar every afternoon.

That first year, something else complicated our search for domestic bliss. My young wife seemed to suddenly notice our twenty-year age difference.

Ron Korkki, my bartending friend at Norman's, became my confidante through these troubled times and almost always could make me smile with one story or another. He had started dating a more than remarkable woman named Dar Tessier. Anyone who has ever watched a relationship build could easily see that this one would go the distance.

As their romance intensified, mine declined. But, as has usually happened through my life, the bars in downtown Duluth provided solace with the sheer humor that ruled every day.

And at home, there was my faithful dog Molly.

1997 brought trouble for Y and me. Most of her father's inheritance was gone, spent on our home, new furnishings, her new truck, and her stunning wardrobe. She seemed melancholy most of the time. When she brought up the idea of a Jamaican vacation with her friends that spring, I encouraged her to go, thinking perhaps when she got home she might be refreshed and agree that we should try harder to make our marriage work.

The Military Ball that year was to be at a hotel in Superior, Wisconsin. At our Reserves meeting the month before, Adam asked me if I planned on going.

"Naw," I told him. "My wife's going to Jamaica and won't get home until late the night of the ball and I'm sure as hell not going stag."

"I'm not going stag, either. I'm going to take my mom as my date."

I laughed till my sides were sore.

"What's the matter with that?"

"Nothing, kid. I'd ask *my* mom, only she's eighty-four and I don't think she can stay up that late."

A month later, at the next drill, with the Military Ball just around the corner, Adam approached me again. "Prince, I have a problem."

"What?"

"Well, ya know, I was going to take my mom to the Military Ball. You remember me telling you that?"

"Yeah. I think that's a very nice thing for a son to do, take his mom to a function like that to show all his friends what a great woman his mother is."

"Well, I have a problem. Three months ago, I'd asked a girl from the Coast Guard Reserve to go with me and yesterday she called and said she would like to go after all. Prince, she's really good looking and she'd be fun to take to the ball but I don't know how to tell my mom. She's kind of counting on it. She's already bought a dress and everything." He paused before continuing. "I was wondering...your wife will be in Jamaica... would you mind giving my mom a ride and...I'll sort of have two dates...only my mom will have someone her own age to talk to?"

"I don't know. I'll ask my wife. If she doesn't mind, I will be happy to give the three of you a ride and I won't look like a loser going to the ball alone."

After explaining the situation to Wynona and finding that she had no objections since it was Adam's mother, for God's sake, the non-date was arranged.

Adam's mom was now divorced but I had no intention of making a move on her anyway. I remembered Sharon Rose— and that she was extremely attractive—but I was, after all, very married and only escorting her as a favor to a friend. My intentions and motives were pure—for once in my life.

Y left for Jamaica, planting a very light kiss on my cheek.

The Saturday night of the ball, I stood in front of the full-length mirror in my dress blues thinking to myself that I looked quite dashing. Over-confidence in our looks runs deep in most Hampston men. My father, brother, sons, and I have never been able to pass a mirror, store window, or glass door without checking out the handsome devil looking back.

Adam *and* his mother *and* his date Marcy were seated at a table when I arrived at R.T. Quinlan's. Adam was dressed in his Class A green uniform and looked plenty sharp himself. Four rows of ribbons decorated his left breast pocket. I was very proud of him that day, thinking that he looked as if he could be on a recruiting poster.

His mother and date were both dressed to kill. We enjoyed a drink or two at the bar to get the evening started and when we left, I could feel the eyes of every male in the place following us as we walked out the door.

It was a quick ride over the Blatnik Bridge to the Androy Hotel in Superior, Wisconsin. The evening was spectacular. Sharon Rose inspired lively conversation and did a pretty good job of dancing my feet off. We all had our photos taken to document the occasion. Once others learned that I was merely her chauffeur and strictly platonic escort, single friends, both mine and her son's, came to our end of the table to talk to Sharon and ask for dances. When the evening wound down, we made the return trip across the bridge to our home saloon. Adam and his date went their own way. Sharon and I shook hands and agreed that the evening had been swell. We thanked each other for the good time and she left for her home in

Hibbing, seventy-five miles away.

Twenty minutes later, Wynona burst through R.T. Quinlan's back door followed by her entourage of fellow vacationers. She had a deep tan and her hair was all done in corn rows like Bo Derek's in the movie 10. I was a little buzzed by now and it didn't go over well when, in a feeble attempt at humor, I told her that she should star in the sequel to the movie. They could call it 5 ½.

Things only got worse at home during the next few months. Wynona brought up the subject of divorce a few times but I fought it off with promises of trying harder to make her life happier. On the first Thursday of June, I was packing my gear for a field training exercise, or FTX, near the Brule River in Wisconsin. As I busied about searching for this item or that, my wife sat on the couch looking quite miserable.

"I want a divorce, Mike, and this time don't try to talk me out of it."

"That's crazy. Just calm down and take the weekend to think it over. I'll be home from the Reserves on Sunday afternoon and together we'll find a way to make this right again."

No dice. The conciliatory speech I'd spent the weekend rehearsing didn't work. Sunday night, she informed me that on Tuesday, two days later, at 3:00, we were both to meet with her lawyer.

I did what I normally do in stressful situations. I went out and got tanked. It didn't seem to help much. We met with the lawyer and I learned that I could keep the dog and the TV. If I paid my spouse half the equity and refinanced, I could keep the house.

Seventy-two hours after the meeting with Wynona's lawyer, she called me at work and informed me that the judge had just signed the divorce decree. Seven short days after she dropped the bomb on me while I packed for FTX, I found myself single again. A quickie divorce and I didn't even get to go to Mexico.

Susan and Tony Hoff agreed to take my dog Molly to their cabin for a month. While they were gone, I could stay at their house in town. Y moved out of our house on the same day the Hoffs came back from the lake. I picked up Molly and thanked Susan and Tony for their hospitality. Molly licked Susan's face to thank her for the lake trip and we headed home.

Molly was ecstatic to be home. She bounded out of the car, her tail going a million miles an hour, and ran up on the deck, jumping at the sliding glass door. I carried my bag to the back door, unlocked, and slid it open. My dog looked confused, seeing only the TV sitting on a media shelf. In the basement, I found the card table we had used for folding laundry and got a plastic deck chair from the garage. "Come on, Molly, let's see if there's still a bed upstairs." There was. Digging through the garage, I found a few more things I could use including a couple of dusty lamps and an old wicker chair. "How do you like our new furniture, girl?"

But so what if I was starting from scratch again? I didn't really have a beef. When we set up housekeeping, I had brought very little dough to the project. And I was grateful; she had left me my old beat up recliner with the beer-stained arms.

A week later, my son Robby and his wife Char moved in with their furnishings. They were looking for a nice place to live and I was looking for help with the mortgage. We all settled into a new routine. The kids became comfortable in their new home. I was glad of the company and, gradually, the memory of Wynona began to fade.

Carl and Arlene

Carl and Arlene, affectionately known around the bar as the "Lockhorns," were transplants from Southern California. Carl was discharged from the Navy after ten years of service. He had decided not to reenlist but instead to try his luck in the civilian world. He was a gifted mathematician and draftsman although he had little formal education. He went into business building and repairing motorcycles in California and he did quite well for some time. It was during that time that Carl joined the Argonauts, a motorcycle club not unlike Hell's Angels, where he quickly became sergeant at arms.

Carl had gotten an extra job as a fry cook at the Navy base in San Diego and Arlene was working as a cafeteria cashier at the base when she noticed the leather and colors-clad Argonaut. It was either love or lust at first sight, I'm not quite sure, but not long afterward they were riding together. One weekend they found themselves in the midst of a hundred or so other bikers thundering into a small Arizona town. Carl and Arlene, both feeling the heady effects of going drink for drink with the gang, got married. Neither one of them really remembered the ceremony but they had the marriage certificate, signed by an Arizona justice of the peace, as verification. From that day on, they assumed that the document was valid and they were indeed husband and wife.

They moved from California to the Duluth—Superior area where Carl had been born, desiring a more stable lifestyle for their growing family. While their children were growing up, Carl worked as a machinist and draftsman for several local engineering companies until, with a partner, he started his own business. Their social life was at the bar. They occupied the first two barstools at R.T. Quinlan's through at least four different names and six different owners. For over thirty years, they were regulars and could usually be found perched on their thrones as the king and queen of Michigan Street. I don't think I've ever known a married couple that spent so much time together. When someone asked Carl why he was always with his wife, he joked, "I'd rather bring her along than kiss her goodbye."

Carl and Arlene bought a cabin on an island in Lake Vermilion. They had spent many happy hours visiting Susan and Tony Hoff at their private retreat, Vagabond Island, and had discovered that the great north woods were a grand place to spend their free time. Like the other island dwellers, they traveled to their cabin by boat in the summer and during the winter they crossed the frozen water by snowmobile.

Winter parties on Lake Vermilion, even when the weather was below zero, abounded. Every weekend there was a wham-jam going on somewhere complete with bonfires, lots of good eats, and of course, plenty of John Barleycorn, snowshoe grog, and other assorted throat-warming beverages sure to numb good judgment and reflexes.

Late one January moonlit night, at the tail end of one of these frozen functions, Carl was speeding across the ice, eager to get back to the warmth of his cabin. Pressure ridges in the ice are difficult enough to see in the daylight and nearly impossible to see at night. Running at seventy miles per hour, Carl saw the ridge a split second too late. The machine and operator catapulted up and over the buckled ice ridge thirty feet into the frigid air, landing ten feet from one another. Luckily, instinct told Carl to let go of the handlebars; had the sled landed on him, he would have been crushed.

He did earn four broken ribs, a separated shoulder, and enough purple and gold bruises to merit a spot on the Minnesota Vikings bench. The sled was totaled.

After his snowmobile accident, Carl slowed down a bit, especially while riding at night, but there were other dangers lurking in the sub-zero north country that Carl hadn't even suspected would reach up to bite him in the ass, as it were.

Carl and Arlene attended the Hoffs' New Year's Eve party where dozens of other cabin owners and guests come each December 31 to say, "So long!" to the old year and welcome in the new one. The Hoffs, who are well-known for the spread they provide at these revelries, outdid themselves that particular year. It goes without saying that the bar was stocked well enough to easily accommodate a Shriners' convention.

Carl wanted to lay down a good base for the booze he planned to consume that night and he dove into the grub—barbecued beef, chicken, beans, meatballs, and pasta salads—like he was going to the electric chair. Fully content, Carl sat on a barstool and watched all the merrymakers at Tony and Susan's that night as they ate, drank, sang, and danced, enjoying the camaraderie of good friends.

Midnight came and a match was touched to a gasoline soaked fifteen-foot-high pile of logs out on the ice, a safe distance from the island. As the bonfire burst into flames, the uninhibited partygoers burst into song with "Auld Lang Syne," their collective voices carrying miles down the frozen lake.

Carl and Arlene were there to hang the last dog.

About 4:00 in the morning, against the sound advice of Susan and Tony, Carl and Arlene suited up, fired up and boarded their snowmobiles to race into the pitch black January morning. They made it back to their cabin without incident and Arlene immediately called the Hoffs to let them know they had made it home safely. Arlene announced to her husband that she was beat to a pulp and was going to bed.

Carl, on the other hand, felt as though at least a couple more cocktails and a half pack of Pall Malls would help him sleep better. As Arlene snoozed away, Carl drained his last drink and decided that it was probably a good time to hit the sack as well. But as he started up the stairs to bed, he realized that his stomach was churning a little, probably a small touch of indigestion, perhaps the result of consuming four large helpings of food and twenty or so Fleishmann's whiskey and waters. He turned, slid on his boots, grabbed his jacket and headed out into the thirty-below night air to the outhouse.

The outhouse was both heated and lit by propane lamps, one adorning each wall. With the help of four layers of insulation in the walls, they kept the facility warm as toast despite the sub-zero temperature outside.

Carl dropped his jeans and long johns and sat down. He lit a Pall Mall and grabbed a *Popular Mechanics* magazine off the rack on the wall to read, but before long, his eyelids grew heavy and he nodded off.

Although the outhouse was a cozy seventy degrees, down below, in the airy business end of the building, no heat was provided other than what recent deposits might produce. This fact left our passed out partier's backside and his "boys" swinging in the minus thirty-degree breeze.

It was a lucky thing for Carl that Arlene awoke to her own urgent nature's call in time to save his boy parts that night. She descended the stairs and not seeing her husband she thought in alarm, *Oh, shit. Carl's fallen asleep in the crapper again. Good thing it's a two-holer.*

By daylight, Carl and Arlene were at Virginia Memorial Hospital where the doc told Carl, "A half hour more out in that cold and you would have more than a medium case of frostbite on your butt and testicles." And further, he added, it was likely that a surgeon would have had to cut his guys off completely.

Carl chuckled. "Big deal, doc. I don't use anything down there anymore except for pissing anyway."

Pocket Sandwiches

Norman's Bar on First Street was experiencing a dip in business, and owner Gary Wizner, the "Wiz Kid," found himself temporarily unable to keep up with the weekly bills coming in from the local liquor and beer distributors. As an emergency measure, he resorted to buying beer, liquor, and wine directly from retail liquor stores on a daily basis, purchased with cash from the previous day's business. Wiz's daytime bartender, Steve Hake, would pick up the day's supplies and haul them in the back of his pickup. This was a labor-intensive task and Steve needed help to load and unload his cargo. He enlisted the help of the King who was usually down on his luck and in need of fresh revenue.

It didn't make too much difference to the King if wages came as money or free alcohol. Once the beer coolers and liquor shelves were restocked, Jack would hunker down on a barstool and swish down his first few vodka waters of the day while Steve set up the bar for the day's business. Before unlocking the front door, Steve would pour his own rations—three full glasses of straight vodka. He positioned one on either end of the back bar and one in the middle, disguised not very convincingly as water. This gave him the advantage of never having to move more than three or four steps when he felt the need of a little pick-me-up. This is how Gary's work team dedicated their mornings, the King getting buzzed on one side of the bar and Steve on the other.

On one of these mornings, Ray was walking out the back door of our bar just as Steve rolled by. Riding shotgun was the King wearing his black cowboy hat. Ray shook his head and pointed them out to the swamper who was dumping mop water onto Michigan Street. "There goes 'Team Vodka!'"

When business picked up again, and after paying a few fines for buying retail, Wiz was able to get Norman's off the distributors' blacklist, drying up the King's source of free vodka like a well in the 1930s' Dust Bowl. But while the King may have lacked ambition, he could be ingenious when it came to priming his pump.

Mom was a wonderful baker and made six loaves of mouthwatering white bread for the family every Monday and Friday. It was the aroma of mom's delicious bread that inspired Jack with a scheme to replace his lost "income." With our mother as his unknowing silent partner, the King launched his new venture—Food for Vodka.

Conveniently for him, Jack did a lot of Mom's grocery shopping and, after carefully searching through the grocery ads in the newspaper, he found a terrific deal on a whole smoked picnic ham. He brought it home and asked Mom if she would like to bake it for supper. She blew her top.

"Jack, have you lost your mind? That's a thirty-pound ham. This family couldn't eat thirty pounds of ham in six months."

The King, pretty sure he could outwit his mother on this one, made the case that, once she baked it, he would cut up the ham and pack it into freezer bags in meal-sized portions. Then they would be able to take it out of the freezer as needed.

"And furthermore," he said, appealing to her frugality, "by buying in bulk like this, you can save a tremendous amount of money."

Mom, not realizing that she had been conned, could see

that Jack had a good point. She baked the ham.

It was delicious.

Early the next morning before Mom got up, Jack made six large ham sandwiches, using one-and-a-half loaves of Mother's bread. He wrapped them in aluminum foil and loaded them into the cargo pockets of his big corduroy coat. Donning his black cowboy hat, he headed out the back door.

His first stop was the Rustic Bar where Bucky was getting ready for his early morning trade. Bucky greeted Jack with a "Mornin', King."

"Mornin', Buck." Jack fished a ham sandwich from his pocket and placed it on the bar. "I made you some lunch," he said with a gracious smile.

"Lunch? Ya nitwit, it's 8:15 in the morning. I just finished my breakfast."

"Well, save it for lunch, then."

"Yeah, okay." Bucky picked up the sandwich and stuck it in the cooler. He poured Jack a vodka water and went about his business.

Jack was very pleased with himself. The plan was actually working. He downed his complimentary drink and two more right behind it.

The next stop on the King's trap line was Curly's Bar in the West End where he found Bimbo, a 280-pound bartender, busy at his work. Jack reached for a ham sandwich. A few more thank-you drinks and Jack was getting well-adjusted to the morning. He headed for the Midway.

When he stopped in at R.T. Quinlan's, I was behind the bar, serving the morning customers who were well on the road to a noontime buzz. Jack swung his leg over a barstool and slurred a "Hi, Muntz. I brought you something to eat." Out from his pocket he wrestled a now badly-misshapen ham sandwich.

"Had a cocktail or two today, Muntz?" I asked as I poured his "va-wa" with no ice. I looked at the damaged goods sitting in front of me on the bar and asked just how long it had been traveling about in his pocket waiting to poison some unsuspecting bartender.

Indignantly, he retrieved the sandwich and started to put it back in his pocket, pointing out that I was an ungrateful son-of-a-bitch and mumbled something about his thoughtful, generous, unappreciated gesture of good will. Guilt ridden, I apologized and held out my hand to accept the thoughtful, generous gift and thanked him.

He handed me the foil package in which the slice of ham had escaped the now crumbly chunk of bread. I set about rebuilding the sandwich. In return I poured him another drink, knowing that once again I'd been had.

As he left, I called to him, "Where now, Muntz?"

"Norman's. I still have one sandwich left."

Jack repeated this scam every day until the ham ran out. That's when the peanut butter and jelly sandwiches started.

It wasn't long before Mom asked him why he thought she was going through so much home-baked bread. She was now baking bread three times a week to keep up.

"I don't know, Mom. I've just been hungry lately, I guess."

"Well, I think maybe we should take you in to the doctor, because eating that much and not gaining any weight...you could have a tape worm."

Every Friday afternoon, the organization that ran our charitable gambling at R.T. Quinlan's had a meat raffle. I bought a raffle ticket even though I knew that as one of the owners I wasn't eligible to win. I gave it to the King. Rather than going home for his customary "over-fifty" nap, he stayed downtown spearing drinks from anyone he could sweet-talk into parting with his brass. Six o'clock came and the girl behind the pull-tab booth began to draw and call out winning numbers. On the table next to the booth sat a large cooler packed full with meat prizes. As participants heard their numbers called, the chops, roasts, and steaks were awarded to the winners.

Jack sat on his barstool, gulping va-wa and complaining that he wasn't winning and the whole goddamned thing was rigged. The grand prize was a hundred dollars' worth of rib eye steaks.

The girl called 672. No one answered. Again but louder, she yelled, "Number 672!" Still no response from the crowd. As she started to reach for another ticket while I was standing in front of my brother pouring him another drink that he had mooched off Steve Bosie, I looked at the raffle ticket sitting on the bar in front of him. It was upside down so I reached out and flipped it over. It was marked 672.

"You screwball, you just won!"

"Number 672!" yelled the King. "I've got it right here!"

He collected his prize of fifteen beautiful rib eyes, chugged down his drink and with his bag of butcher-wrapped steaks tucked under his arm, started for the door, weaving wildly.

"What ya going to do with all those steaks?" called Bosie.

"Pocket sandwiches," slurred the King. "Pocket sandwiches."

When he got home, he noticed the kitchen light was on and he could see Mom moving about. He hoped it wasn't too late to get something to eat.

I'd better hide these, he thought. *Mom will want to have a dinner party or something equally silly and I'll lose out on a hundred bucks worth of pocket sandwich meat.*

He was lucky in the fact that although it was only late September, the weather had turned unseasonably cold and the mercury was forecast to dip into the low thirties that night. He stashed his goods in the shed using Mom's gardening pots for camouflage. He smiled, pleased with himself that once again he had bested his mother in the never-ending war of wits.

Coming in the kitchen door with a "Hi, Mom," he noticed

a slightly aggravated tone in her voice as she pointed out that he was over an hour late for supper and she was not a short-order cook waiting patiently for an unemployed son who comes home drunk and expects to be fed at all hours of the day and night.

"You're just like your father," she scolded. "John Barleycorn!"

"Jesus," he pouted, "all I said was 'Hi, Mom.'"

Jack ate his supper while Mom apologized for chastising him. She pointed out, however, that she had spent thirty years of her life waiting on our alcoholic father and was growing very tired of that job.

The King finished his supper in silence. He announced that he was a little tired and thought he would turn in early. He bid Mother goodnight and climbed the stairs to his room, making a mental note to put those steaks on the grill tomorrow after Mom and our stepdad Frank went to the lake to close up their camper for the year.

A mental note written in vodka rather than a No.2 black pencil almost always will evaporate. The following morning, as Mom and Frank loaded the car getting ready for their trip to the lake, Jack slipped out the front door, forgetting that he had left fifteen beef steaks hidden in the shed.

The temperature that next week climbed into the lower eighties.

Two weeks later, Mom took advantage of a delightful Indian summer day and began preparations for putting her garden to bed for the winter. She pushed the shed door open. That was as far as she got. She was stopped in her tracks by a smell that seemed to come from the bowels of hell itself.

Mom called Frank from the house, telling him that she thought an animal had got into the shed and died because there was a God-awful smell coming out of there and she couldn't imagine what else could cause such a foul odor.

Frank put a handkerchief over his face and forged ahead to

investigate.

After a short search, he came out, holding Jack's package of steaks at arms' length with an old rag. He put them on the sidewalk at his wife's feet. "Phew!" gasped Mom. "What in the world is that? It stinks to high heaven."

Unwrapping one and examining a hunk of something crawling with maggots, Frank answered that he thought they used to be steaks. "But why in the world would anyone put a full bag of meat in our garden shed?" They looked at each other, silent for several seconds...and then exclaimed together, "Jack!"

When Mother confronted him that night, his eyes lit up with recollection. But he recovered quickly and insisted that somehow, some phantom meat thief ("Didn't you hear about him on the TV news, Mom?") must have stashed his plunder in our open shed.

"Really, Mom, you and Frank should start locking that shed door..."

50

Sharon Rose

September of 1997 brought R.T. Quinlan's seventh annual golf tourney, followed the next day by the Viking regular season opener.

Adam mentioned to me that his mother wasn't a golfer but had volunteered to help on golf day, thinking that she would probably be bartending. At the time, she was supplementing her insurance company income by tending bar at Valentini's Restaurant in Chisholm, Minnesota. In years past, she had co-owned her own small tavern for eight years and she knew the business. But business at our bar might be very slow during the tournament since everyone would be on the course. I thought she'd get pretty bored so I suggested she help Jeanette who traditionally ran the sign-up table out at the Nemadji Golf Course.

It hadn't occurred to me that after all the players teed off, there would be nothing to do until much later when everyone returned from eighteen holes of golf with their scores. Jeanette was a golf tourney veteran. She had wisely brought a paperback and even though she was up for conversation, it was still an uneventful six-hour wait for the golfers to return. They were both good sports about the long day, and I reminded myself to give them a big thank-you at the awards ceremony back at R.T. Quinlan's.

Later that night, I sat with Sharon at the bar. We talked mostly about her son Adam, the golf tourney, and our experiences in the Broken Hearts Club. Karaoke was the entertainment that night. I remembered that Adam had told me his mother had sung professionally for many years and had a "pretty good" singing voice. So I asked her to do me a favor. "I'd really appreciate it if you'd write down the name of a tune you'd be willing to sing and slip it onto the Karaoke guy's table." It took a little convincing, but she finally agreed. Adam joined me at the bar as his mom took the microphone up on RTQ's historic stage.

Sharon Rose dedicated her song to me. She began singing "Danny Boy" so beautifully that my Irish eyes welled up with tears. I looked at Adam as the high notes toward the end neared and whispered, "Oh, God, please let her make 'em," just as her rich voice easily lifted to sing these final words.

And I shall hear, tho' soft ye tread above me,
And och, my grave will warmer, sweeter be,
And if ye'll kneel and tell me that ye love me,
Then I shall sleep in peace until ye come to me.

No one in my family can hear "Danny Boy" without going all gooshey. I grabbed for my handkerchief and blew my nose.

At the end of the evening, I once again told her how much I appreciated her coming to Duluth to help with the tournament. Then we did our usual drill, a kind of formal old-fashioned goodnight. We shook hands and thanked each other for a great time. I watched, feeling a little happy and a little sad, as she got in her car to drive the seventy-five miles back home to Hibbing.

51

Molly, the Football Fan

With another successful golf tournament now in the can, we all set our sights on football. Rob and Char and most R.T. Quinlan's regulars are loyal Vikings fans. I've always been more interested in putting asses on barstools than in the outcome of a football game. But we agreed that Viking wins kept those cheering crowds around to celebrate. That meant Ray and I would be able to pay our bills that week. In that way, we all won.

Every Sunday, I joined the throng of screaming, cheering, arm-waving fanatics at the bar to watch the purple gang take on that week's opponent. Fans at our place take turns cooking on football Sundays, each trying to outdo the other with a steaming pot of grub spiced up to bring on wows from the competition. On game day, big roasting pans, crock pots, and trays of culinary wizardry are hauled in before kick-off.

Rob and Char always left home early to claim their favorite barstools, buzz about their game predictions, and along with the other mad hatters, toss a shot glass of favorite hootch down the hatch just as the first kick popped the ball into the air.

They would usually let my dog Molly out before leaving the house, but on one particular rainy Sunday, Rob reported that Molly wanted no part of getting her paws wet. She refused to brave the downpour. A bit later, when I went to the Michigan Street door to check the weather, I saw that the rain had stopped, the clouds had parted and the sun was shining with good cheer. *Gosh*, I thought, *Molly must be desperate to relieve herself by now, especially looking out at all the water puddles on her lawn.*

I called the Yellow Cab Company, and promising a handsome tip, I asked the dispatcher to send a cab driver over to my house, open the door, let Molly do her business, and then drive her over to the bar.

"I don't know," said the dispatcher dubiously. "I'll have to see."

The food arrived with that week's chef who would serve enchiladas at half-time. I stationed someone at the bar's back door to watch for Molly's taxi and ten minutes later, the guy yelled, "Here she comes!"

I walked outside to see my dog in the cab's back passenger seat, riding with regal elegance. When she saw me in the doorway, she started bouncing around like a Mexican jumping bean. I paid the cabbie and opened the door. She leapt out, racing right by me and into the bar. Molly got down to the business of greeting everyone in the place. She gave as many tongue licks as she could manage to every hand and face made available to her.

I went back to pouring drinks. Molly was right on my heels. I think customers paid more attention to my dog that afternoon than they did to the football game. Halftime came and the enchiladas were served. No matter how much I discouraged the idea, people shared more of their food with my pooch than was prudent. When we got home and I scooped her food into her dish, she totally ignored it, looking up at me as if to say, "You don't really expect me to eat that crap, do you?"

Molly was the only girl in my life at that time, and appropriately, we shared a bedroom. But that night it wasn't just cuddling, scratching, and snoring. If you have ever slept in a room with a dog that has gorged herself on bean-rich enchiladas, you can imagine my plight—"Pfffft" every five minutes. In a small room with the door closed (to give Rob and Char privacy), "Pfffft" created a powerful emission. The aroma was strangling.

I finally gave up and went downstairs to sleep on the couch, leaving Molly to her dreams of Milkbone-filled piñatas and Mexican chihuahuas. Later I heard Robby get up in the middle of the night for a bathroom call. Maybe I'd left the door ajar as I headed downstairs carrying my pillow in one hand and holding my nose with the other, because the "Pfffft" clearly hit him with full force.

Passing my bedroom he wailed, "Jesus Christ, Molly, it smells like the gut pile at deer camp!" He mumbled, "Damn dog," and slammed the door.

I forgave him. After all, she wasn't his best girl.

52

The Actor

Tor was a fixture in Duluth bars for almost as long as I can remember. When I first met him, Tor was married to a grocery owner's daughter. They were both intellectuals and had several college degrees to their credit. Tor and I met each other in the late 1960s. He had recently been discharged from the Army where he had been assigned to the crew of a Davy Crockett short-range nuclear device.

He was a smart guy. After his initial training on this nuclear contraption, he learned that, once fired, the crew would be too close to the nuclear blast to have much hope of surviving. From this, Tor made a clear deduction. As soon as humanly possible, he should get the hell out of the Army.

A civilian once more, he grew his curly hair until it was bushy and long and also let his beard grow down to his chest. With the addition of beads and sandals, he was ready to join the hippie drop-out society of the 1960s that arrived in Duluth in the early 1970s. Tor was an artist and an actor, but when it came to conventional work of the kind that puts bacon on the table, he did as little as he possibly could.

Bill Anderson, the grocery's owner and Tor's father-in-law, tried his best to make a grocer out of his daughter's new husband. Tor was a small man but showed surprising strength in his resistance, fighting Bill tooth and nail every step of the way. Neither his job nor his marriage lasted long.

The energy he was unwilling to put into work, Tor lavished on his art—acting, in particular. He became very active in community theater, appearing in many Duluth Playhouse productions. He played George to my sister Claudia's Martha in *Who's Afraid of Virginia Woolf?* The gutsy and controversial script combined with superb acting caused a sensation in Duluth. This role prepared Tor for other "crusty old man" roles such as the farmer in *Of Mice and* Men and Colonel Potter in *M*A*S*H*. Tor excelled at playing drunks. In *Sly Fox* he played a lascivious old codger who had the pleasure of falling asleep on my sister Kitty's chest, she playing the role of the buxom Miss Fancy. Tor was heartbreaking in *The Potting Shed*, cast in the role of the whiskey-priest.

R.T. Quinlan's fans sometimes filled an entire row at the Playhouse. One of Tor's fans was my son John. Despite their age difference, they became fast friends, both being hardcore movie fans and sharing their encyclopedic knowledge of cinema lore. As the years passed, Tor's friends at the bar became his family and he was welcomed into their homes and my home to be part of holidays and celebrations. He was good company, well-informed, and boy, did he love to talk.

Central Casting could not have provided a more non-confrontational character than Tor. As long as he wasn't expected to have an actual job, Tor was a completely agreeable fellow.

In any conversation at the bar in which an orator might require a confirmation of fact or opinion, Tor would raise his voice heartily with a resounding, "Of *course!*" and "Why *certainly!*" Had Tor found himself sitting on a barstool flanked by Rush Limbaugh on one side and Ted Kennedy on the other, I am sure he would have found a way to be in agreement with everything said on both sides. "You're *right!*" and "Why *certainly!*" would have rattled the bottles on the back bar.

One warm October Sunday afternoon, Robby found himself sitting next to Tor at the bar which, in itself, was unusual because Tor seldom got out of bed before the sun went down. Rob remarked, "What the hell are you doing out during the day? Did someone throw holy water on your coffin?"

Tor laughed and, of course, agreed that it was totally out of character for him to be anywhere other than his bed whilst the sun shone. Tor jabbered in Rob's ear, interrupting the televised football game time after time with talk, talk, talk that had nothing whatsoever to do with the Vikings and their battle with the Chicago Bears.

Finally fed up, large, muscular Robby told small, skinny Tor, "Don't talk to me again unless it has something to do with this football game or it's during a commercial!"

"Of *course*! I apologize. I won't do it again."

Two minutes later, he once again butted in, this time exactly at the moment the ball was snapped for a forty-five-yard field goal to win the game.

Five minutes after that, the "Lockhorns," Carl and Arlene walked in, and Carl asked why Tor was duct-taped to a parking meter, hand and foot, with another piece of tape across his mouth. Robby explained. Arlene turned to Carl, "Goddammit, Carl, they can't do that! It's against the law!" Carl stormed out the door. A minute later he returned, but without Tor.

"I thought you were going to let him go," said Robby.

"Oh, no. When I pulled the tape off his mouth, he wouldn't shut up—so I just plugged the meter again. He's good for an hour."

53

Paul Revere and the Raiders

Spring came early to northern Minnesota in 1998. At least it did for me.

Adam mentioned that his mother and aunt were driving down from Hibbing on Saturday afternoon to see a Paul Revere & the Raiders concert. He was planning to go as well. Adam asked if his mom and her sister could spend the night in the guest room at our house rather than make the long drive back to Hibbing so late at night. Out of the blue he said, "Ya know, Prince, my mom likes the way you dress."

What the hell does that mean? I wondered. Maybe, just maybe, the good-lookin' mother of my swamper (bar-maintenance commando) had a shine for me. I was terrified—I had been single for almost a year now and hadn't even considered dating.

Saturday afternoon, dressed in a folded, cuffed, starched and pressed white shirt with my favorite beige sweater vest and a pair of tan slacks sporting a dangerously sharp crease, I waited for Adam's mom while considering the possibilities. *What the hell? I'll make my play. If she isn't interested, it certainly won't be the first time I've gone down in flames.*

Precisely at 5:00, she walked into R.T. Quinlan's, her pretty blonde hair back-lit by the sunlight coming in the back door. She was smiling when she announced that her sister had

297

experienced a last minute crisis that prevented her from attending the concert and that Sally's ticket was now available. Sharon was quick to offer me a spot on the guest list.

"Yes!" I exclaimed. But first, I asked her to step over with me to the "Ex-Wives' Table" where Wife Number Two, Susan, was sitting with her husband Tony and some friends, to ask their approval for this "date."

Another resounding, "Yes!"

The concert was loads of fun. We had grown up listening to songs like "Louie, Louie" and sang right along with the band. After the concert, the three of us stopped at an out-of-the-way bar for some drinks, not wanting to share the rest of the evening with the crowd at R.T. Quinlan's. Sharon and I were attracted to each other and we laughed and talked the night away, with Adam as chaperone. She told me her life story and I gave her an account of my stagger-step through life.

When it was time to head home to my house, I assured her that her car would be perfectly safe parked in back of R.T. Quinlan's and that we could pick it up in the morning. She needed to leave by 8:00 in the morning to be back to Hibbing in time to play the organ for her church's 10:00 service.

At home, while having a nightcap, she told me that she had never felt comfortable with the name Sharon, that when people said her name, she tended to look around to see who they were talking to.

"Well, what do you think your name should be?"

"Well, I was named Sharon Rose, but I've always felt more like a Rosie."

I never again called her Sharon. From that moment on, she was simply my Rosie.

We climbed the stairs together, stifling laughter. I showed her to the guest room, tiptoeing past Robby and Char's closed bedroom door. A kiss goodnight in the doorway left my head spinning. I suppose the cocktails could have had an effect but in any case, I was definitely smitten.

This is how Rosie tells the rest of the story.

I went to J.C. Penney's and bought a pair of men's classic cotton pajamas in pale blue. Doris Day pajamas. I'd been invited to stay at the Hampston house and I didn't want this guy everyone called "Prince" to think I was coming on to him if we met in the hallway. We went to the concert and had a fabulous time, the three of us, Adam, Prince and me, laughing and talking and loving the music. Afterward, we all went to a little bar and Princie won me a white teddy bear out of one of those games-of-chance machines.

Adam had written letters home from Saudi Arabia about his nutty sergeant and the rest of the madcap soldiers in his medical unit and suggested that some of the goings-on of the 477th resembled the lunacies portrayed in the *M*A*S*H* 4077th sit-com.

I gratefully thanked Sergeant "Prince" for having taken my twenty-two-year-old soldier under his wing in a foreign land during a time that was plenty stressful for his mother.

Prince laughed. "You and I *have* to get together. We share a son!"

When we got to his place, Robby and Char were already in bed. We sat on the couch talking for a bit and I asked him about his nickname, Prince.

"That's someone I used to be," he said quietly. So he became Mike to me.

With our new names decided upon, we headed up the

stairs and shared what I hope was a quiet kiss at the guest room door. My night was spent in a charming little bedroom that the menfolk of the house had named "The Bad Girl's Room—where mouthy women are sent to sleep."

I woke in the morning to hear rain spitting at the windows and thought, *Oh man, I've got to get going.* I was scheduled to provide the music for my church's Sunday morning service. It would take an hour and a half to drive home and my car was still downtown where we'd left it at R.T. Quinlan's.

I got dressed in a jiffy, tiptoed out and peeked in the bedroom door of Michael Hampston's room. He was sleeping soundly. It had been a late night and I didn't want to wake him so I eased my way downstairs to the kitchen and found a telephone book.

"Yellow Cab? Yes, I need a taxi sent to...ah, just a minute. Ah, I'll call you right back."

Mike's number wasn't listed in the phone book so I looked for a stack of mail with an address. None. I looked at the cards magnetized to the refrigerator. Nothing.

I threw on my jacket and walked around to the front of the house, rain spattering my face as I peered up at the numbers on the porch column. Got 'em.

I hurried to the end of the block to read the street sign. Got it.

"Hello. Yellow Cab? Yes, I'm in a hurry and the address is..."

I stood out in front of the house getting soggier every minute until the cab stopped at the bottom of the front stairs. "Hi. Thanks for being so speedy."

"Where to?"

"Ah, I don't know the address but it's a bar downtown called R.T. Quinlan's."

The cabbie looked at me in his rear view mirror as if to say, *Yup, another one.*

"And please hurry," I snapped. "I have to play organ in my *church* in Hibbing in two hours!"

54

Seventy-Five Miles Isn't That Far

A few days after the Raiders' concert, Rosie and I decided we should meet again. This next date was to be in her town, Hibbing, the following Thursday. With the directions to her house in my pocket, I drove the seventy-five miles up US Highway 53 in a quick hour and fifteen minutes. I was in a hurry.

I walked through her iron gate and was heading across the back yard carrying a small red canvas overnight bag, just in case I didn't get thrown out right away, when I spotted Rosie. She was sitting at a large round picnic table next door in her neighbor's back yard. Along with neighbor Elaine sat no fewer than three other ladies. As Rosie registered my arrival, I saw a look of repressed horror come over her face that said, *Oh, God. He has luggage. Luggage! He thinks he's going to get lucky!*

Her face pink with embarrassment, she waved, as Elaine called, "Michael, drop your bag and join us for a drink."

I did as she asked and plopped down the blush red bag before I crossed the yard. Rosie introduced me to her friends, all about twenty years older than she. I know women well enough to realize they were giving me the once-over, sizing me up and trying to determine if I were an acceptable candidate to cozy up to their friend. I turned on the charm and dazzled them with B.S. and bartender's wit. Elaine's face glowed with glad acceptance.

I'm in, I thought, pleased with my ability to make friends quickly with Rosie's best pal and neighbor. I'd been forewarned that Elaine was a shrewd judge of bullshit.

Later, seated in her kitchen, Rosie made it plain that I had put her in a bad light with the red overnight bag. "Red!" she exclaimed. "This *is* only our second date."

"Well," I scrambled for an answer, "if you count the Military Ball last year and the golf tournament last fall, this is our fourth date, I'd say."

The grin on my face must have defused the situation because she laughed as she pointed her finger at me, "Don't count your chickens, buddy."

I'd figured she'd be making me dinner and she'd figured I'd be taking her out to eat, but it didn't matter. Instead we feasted on crackers and her homemade antipasto and never stopped talking. In the weeks and months that followed, we found that conversation came easily between us. Every Thursday and every other weekend, I went to see my new gal in Hibbing. On the odd weekends, she came to Duluth. And before long, our relationship grew from like to love.

I liked her family and friends, and everyone in Duluth fell for her just as I had. They saw what I did—beauty, brains and talent. My sisters were the first to point out that she was way too good for me and if I screwed this up, they'd never speak to me again. Harsh, I observed, but assured them that this was the one—and I had no intention of letting her get away.

55

Whiskey for Free and Money for Nothin'

Jack and Mom continued their war of wills. Mom tried desperately to keep her fifty-seven-year-old teenager on the straight and narrow, and the King fought responsibility at every turn. He used every trick he could devise to maintain his royal right to do exactly as he pleased.

Mom had noticed that his hair had grown far too long and told him, "Either put it into a pony tail or get a haircut." When we were growing up, she always cut our hair but her vision was fading so she decided to throw some money at the problem. She opened her purse, handed him fifteen dollars and sent him to the barber's while she went shopping.

The barbershop was next to Curly's Bar. With fifteen dollars cold cash in his pocket and temptation overwhelming him, he marched by the barbershop and turned in to Curly's.

Two hours later, half in the bag, he boarded a bus for home, needing to get there before Mom returned from shopping. He found Mother's sewing scissors and with unsteady hands cut his own hair. Admiring his handiwork in the mirror, he thought, *Not bad. I could make fifteen bucks drinking money a month like this.* Retrieving his shorn locks from the sink, he hid them in the bathroom wastebasket by covering them up with toilet paper. Then he toddled off to his room for a nap.

"Jack, that's the worst haircut I've ever seen in my life," Mom exclaimed on seeing his hacked up hair.

"I don't know. It looks okay to me."

"That barber must have been drunk or blind or something. Here's another fifteen dollars and don't go back to that hair butcher. Find another one that actually knows how to cut hair."

Believe it or not, the knucklehead did the exact same thing the next day. By now, Mom had had it with these so-called hair-cutting professionals. Even though she couldn't see very well, she could do a better job than these sorry excuses. She'd go back to cutting his hair herself.

Two days later, while cleaning the bathroom, Mom discovered the clumps of Jack's dyed black hair hidden in the wastebasket. From then on, she resolved, he would have to find another way to raise haircut money because he sure as hell wasn't going to get it from her.

Our stepfather Frank died in 1999. When he got sick, Mom and Jack took care of him at home as best and for as long as they could. Considering all his shortcomings, Jack was soft-hearted and took Mom's cue when it came to helping out neighbors and looking after their pets. He was devoted to Frank in a way that surprised my sisters and me. We had all come to love Frank especially since he and Mom had such a happy marriage together. Mom was glad to have Jack at home after Frank died. Though he hadn't changed his stripes, he was a voice in the house and someone to cook for and look after.

With her eighty-sixth birthday right around the corner, it occurred to Mother that if something should happen to her, Jack would be unable to keep up with household expenses until the insurance money came through. With this in mind, she opened the family Bible to show him the one thousand dollars she had put away for him.

"There's $1,000 here. It should be plenty to pay the bills for a month or two and provide you with money for food until my life insurance settlement becomes available."

Mom was a person who always tried to focus on the positive. She always held out hope that in a crisis, good sense would overcome Jack's irresponsibility, but she knew better than to show him the larger stash which was safely hidden in her sewing machine. Good thing, too.

That week the Powerball Lottery for the first time totaled $145 million, before taxes.

Jack came up with one of his over-the-top cockamamie schemes. He would take the $1,000 from the Bible and buy a thousand lottery tickets. After he won the lottery, he would simply return the borrowed grand to the Bible, thanks be to God, and Mom wouldn't even know it had been gone. He'd make a more than tidy profit from his investment.

"Brilliant!" That's what I said a week later when he asked for a thousand bucks to replace Mom's embezzled dough.

I guess if you ever really tried to mathematically figure the odds of my Einstein brother's winning $145 million with a thousand dollar investment, you would find that he really did have a pretty good chance. It was somewhere in the neighborhood of 121 million to one.

"No, goddamn it, Jack. Not only am I not going to give you $1,000 but I'm gonna call Mom right now and tell her what you've done."

"Stool pigeon! After all I've done for you!"

I think the King was the only fifty-seven-year-old in history to be grounded by his mother.

He paid the money back at the rate of one hundred dollars a month from his Social Security disability check—with an additional 8 percent interest.

56

My Dear Brother

In the spring of 2001, Jack was diagnosed with liver cancer. He endured the chemotherapy treatments like a hero, but in late summer came the dreadful day when we were told there was nothing more to do. The doctors told us we should make arrangement for St Mary's Hospital Hospice care. With their help, our family cared for Jack at home until December. My nephew Sean Daly kept watch for the last couple of months. He camped out on the sofa next to where Jack's hospital bed was tucked into a corner of the living room in our family's home on Chestnut Street.

At 5:30 on Monday morning, December 17, Jack died, lying below his own portrait, a painting of him done by an artist at the Tri-State Fair when he was a handsome boy of eighteen.

His death left a huge hole in our family, especially for our mother. She mourned his death in a quiet, lonely way. Outwardly, she seemed to accept his passing, but I could tell that she was different somehow. My sisters and I tried as much as we could to fill the empty space, but Jack was Jack, her stay-at-home kid all of his adult years and most of hers. She missed him, plain and simple.

A day never passes that I don't think about my brother. Whenever I turn off Seventh Street onto Mesaba Avenue and see the panorama of Lake Superior and St. Louis Bay sparkling in the sunshine, I'm reminded of the morning I was giving Jack a ride home. When we started down the hill, Jack said to me. "What a great day. Aren't we lucky to live in such a beautiful city, Muntzie?" I see him wearing his big, black Clint Eastwood cowboy hat, the collar turned up on his jean jacket, stuffed with pocket sandwiches, and that grin. Oh, God help us, that grin—a sure sign of another scam to make a bundle with little or no effort on his part.

Stories of the King's nutty exploits still pour out whenever a group of his friends gather at their usual corner of the bar. Rounds of drinks are delivered at a dizzying rate as someone laughs, "And remember the time Jack decided to..."

Sooner or later, someone will hoist his glass and toast, "Long live the King!"

I will always raise a glass to that.

57

Mike and Rosie

Rosie had worked for twenty years at a major insurance company in Hibbing. After the company restructured and closed her office, she was free to come to Duluth more often. Around the same time, Robby and Char had found their own place and the following summer, Rosie moved in with me, bringing her little dog Meg with her.

The house seemed alive again with Rosie, me, and our two dogs. She enrolled in the fall semester at the University of Wisconsin to take sixteen of the last twenty-four credits she needed for her degree, intending to enhance her qualifications to get an interesting part-time job. I pointed out that it had long been a dream of mine to live with a beautiful college girl but had somehow imagined her being about thirty years younger.

I worked five shifts a week at the bar while Rosie made the house cozy and studied her heart out, scoring straight As of course.

Shortly after moving in with me, Rosie started singing with a choral group at a music conservatory located on the grounds of a magnificent estate in Duluth. A month after the end of the college semester, the director of the conservatory asked her to fill an opening as her assistant, and Rosie accepted.

She loved the work. The people she worked with were kind and gracious. Especially touching her heart were the hundreds of children who came through the elegant doors of the mansion each week to take music lessons. Rosie had all the right stuff for her job. She had the secretarial skills, a love and knowledge of music, and she knew kids—she was the mother of four sons. She had found a home.

We sat on our deck one July evening in 2005, enjoying each other's company. I looked at Rosie quite seriously. "I think we should get married."

She looked back at me with a warm smile. "I think so, too."

We visited Ireland in 2002 and had come home seriously enchanted. Now we planned to return to be married there on December 23, 2005. We would not tell our families until the day before we left. We knew that the nuptial parties would be endless if our friends got wind of it. We didn't have time for that. There was a lot to do.

E-mails and sheaves of certified documents proving that we were both single flew between Minnesota and Dungarvan, Ireland, one of our favorite places on Earth. Overnight mail delivered the final necessary papers to Mary, our new friend at the registrar's office in Dungarvan. Our flight was scheduled for December 21 and it wasn't until Friday, December 16, that we received the joyous news that yes, the Republic of Ireland had approved our request to marry in their country!

Later that day, our joy was washed away when we learned that the Anglican priest who had agreed to perform our service had forgotten about it and "besides, did no one tell ye that if ye're not Catholic or Church of England, ye need to be in country for twenty-nine days before the ceremony?"

No. No one had told us. We were disappointed but far from

defeated. Rosie called her own minister in Hibbing. We got a license at the very last minute on that Friday afternoon and on Sunday, December 18, with her eighty-five- and eighty-six-year-old parents as best man and matron of honor, we were married in Hibbing's Holy Trinity Lutheran Church next to a twelve-foot Christmas tree. A dozen rather dazed family members and one close friend were in attendance. They were all sworn to secrecy until our plane took off at noon on that Wednesday, as planned.

What was to have been our wedding day, December 23, was cold and damp in Dungarvan, Ireland. That afternoon, we stood high atop a hill overlooking the Irish Sea in front of the iron-barred door of St. Mary's Church where we were to have tied the knot. There, sun shining through the misty air, Rosie and I again exchanged our personal vows.

At last, I felt married.

We spent Christmas Day in a third-floor room of the Moorings, an ancient tavern adjacent to Dungarvan Castle and overlooking colorful fishing boats made fast to the quay below our tall lead-paned windows. Except for the two of us, the inn was temporarily abandoned and unheated as the entire staff had gone home to spend Christmas with their families, not taking into account that the kitchen fires normally heating the building would die out. We sat in stocking caps and mittens at a table that had been laid for us the night before. There was champagne to drink and bottles of Guinness. Then we ate a hot turkey dinner delivered in the early afternoon by a bar maid who wished us the merriest of Christmases. It was the best Christmas of my life. It was also my sixty-second birthday, and that year I finally got what I wanted for Christmas. I got Rosie!

Although we had expressly requested neither a party nor wedding presents from our friends, they had made their own plans for our return home. I parked the car outside R.T. Quinlan's and took my bride's hand.

"We may as well go in and face the music."

They were all there, golfing buddies with their wives and girlfriends, family, and assorted well-wishers. A chorus of "Congratulations!" rang out from the crowd. After the hand-shaking and hugging and kissing subsided, I caught notice of a table toward the back of the bar loaded with brightly wrapped packages, oddly, all of a similar size and shape. I pointed them out to Rosie and whispered, "Toasters."

Our goofy friends had cooked up a good joke and they gave us eleven cheap white toasters. The last two packages opened were a loaf of bread and a package of bagels. They made us promise not to re-gift any of our ample supply of small kitchen appliances. We "toasted" each and every one of our friends with great thanks for their generosity.

As the weeks, months, and now years have passed, I have learned that marriage makes a difference. Trust me. It is good.

58

Mother Marguerite

Mom's eyes began to dim with the macular degeneration that slowly stole her independence. For a while, grandson Sean stayed with her, and after Sean, Stephanie Richards, a young college student. Mom always liked having young people around. She loved her grandson and looked on Stephanie as another daughter. Eventually, she went to live with my sister Kitty and her husband Ben in Minneapolis, but in the spring she fell when getting out of a car and fractured her pelvis. For her recuperation she became a resident at the Benedictine Health Center, a top-of-the-line nursing care facility in Duluth, half a mile from my house.

My mother's loss of eyesight, in addition to having to leave her beloved home, took its toll. My sisters and I tried our best to see to it that she not only had everything she needed but we also made sure that one of us would visit her nearly every day.

Even so, Mom became melancholy and asked us repeatedly to let her go back home. One day, she appeared at the nurses' desk and asked regally, "May I pay my bill? And then please call a cab to take me home."

We all tried our best but she seemed to need something else, other than just visits. We fell into what became our regular schedule. I lived nearby and would go to see Mom five nights a week. Claudia's oldest son Patrick would stop by one night a week and Claudia and Kitty would break it up with visits from the Twin Cities as often as they could.

Visiting with Mom as often as I did meant that conversation would begin to lag after we'd got caught up on whatever had happened that day. We'd talk a little politics and then I would help her with supper. But something was missing.

One night at home, Rosie and I were talking about Mother's downward spiral. Rosie suggested, "Why don't you try reading to her? You know how you like to listen to me read aloud to you in the evening."

She walked over to the bookcase, picked out a book and placed it on the table. It was Richard Llewellyn's *How Green Was My Valley*, the first book she'd ever read to me. The next night, I began to read to my mother.

She loved it. Her days were brightened by the stories I read. I saw a change in her. She seemed interested in life again. Even into her late nineties, Mom would lean forward in her chair, anticipating each twist and turn in the story. Five nights a week, at 5:00, I'd say goodnight to my friends at the bar. "Gotta go see Mama." It was usual for at least two or three of my buddies to answer back, "Say 'hi' to Marguerite for me."

Tomorrow we will start our sixty-first book, spanning eight years of family stories, tales of children and dogs, and high adventure. Tonight we finish *Oliver Twist*—and *Great Expectations* is waiting in the wings.

I'm still not a very fast reader.

Afterword

The day I sat down at my kitchen table during a Minnesota snowstorm and wrote the first line of this book, I had no idea where the story would lead me. The original intention was to pass on tales of the taverns, told by and about people who gather in their favorite public houses, relying on each other for conversation, laughter, and occasional sympathy. My thanks go to all those characters, both living and gone, who provided inspiration for these memories. When memory failed, well, I wouldn't be a true Irishman if I couldn't embellish a good story.

As the chapters wove together, I realized I was also telling the story of my life. There were many bumps in my road, but for every person I met who took the smile from my face, there came many others who could put dimples on the faces at Mount Rushmore. I thank all who extended a hand, gave me a pat on the back, wished me well, and before sending me on, gave me a story to carry with me.

My great wish was that I could place this finished book in my mother's hands but she died just one month before the preliminary galleys of *Swinging Doors* went to print. It was her rich humor, good sense, and great heart that saw me through every difficulty in my life. She had extraordinary love for her family and she held her friends close—they were part of her family, too. She brightened the lives of all who knew her.

I am not a writer, but I tried to tell these stories as if I were sitting on a barstool flanked by a few good listeners. It was a learning experience going through the editing process with three capable and strong-willed women—my wife and my two sisters. Their job was to knock the rougher edges off my untaught writing style. My manuscript is better for their help and I'm glad to say we made it through with our love and respect for each other intact.

To the youngest member of our team, our friend and publisher, Jay Monroe: for each time you helped us get back on the bike, "Thanks, Dad."

I've always enjoyed stories, both telling and listening to them. During the writing of this book I've come to an even greater appreciation of how stories told friend to friend and family to family help us understand those who have died and those who are still with us. Wherever friends get together to share a good drink and lively conversation there will be old stories and new stories. Some will be hands-on-the Bible true and some may have evolved through the years. That doesn't really matter. The good ones will live on.